WHISPER
NO
LIES

Cindy Gerard

POCKET STAR BOOKS

New York   London   Toronto   Sydney

Pocket Books
A Division of Simon & Schuster, Inc.
1230 Avenue of the Americas
New York, NY 10020

This book is a work of fiction. Names, characters, places, and incidents either are products of the author's imagination or are used fictitiously. Any resemblance to actual events or locales or persons, living or dead, is entirely coincidental.

First Pocket Star Books paperback edition January 2009

POCKET and colophon are registered trademarks of Simon & Schuster, Inc.

For information about special discounts for bulk purchases, please contact Simon & Schuster Special Sales at 1-800-456-6798 or business@simonandschuster.com

Cover design by Lisa Litwack.

Manufactured in the United States of America

10 9 8 7 6 5 4 3 2 1

ISBN-13: 978-1-4165-6675-5
ISBN-10: 1-4165-6675-9

"I can't believe you bought into that guy's hand-kissing, smooth-operator bunk," Johnny said.

Crystal smiled. "Never had my hand kissed before."

"Never knew you wanted it kissed," he muttered, finally looking at her. That's when he realized she was messing with him. "You know what they say about playing with fire, don't you?"

"No, what do they say?" she asked, laughing when he rolled her beneath him on the bed.

"You're gonna get burned, baby."

Then he set about lighting a fire.

Also by Cindy Gerard

This book is dedicated to the men and women of the United States military—both active and retired. There are no words to adequately express my gratitude and respect for the sacrifices you and your families have made and for the losses many of you have endured to protect and defend our nation and our way of life.

And to Tommy, who is always there for me.

ACKNOWLEDGMENTS

Heartfelt thanks go to the following individuals whose gernerosity made such a difference in the writing of this book.

Marjorie Liu, Ki Dei Liu, and Stacey Purcell for sharing such riveting information on Indonesia and specifically Jakarta.

Jennita Low—amazing author and friend—many thanks for the Indonesian translations. You rock!

Joe Collins—what can I say? These books wouldn't go *boom, bang,* or *blam* without you!

Susan, Glenna, Kim, and Leanne—thanks, again, for being there.

Live for something rather than die for nothing.
—George Patton

1

It was business as usual tonight at Bali Hai Casino on the Vegas Strip, which meant that every nut job and wacko who could arrange bail was on the prowl. Crystal Debrowski figured that in her seven years working casino security she'd pretty much heard every come-on line written in the casino crawlers and lounge lizards' handbook. That was because Crystal was what her friend Abbie Hughes Lang referred to as a man magnet and yeah, Crystal knew what men saw when they looked at her: sex on a stick. Pixie features, spiky red hair, and fairy-green eyes. Showgirl breasts and round hips that swayed to a sultry beat when she walked and drew heartbreakers and bizarros from the four corners of the earth.

In her twenty-seven years, she'd been lied to, cheated on, hit on, and proposed to. Just when she'd thought she'd heard it all, this guy sweetened the pot. Her latest admirer—a Mr. Yao Long, according to the business card sporting an embossed Komodo dragon emblem—had come a long way for a letdown.

Wait until she told Abbie about *this* joker.

She glanced from Mr. Yao to the man who appeared to be his assistant. "I don't believe I caught *your* name."

"Wong Li."

Wong, a Jackie Chan look-alike, did most of his boss's talking for him. Talking that included propositioning Crystal at a one-hundred-dollar-minimum blackjack table where she was filling in for a dealer who'd gone on a quick break. Crystal was about ninety-nine percent certain that the gist of Yao's offer ran somewhere in the neighborhood of: Him, lord and master. Her, concubine and sex slave.

"Please tell Mr. Yao, thanks, but no thanks," she told Wong, who hovered at her amorous suitor's side like a pet gnat.

Because she perpetuated the sex kitten image—a girl had to have some fun, especially if that girl lived in a world where few people took a woman seriously who wore four-inch platforms that topped her out around five-four—Crystal cut Yao a little slack.

That didn't mean she was going for his insulting proposition. And it didn't mean she liked it. She'd pretty much had it with the opposite sex. Recently promoted to Gaming Manager at Bali Hai, and with several heartbreaks under her belt, Crystal's newly adopted motto was: Men. Can't live with 'em. Can't tie 'em to a train track and wait for Amtrak to do the deed. Chalk her disenchantment up to a string of bad relationships with men who had basically "gotten into her" because she jiggled when she walked.

Johnny Duane Reed was a recent example. That cowboy had heartbreak written all over him and she'd be damned if she knew why every time he blew into town she ended up naked before he ended up gone. Reed always ended up gone.

The latest case in point, however, stood before her tonight. Mr. Yao Long did not look happy. But then, it was hard to tell for certain. His expression hadn't altered since he'd appeared thirty minutes ago with Wong.

"Did he understand that my answer is no?" Crystal's gaze darted from Wong to Yao as she turned the table back over to the dealer. "Because, I'm thinking that if he did, now would be a really good time for him to leave." To stress her meaning, she made walking motions with her fingers.

Mr. Yao, all five-foot-four inches of salt-and-pepper hair, Armani suit, and Gucci loafers, continued to stare at her through narrow eyes the color of onyx. His expression never wavered.

Was it anger? Disappointment? Gas? she wondered, as a frisson of unease tickled its way down her spine.

"Did *you* understand that my answer is no?" She averted her gaze from Mr. Personality to Wong, hoping to make it clear that it was time for the two of them to shuffle on back to Laos or Cambodia or Hong Kong—wherever—and out of her face so she could get back to business.

"Mr. Yao understands your response but respectfully rejects your answer."

She blinked. "He said that?" She hadn't heard a word.

"Mr. Yao is quite taken with you. He expresses regret that you are reluctant to allow him the opportunity to get to know you better but must insist on your cooperation."

"No, seriously. Is he like texting you or something because I never saw his lips move." This was so ludicrous it was almost funny. The next words out of Wong's mouth, however, sobered her like a judge in night court.

"Miss Debrowski, please understand it would not be wise—"

"Wait." She cut off Wong with a hand in the air as unease shifted to alarm. She didn't wear a name tag and as Gaming Manager, practiced anonymity with the fervor of a religious zealot. Yet this man knew who she was. "How do you know my name?"

"Mr. Yao makes it a point to know everything. He is a very important and powerful man in our country."

"Yeah, well, this is *my* country," she informed Wong, searching the sea of gamblers and finally getting the attention of the security muscle on duty this shift. "And in my country it's neither polite nor acceptable for any man—important or otherwise—to impose his attention where it isn't wanted.

"Max," she said when the twenty-something body-builder walked to her side, pecs and biceps bulging beneath the navy T-shirt with a Bali Hai Security Force logo printed on the breast pocket. "Please escort these gentlemen out. Their business here is concluded."

It wasn't that she couldn't handle the situation—her daddy had been one of Las Vegas Police Department's finest before he'd retired last year. He'd taught her to handle *any* situation—but Max's sheer size was enough to prevent any potential ruckus. She just wanted them gone without incident. Harmless or not, ridiculous or not, the two of them spooked her and Crystal wasn't easily spooked.

"You will regret this," Wong said softly.

"Already do," she muttered under her breath, relieved when they bowed to Max's muscle and allowed him to walk them across the casino floor toward the exit without a protest.

"Tip, boss," Sharon Keiler announced, drawing Crystal's attention back to the table action.

She nodded permission for Sharon to pocket the five-dollar toke, then went on about her business of scanning the action on the casino floor.

Crystal had work to do. Promotion came with a price. Because she was who she was—a very small woman in a man's world—she'd had to work twice as long and twice as hard to earn her current position. She was two weeks into her Gaming Manager post and still learning the ropes. The last thing she could afford to have happen was to let these jokers distract her from doing her job.

Everyone wanted to score in Vegas. Everyone had an angle. For every hundred no-luck and good-time gamblers, there was at least one among them intent on upping the odds in their favor. It was her job to spot the cheaters—card counters, past-posters, hand-muckers, palmers, and techno wizards—whether they were on the payroll or on a weekend junket from Podunk, Missouri.

A war whoop sounded from a bank of Lucky Seven slots. Someone had hit it big. She ambled over that way, prepared to offer the casino's congratulations and assistance with the haul when that unsettling curl of awareness skittered down her spine again.

She stopped, spun around, and found herself staring straight into eyes as cold as chipped ice. The man was Asian, midforties, impeccably dressed in a black suit and blue silk tie—almost indistinguishable from Wong Li's attire. He held her gaze for a long menacing moment, then turned and melted into the crowd.

"Spooky," she muttered, then resumed walking—and ran headlong into a wall of muscle.

"Excuse me." She backed up and encountered yet another Asian man. Identical suit. Similar tie. Same hard, intense stare.

This man, too, impaled her with an ominous look before he turned and walked away.

Damn, if her knees weren't shaking when she forced herself toward the slot that was still dinging and whistling for the crowd that had gathered to see exactly how much money the lucky player had won.

And damn if she'd knuckle under to yet another urge to turn and see if someone else was watching her.

Screw them and the Komodo dragons they slithered in on. No way was she letting them see her sweat, because by this time tomorrow, Mr. Yao Long and his ninja squad—and yeah, she figured those guys were with him—would most likely be sailing on a fast boat to China and her life would be back to normal.

Normal. Right. What was she thinking? This was Las Vegas.

Three weeks later, Crystal knew she was in trouble. There was no question and no doubt that she was in deep, mucky doo-doo and she didn't have one single clue how it had come to this.

Ten days ago the counterfeit chips had shown up on the floor. Each casino had a unique set of chips, distinguishable from those used at other casinos and backed up with the appropriate amount of cash. The counterfeit chips that had made their way into the inventory had been identical to the Bali Hai chips so no one had spotted them until random UV testing had discovered the fakes, whose appearance had been traced to her section and her shift.

Initially, there was no reason to blame Crystal, but then things started to snowball. Her section came up short for the evening shift's take. Tens of thousands of dollars short. Then hackers breached computer security codes. Dozens of other little yet vital security glitches—all on her watch—had her pulling her hair out.

So yeah, she became a subject of intense scrutiny. And no, she had no explanation, just a lot of sleepless nights trying to figure out how this was happening on her watch.

She'd since triple-covered all of her security measures and prayed to the gods of roulette that she had a handle on things. That's when the unthinkable happened. Last night, twelve of the thirteen gaming tables under her direct supervision had been flooded with counterfeit twenty-dollar bills. Whoever distributed them had taken the casino for close to two hundred K.

Now here she was, standing in her boss's office listening to him tell her that someone had made an unauthorized entry into the vault using her access card.

For the first time since he'd called her in, Crystal breathed a sigh of relief. Cameras monitored the vault twenty-four/seven, three-sixty-five. If someone had used her card, it would be clear that it wasn't her. "Check the videos."

"We did." Mark Gilbert, the director of casino security, looked grim. He was fit, forty, and the model of corporate efficiency. "The digital video surveillance system developed a glitch during the time in question. Nothing was recorded. The computerized archiving just mysteriously came up empty. Convenient, wouldn't you say?"

Her heart dropped to her knees. There was no way a secure computer system like Bali Hai's could have been hacked into. Yet, it had happened. "You don't seriously believe I'm stealing from you?"

Gilbert sat behind his massive mahogany desk and stared past her rather than at her. "I don't want to, no. But given the circumstances, Miss Debrowski, we have no choice but to place you on leave without pay."

She swallowed back anger and frustration and tears. Gathered herself. "I understand." Actually, she didn't, but given the fact that the only case she had to plead was ignorance, what else could she say? As Gaming Manager, Crystal was the last line of resistance. The security breakdowns had occurred on her watch. That not only made her negligent, it made her suspect.

Gilbert pressed the intercom button on his phone. "Send them in."

The door opened. Crystal looked over her shoulder and saw two uniformed LVPD officers walking in.

The blood drained from her head, swamping her with dizziness. *Oh God.* She'd been waiting for the other shoe to fall. It hadn't just fallen, it had stomped, then ground into her with attitude.

She turned back to Gilbert, her heart pounding. "You're having me arrested?"

Her boss had the decency to look remorseful. "I'm sorry."

He was sorry and Crystal was scared to death as the officers Mirandized her and charged her with suspicion of grand larceny and embezzlement before they handcuffed her and led her out the door.

"And here I thought I was the only one who got to use handcuffs on you."

Crystal looked up from the corner of the white cement-block jail cell four hours later to see Johnny Duane Reed grinning at her from the other side of the bars.

Perfect.

Grinning and gorgeous, Reed was the last person she wanted to see specifically because until today he *had* been the only one who had ever gotten to use handcuffs on her.

A vivid memory of her naked and cuffed to her own bed while Reed had introduced her to a new way to enjoy Ben & Jerry's Jamaican Me Crazy Sorbet was not the diversion she needed at this point in time.

"Abbie called you," she concluded.

Abbie Hughes—now Abbie Hughes Lang—was Crystal's best friend. More than friend, actually. They were as close to family as it was possible to be without benefit of blood ties. Crystal and Abbie had been through it all together. All, possibly, except imprisonment.

"I was visiting the ranch," Reed said. "I was there when she got your call."

It figured that Reed would be back in Vegas and not bother to come and see her. Not that she wanted him to. Not that she cared.

"I need a lawyer, not a . . ." She paused, groping for the word that best described him.

"Lover?" he suggested with that cocky grin.

"Not the word I was searching for," she grumbled, but let it go at that because Reed would take further protests as encouragement.

"If you don't want him, sugar, I'll be happy as hell to take him."

Her cell mate, Jasmine, shot Reed her best come-hither hooker smile. Reed, of course, couldn't help himself. He winked at the ebony-skinned working girl, flirting outrageously.

Jesus, would you look at him. Hair too long and too blond. Eyes too sexy and too blue. Body too buff, ego in danger of liftoff. Standing there in his tight faded jeans, painted-on T-shirt, and snakeskin boots, he looked like God's guilty gift. Trouble was, he knew it.

So did Jasmine. So did Crystal. What she didn't know was why she was so glad to see a man who played at life, played at love, and played at caring about her. That was the sum total of Reed's commitment quotient. He played at everything.

"How you holdin' up, Tinkerbell?" he asked gently.

Oh God. He actually sounded like he cared.

"Careful, Reed. You might get me thinking you give a rip."

He had the gall to look wounded. "Now you've gone and hurt my feelings."

"Just get me out of here," she said, rising and meeting him at the heavy barred door.

"Working on it," he said. "Abbie and Sam are right behind me. They'll arrange bail as soon as they can."

"Bail's already made."

The jailer approached them with a set of keys and a sympathetic look. Crystal had gotten a lot of those looks during processing. It hadn't taken long for word to spread that she was Phil Debrowski's daughter. Thank God her mom and dad were on a three-week tour of Italy and weren't here to witness this.

Crystal backed away from the bars when the barrel-chested and balding deputy slipped the lock and slid open the door with a hollow, heavy *clunk*. "Hey Jake. Someone made my bail? Who?"

The deputy, who was clearly uncomfortable with the situation, shook his head. "You'll have to ask at processing, Crystal. They don't tell me that stuff down here."

"I've always had this prison chick fantasy," Reed said confidentially as Crystal slipped out of the cell. "You know—sex starved, man hungry."

"Stow it." Crystal marched past him, ignoring his warped sense of humor. She was tired and terrified and doing her damnedest not to let either show.

"Hey, hey," he said gently and caught her by the arm. "Looks like someone could use a hug."

Yeah. She could use a hug. She could use a hundred hugs but now was not the time, this was not the place, and *he* was not the man she wanted to show the slightest bit of weakness to. "What I need is fresh air."

"Sure. But first, do a guy a favor." He leaned down close and whispered in her ear. "Make my fantasy complete. Tell me that you and the sister there had a hairpulling, nail-scratching catfight and I'll die a happy man."

"Screw you, Reed."

He dropped a hand on her shoulder, squeezed, and poured on his Texas drawl. "Now you're talkin'."

2

More shaken than she'd ever let on to her friends, Crystal sat in the corner of a plush leather sofa in Abbie and Sam Lang's family room. Her feet were curled up under her hips and a glass of wine sat on the end table by her elbow. Across the richly paneled room Reed flirted outrageously with Sam's six-year-old niece, Tina.

No woman, it seemed, grown-up or otherwise, was immune to Reed's charm. He was really quite wonderful with her, Crystal acknowledged grudgingly. Grudgingly, because she didn't want to see Reed in any light that wasn't a self-serving spotlight shining on his poster-boy persona.

Tina didn't care that the tall Texan was a playboy. She only cared that at the moment, he was sitting patiently, faking the right amount of pain, making the right noises as Tina wound yards of gauze around Reed's "broken" leg as she played out her Florence Nightingale fantasy. Only in Tina's current scenario, Florence was a veterinarian, not a nurse, and Reed was a horse, not a human. And yes, it really was very sweet.

Tina needed sweet. Only months ago the poor baby had lost her mother and father in a car bombing meant as a warning for Sam. Crystal's heart broke for the little girl, who was coping amazingly well thanks to Abbie and Sam and yes, even Johnny Duane Reed's patient and loving attention.

"How you doing, toots?"

Crystal glanced up as Abbie joined her on the sofa with a glass of sparkling grape juice in her hand.

No wine for the momma-to-be.

It was still hard to fathom. Crystal and Abbie had been buddies since forever. They'd grown up together, helped each other through heartbreak, cheered each other through triumphs. A couple of months ago, Crystal had crawled out on a very shaky limb for Abbie and hidden a stolen, priceless necklace while Abbie and Sam had raced across the slippery slopes of Honduras on a mission to rescue Abbie's brother from the same man who had killed Sam's sister.

Now here Abbie was, married to Sam-the-mystery-man Lang with a baby on the way. Life was full of surprises. Some of them not so good. Crystal's losing her job and getting arrested led the not-so-good list.

"Crystal?"

The concern in Abbie's voice had Crystal reaching for her wine. But it wasn't until she caught sight of the ink stain on her fingers from her booking down at the police station, that tears gathered. She stubbornly blinked them back. "I'm okay. Frustrated. Royally ticked off. But okay." So she lied—compared to the laundry list of criminal charges filed against her, a little white lie to protect her friend hardly merited a mention.

"We'll figure this out," Abbie assured her. "Sam's working on it."

If Sam Lang was working on something, Crystal had every reason to believe that he *would* figure it out. Crystal didn't know exactly who Sam worked for when he wasn't running the ranch here with his father. She did know that the operation was based out of Argentina, that Reed, along with several other buff paramilitary types, still spent the bulk of their time south of the border in Evita Perón territory, and that none of them were men whose bad side you'd want to be on.

They had certain . . . skills. Skills that involved weapons and advanced communication devices and covert operations and a tight-lipped brotherhood that would rival any secret order's code of silence.

Watching Reed now with Tina, remembering him naked and needing her in bed, it was hard to reconcile what he did for a living with the way he lived his life off the clock. Maybe that's why she'd let herself become so intrigued by him. And yes, dammit, she was intrigued.

It didn't mean anything would come of it, though. Actions spoke louder than any words and Reed's actions made it clear that he was as commitment phobic as she was. Thanks to her track record with men, Crystal had a problem with trust. Reed had a problem with intimacy. Ask him a personal question, and you got a change of subject or a joke for a response. Figure him for a sleepover, wake up to cold sheets and no word for over a month.

Nope. No future. Not with Reed in it.

No future at all without prison in the offing if she didn't get to the bottom of what was going on with the casino. She suppressed another shiver.

"Let's not call the folks, okay?" Crystal met Abbie's eyes. "I don't want them to know about this. They've been saving for this trip all their lives and I don't want to ruin it for them."

Crystal's parents and Sam's parents, who had become fast friends over the past few months, had boarded a plane for Italy only four days ago.

"Agreed," Abbie said. "We'll just see how this plays out first."

Sam limped into the room, his foot bound up in a walking cast. He was a big man. Like Reed, an inordinately handsome man, but in a competent, confident, yet humble way that spoke volumes about the depth of his character. Oh, and those surprises life was full of seemed to extend to Sam as well. Two weeks ago he'd rescued Tina's kitten from a tree and ended up with a broken foot when the ladder slipped and he'd made a twelve-foot drop to the ground.

The man dodged bullets for a living and a little calico kitten with blue eyes and a soft purr had taken him down. Reed had been having a field day with that one.

"Took a while but I got a name," Sam said.

"You found out who put up my bail?" Crystal uncurled her legs. Her bare feet hit the floor as she sat up straight. She could have called her dad and asked him to check with his pals on the force to get the information but the longer she kept her arrest from him, the better. It would devastate him and her mom. Just like it had devastated her dad when she'd failed the LVPD physical five years ago.

It had destroyed her, too. She didn't remember a time when she hadn't wanted to be a cop. It seemed like she'd been in preparation for the job all of her life, only to have a series of ear infections leave her with a hearing loss in her left ear that had taken her out of the running. She'd passed every test but that one.

But she'd moved on, put it behind her until this had stirred up all the old disappointments again.

"Crystal?"

Sam's voice jarred her out of her thoughts.

"Yeah. Sorry. You've got a name?"

"Yao Long. Mean anything to you?"

Crystal felt her heart stop as images of a night around three weeks ago flashed through her memory. Little Yao Long in his Armani suit. Wong Li at his side. Shadow ninjas materializing left and right. "Shit," she muttered.

"I'll take that as a yes," Sam said with a sharp look toward his wife.

"Shit," Crystal repeated and lifted her wine with a shaking hand. "Guess Yao and his ninja squad missed the boat back to China."

Reed was on his feet now, exchanging a hard glance

with Sam. "Sounds like you'd better tell us what you know about this guy."

"Other than the fact that he thought I'd make a good mistress?" Crystal glanced from one man to the other. "Not a damn thing."

Then she downed her wine in one huge swallow.

Sam had long ago put Tina to bed and returned to his office to do some more digging on Yao. Abbie had fallen asleep on the sofa. Preggers people—even those who were barely showing—needed their rest. Crystal needed to sleep, too, but she was too wired, despite several nights when she'd lain awake trying to figure out what was happening to her life.

She prowled restlessly around the dark, quiet house and for more than one reason, wished she'd gone home to her apartment in town instead of bowing to Abbie's insistence that she stay with them tonight.

Reason number one, Johnny Reed dogged her step for step, like he was afraid to leave her alone because she might do something stupid. The closest she came to stupid, however, was when she let him get the drop on her and pull her into his arms.

"What are you doing?" she sputtered as he backed her up against the fridge and pinned her there with his big, hard body.

He nuzzled her neck, nipped her lightly. "I must be slippin' if you haven't figured that out."

"Reed . . ." She flattened her palms against his chest. Trouble was, what he was doing felt so good that she ended up gripping his shirt in tight fists and put more muscle into keeping him exactly where he was instead of pushing him away.

"At your service, darlin'." He knew exactly the effect he was having on her. Her groan of pleasure as he pressed his hips against hers and rocked, might have tipped him off. And when he lowered his head and kissed her, fool that she was, she let him.

Lord, the man could kiss, she thought, melting into him as his tongue slid past her lips, bold and wet and hot, and he made that deep humming groan low in his throat that told her he was as turned on as she was and thoroughly dedicated to taking things to the next level.

Only with Reed, there was no next level beyond sex, fantastic, blow-the-top-of-your-head-off sex, granted, but that's where it ended. For reasons she had yet to figure out, Crystal needed more from him. More, however, just wasn't in the cards. Not from this blue-eyed boy. That certainty finally gave her the presence of mind to put on the skids just about the same time Reed reached his big, busy hand between them and flicked open the snap on her jeans.

"This isn't happening," she told him, marshaling a shallow breath, cursing her stupid libido that had risen to the occasion the same way the bulge in Reed's pants had risen against her belly.

"Come on, Tink." His breath fanned against her cheek, his clever fingers working their way into her jeans. "It'll relax you."

"I don't want to relax," she grumbled, finally managing to push him away. "I like hovering on the edge of manic depression. Keeps me sharp."

He chuckled, of course, because he didn't buy it any more than she did, but she'd be damned if she was going to let Reed seduce her while she waited out the biggest trouble she'd ever been in in her life.

"I know this will shock you, but sex isn't the answer to everything," she added for good measure and headed back to the family room.

"But you have to admit, it is a *good* answer," Reed argued, following her.

Not tonight it wasn't. If she had the sense God gave a neon light, not any night with Reed ever again. She glanced at the mantel clock when she walked back into the family room. Almost midnight. It had been one long ugly day.

When Sam joined her and Reed in the room, it got a whole lot longer.

"My sources came through with more information on Yao. It's not good."

"Tell me." Crystal had never been one to want to ease into anything. She liked her Band-Aids ripped off, not slowly peeled away. She dove into cold water, didn't wade in slowly to gradually absorb the freezing shock.

"Yao is purportedly the head of a crime syndicate based out of Jakarta."

Rip!

"Crime syndicate?"

"In Indonesia."

"Yeah, yeah. I know where Jakarta is. I just figured him and his goons for China or Cambodia or something."

"However you figure him," Sam said, cupping his nape, "figure him trouble."

"As in *angry*, mafia-type, crime syndicate trouble," Reed said after thinking it through. "Apparently with a real hard case for red hair and big boobs. I'm betting he's determined to either have you or ruin you—take your pick."

Under other circumstances, she'd never let the big boobs remark pass. "He bailed me out. That doesn't say angry to me."

"It does if Yao was responsible for setting you up."

"Setting me up? At the casino?" She cut her gaze from one man to the other. "You think he . . . oh, man. You think he's behind the counterfeit chips? The fake twenties? Seriously?"

"Unless you know another crime lord who has the hots for you and apparently the network capable of pulling off the crime spree at Bali Hai, yeah," Reed said, clearly implying she needed to pull her head out of the sand, "we're damn serious."

"As a heart attack," Sam added when she turned to him for confirmation.

"Well." She dragged a hand through her short, spiky hair. "Well."

"Deep subject," Reed said with a grim scowl.

Crystal glared at him. "Old joke."

He held up his hands. "Hey. I just call 'em like I see 'em."

She turned back to Sam. "Given that becoming Yao's mistress, whore, or sex slave is off the table, what do I do now?"

Sam looked at Reed. Reed, for once, didn't have a joke, which translated loud and clear: she was in a whole lot of trouble.

Prostitution, human trafficking, illegal arms shipments, counterfeiting, corporate espionage. Those were just a few of Yao's sterling enterprises. Johnny tossed aside the report Sam had shared with him, and pushed away from the fireplace. Then he simply watched Crystal where she'd finally fallen asleep, curled on her side in an oversized leather chair. Tinkerbell was in a world of hurt with this creep, Yao.

She was also tapped out. An unexpected and irrational curl of tenderness wound through him as he watched her. The same tenderness that always blindsided him when he thought of her.

What was it with this chick, he wondered, that kept him coming back for more? It didn't compute and it frustrated the hell out of him. She was so not his type. He went for long leggy blondes with shy smiles and come-hither looks. Or give him a willowy brunette without too many opinions and even less of an agenda. Crystal was a short, stacked redhead. Sexy as hell, yeah, but she was too smart, too opinionated, and too perceptive to suit him. Give her a little more time and she'd have him figured out, and that was something he just wasn't prepared for.

Besides, the woman never smiled—at least not at him—plus she wouldn't know demure if it snuck up and bit her in her cute curvy ass.

So no, he didn't get it. It was not his MO to return to the scene of a crime or, in Crystal Debrowski's case, the scene of the good time. Maybe it was because of the size of the heart beating inside the pint-sized little pixie. She had guts and she had grit. Truth was, she reminded him of Jenna. Although, except for the red hair, there was absolutely no physical resemblance between Crystal and Gabe Jones's wife.

Jenna wasn't blond or demure but she was absolutely a woman he could get into. There had been a day when he wouldn't have let a simple thing like friendship stand in his way of making that happen. A day when he'd been young and stupid and selfish and mean, both before and after he'd escaped a stint in juvenile detention by "voluntarily" enlisting in the marines.

Yeah, there had been a time before Force Recon had made him a man and Task Force Mercy had made him a brother to men like Sam and Gabe Jones and a dozen others, when he would have moved in on another man's woman and congratulated himself for the dirty deed.

Thank God he'd grown past that kind of crap years ago. He still made it a point to be a one-night-wonder kind of man, though, and yeah, a shrink would have a field day with his dodge-and-fade tactics and his no strings, no strain game plan. Monogamy just wasn't his thing; the idea of commitment made him break out in hives. He wasn't good at it. Didn't want to be good at it. He loved women, plural, and there were a whole lotta fish in the shallows that he had every intention of splashing around with.

He glanced at Crystal, her head resting on folded hands, her heavy lashes dusting her cheeks, her round hips emphasizing her tiny waist and thought again, no. He was not a one-woman kind of man. Yet this *one* woman had been messing with his head since the first time those wild green eyes of hers had sized him up like he was a cut of beef and she found him way short of prime. Talk about an ego hit.

And talk about trouble. She was in it neck deep. Because she was Abbie's friend, and because Abbie was Sam's wife, that meant only one thing. Sam would move heaven and earth to get Crystal out of this fix.

Because Sam was *his* friend, Johnny was in the thick of it, too. At least he tried to convince himself that was the main reason he was sticking around and relishing the idea of taking a big swing at Yao Long.

"What's the plan?" he asked when Sam wandered back into the family room after rousing Abbie and coaxing her to go to bed.

Sam glanced at Crystal, shook his head. "Damned if I know."

"Yeah." Johnny scratched his head. "I pretty much see it that way, too."

The pixie was caught between a boulder and a battleship. One was a rock. The other was a very hard place.

"Unless we can come up with concrete evidence to tie Yao to the thefts and counterfeit schemes at the Bali Hai and prove he set her up, she's a sure guilty verdict," Sam said, looking grim.

Johnny nodded. "By the time she gets out of prison, she'll bear more resemblance to a fairy godmother than Tinkerbell."

Sam cut him a look full of speculation and a healthy dose of "so that's the way it is."

"Well, she will," Johnny said, defensively.

Sam grinned. "I'll be damned. You've got a thing for her."

"Hell I do," Johnny said with a snort. "I'm just sayin'."

"I know what you're saying. And I'm going to love gloating about it."

"Whatever," Johnny said, irritated that Sam had seen through him, pissed that Sam was right. So he had a little thing for her. Didn't mean he was going to do anything about it.

"What do you figure?" he asked, steering clear of those deep weeds. "Yao's so ticked that Crystal turned him down that he'll leave her to rot in jail? Or is he using the threat of jail time for leverage to get her to agree to his proposition?"

Sam yawned, shook his head. "Criminal minds. Who can figure what they're thinking? Best guess, he set her up then bailed her out figuring he'd convince her she had no future where she was and she'd run away with him."

"He don't know her very well, do he?" Johnny's intentionally garbled grammar made Sam grin around another yawn.

"Look. I'm hitting the sack. Mendoza may have something more for us on Yao by morning. We'll look at things with fresh eyes then."

Raphael Mendoza was one of the BOIs—Black Ops, Inc.—team members based out of Buenos Aires. Mendoza, Colter, Savage, Green, and Jones, to name a few, had signed on with their old Task Force Mercy CO, Nathan Black, when they'd parted ways with the military several years ago.

The split from Uncle, however, hadn't been all that wide. BOI did contract work for the government now. Some would call them mercenaries, but it couldn't be further from the truth. Mercenaries hired on to the highest bidder because their loyalty was to the almighty buck or Euro or currency with the highest conversion rate. BOI fought exclusively for Uncle Sam. They fought the same kind of bad guys they'd fought in uniform but with a different set of rules and with absolutely no culpability on the part of Uncle Sam. The BOIs were what the spy books referred to as shadow warriors. They operated so black a football field full of floodlights wouldn't be enough illumination to get a fix on their activities.

Until recently, Sam had been an integral part of the BOI team. Then a rat bastard by the name of Fredrick Nader had killed Sam's sister—little Tina's mom—and her husband, as a warning for Sam to get off his back. It had been the last warning Nader had ever issued. Tracking Nader down and helping Abbie rescue her kid brother, whom Nader had abducted, had also been the last official act Sam had completed for BOI.

Time, Johnny hoped, would bridge that gap and Sam would eventually come back on board again. Back with his brothers who tried to make the world a little less cluttered with bad guys.

Yao Long was a very bad guy. And yeah, Johnny figured that by morning, Mendoza might have a lead on how they could take the Indonesian crime boss out of play and get Crystal's life back on track.

3

Crystal liked her bed. She liked the pretty brass head-board. She liked her 800-thread-count Egyptian cotton sheets and the nice queen-sized mattress. She liked to sleep on her stomach, her arms spread wide, her legs stretched out.

So when she woke up wedged between leather and rock-hard *something,* it didn't take her long to figure out she hadn't fallen asleep on her own pillow-top mattress.

She opened her eyes slowly. Got a bead on dark pan-eled walls, a beautifully woven Couristan rug in rich saturated colors, and a scent that could never be mis-taken for anything but Johnny Duane Reed. Dark and musky and sexy as sin.

They were on the sofa, she realized. She'd fallen asleep in a chair in Sam and Abbie's family room. Evi-dently, sometime during the night, Reed had dragged her to the sofa and joined her there. He was stretched out beneath her—fully clothed, thank God—and she was plastered against the long, hard length of him like butter on a muffin.

Sweet, she thought, and snuggled until she was comfortable against him.

Not sweet, she amended when she felt the length and thickness of his erection rise between them.

Not happening.

She lifted her head and saw that he was still sound asleep with one hand splayed over her hip and the other forked into her hair. Just like a boy scout, he was ready at a moment's notice, she thought, trying to muster some degree of disgust when in fact, it felt mighty fine to be nestled up against all that hard, male heat.

Mighty fine, but not the time.

On a deep breath, she eased up off him. He mumbled something unintelligible, shifted onto his side, and plunged a little deeper into sleep. Crystal checked the mantel clock. It was almost five a.m. It would be daylight soon. Daylight of the second day of her life as a criminal.

The thought made her weary. Frustrated. And wondering how she'd look in an orange prison jumpsuit. With her red hair? *Eeeeeww*.

Fully awake now, she glanced around the room, feeling closed in and restless. Her friends were wonderful, protective, supportive, and kind, but she needed a little time alone. Raking her fingers through her hair, she searched for her purse and snagged it on her way to the door. At the last second, she stopped, considered, and gave in to guilt.

"Needed a little space," she scribbled on the back of a deposit slip from her checkbook and left it on the kitchen counter. "And a change of clothes. Call you later. Thanks for just about everything in the world."

Thirty minutes later, she hit the outskirts of Vegas.

Ten minutes after that, she let herself in to her apartment.

One second after she closed the door behind her, she felt the presence of another person. It had barely registered that she was not alone when she was grabbed from behind. One hand covered her mouth, another arm hooked around her throat.

Five years of karate training kicked into overdrive. She knew she had to protect her airway. She immediately grabbed on to her attacker's arm with both hands, shrugged her shoulders, and sank her chin toward the crook of his elbow. Then she sank down, bending her knees, and swung her foot behind her, trapping his right leg behind his calf and pulling him off balance. Turning one-hundred-eighty degrees, she jerked diagonally on his arm, flipping him to his back on the floor.

Then she ran like hell for the door, barely aware of a table lamp crashing to the floor behind her. She'd just reached the knob when she was grabbed from behind again. A second attacker. He was ready for her, countered her moves. She stomped on the top of his foot, heard the crunch of bones, and jabbed her elbow into his solar plexus. His wind rushed out on a hard grunt and she spun, kicked hard at his knee. She heard the pop and he went down with a roar of pain. Before she could move, the other guy was on his feet again. He tackled her. They fell to the sofa and rolled to the floor. She hit hard with him on top of her. The landing knocked the wind out of her and for a frozen, terrified moment, she couldn't breathe.

She writhed in agony as the two of them pinned her down, flipped her over, and pressed a cloth over her mouth and nose. She bucked and kicked and gulped in air pungent with the scent of ether as her world went hazy, fuzzy, then black.

Johnny woke up to a warm, wiggling female bouncing on his chest. It was not, however, the female he'd gone to sleep with.

"Hey, half-pint." He tickled Tina's ribs until she shrieked. "What are we playin' today?"

"Nothin'," she said, sounding put out. "I gotta go to school."

Johnny lifted Tina off his chest, set her down beside him on the sofa, and eased himself upright. "Well, that sucks," he commiserated, rubbing the sleep from his eyes.

Face long, Tina nodded in agreement. He grinned and tugged on her ponytail. "Where's Crystal?"

Abbie walked into the room carrying a mug of coffee. "She drove into town for a change of clothes."

He frowned, then thanked her when she handed him the mug. "And Sam let her go?"

"Sam and I were still sleeping. She left sometime before five-thirty."

Dammit. He'd known that they shouldn't have let

her drive her own car out here. It wasn't as if there was an immediate threat, but it wouldn't hurt to keep an eye on her until they nailed this down.

"What time is it now?" Johnny buried his nose in the amazing aroma of Abbie's coffee, which she ground fresh every morning.

"Almost seven. I just tried to reach her on her cell. She didn't answer. Didn't answer her landline either or the text message I sent her. You think we should be worried about her?"

"Maybe she just wants a little space," Johnny said reasonably. He didn't buy it, though, and he could tell by the concern on Abbie's face that she didn't either.

"So she said."

He shook the remaining cobwebs from his head. "Where's Sam?"

"Finishing up chores."

He took a careful, savoring sip of the hot coffee. "I'll go check on her."

"Thanks." Abbie forced a tight smile. She was worried. He didn't want to be, but he was worried, too.

Forty-five minutes later Johnny knocked on Crystal's apartment door. It eased open a crack when he did, and he shot past worried to red alert. Experience, training, and instinct had him backing away from the door and up against the wall beside it. If someone were inside, someone who, say, liked playing with guns, too much time spent in the fatal funnel—the frame of the door-way—and he'd be out of commission or dead.

Because he was who he was and because he did what he did, he'd dug his Sig out of the glove box of his rental car—screw the legalities of carrying concealed—and tucked it into the waistband of his jeans, covering it with his shirttail before entering Crystal's apartment building. He reached behind his back now, drew out the pistol, and held it in a two-handed grip. The gun felt comfortable in his hands.

He'd grown to appreciate the Sig when his buddy, former SEAL Luke Colter, had sung its praise. Colter had taken exception to his standard issue Beretta 92F in the navy because he'd seen the backlash on one of his buddies. The Beretta had a tendency to blow the slide off into a guy's face when he shot the hotter loads. The single-action Sig, however, was a sweet and crisp 3.5 pounds. Like a state-of-the-art camera—all he had to do was point and squeeze and bye-bye bad guy.

Very quietly, he nudged the door all the way open. Then he shot into the apartment fast and hard, the business end of the Sig sweeping the room.

Nothing.

No one.

With the precision honed by years of practice at armed entries, he cleared each room, one at a time. It didn't take long. The apartment was small. One bedroom. Bath. Living room. Kitchen. Crystal wasn't in any of the rooms.

Her purse was. She'd dropped it just inside the door. A lamp had been knocked to the floor. The sofa cushions were in disarray. All signs of a knock-down, drag-out struggle.

Heart stalled, chest tight, Johnny reached down and picked up a business card that had fallen out onto the floor beside her purse.

His blood went cold when he saw the embossed Komodo dragon logo in the upper corner of the card. Yao Long's name was printed beneath the dragon in blood-red ink on pricey white card stock.

The closest thing Johnny had felt to fear in a very long time knotted in his gut and fisted as he flipped open his phone and dialed Sam. "The sonofabitch has her."

She watched with narrowed eyes as the woman on the bed began to wake up. Another American. A redhead this time. Once, she would have felt sorry for her. Once, she had felt sorry for all of them who ended up here.

But no one had felt sorry for her, no one had cared about her, so she'd stopped caring, too. Stopped hoping. Stopped believing that someone was looking for her. That someone would save her and take her home.

Home. Sometimes she wished she could forget about home. Most of the time she wished she could just die, but they wouldn't let her. So she existed. And tonight she waited as she'd been told to and the only thing she allowed herself to feel for this new girl's arrival was relief. The master had a new toy to play with. Tonight, at least, he would leave her alone.

* * *

Crystal's head hurt. Her tongue stuck to the roof of her mouth, which was as dry as cotton. Her eyes felt like they were strung with cobwebs and sand. The light burning away at her closed lids seared all the way to the back of her skull.

She heard someone groan, realized the sound came from her about the same time she realized she wasn't alone. Fear—reflexive and instantaneous—had her forcing her eyes open, only to recoil against the light when a low-riding sun burst through a bank of floor-to-ceiling windows.

She covered her eyes with her forearm, only then realizing that her right wrist was bandaged and that the skin under the dressing burned beneath the layers of gauze.

"He must have really dosed you."

It was a woman's voice. One she didn't recognize.

"Take it easy. Give yourself some time."

Definitely female, at any rate, but not a woman. She sounded young. Too young to impart such weary wisdom in those few words. With a small measure of relief, Crystal also decided the voice was too indifferent to mean her harm.

"Where am I?" Crystal would have laughed if her head hadn't hurt so badly. Her question sounded like a line of bad dialogue from some low-budget movie and yet it was the first thing that came to her mind.

"Jakarta."

She dropped her arms. Opened her eyes and fought

through the blinding light. Then she made herself focus on the wall of windows across the room before finally shifting to the face regarding her impassively.

"Jakarta? As in Indonesia?"

The young woman nodded.

Crystal jerked upright. Immediately regretted it when the room spun. She lay back down, willed her stomach to settle.

Jakarta?

Jesus.

Jesus!

It couldn't be. She'd just left Abbie and Sam's. She'd driven back to Vegas. Unlocked the door to her apartment, then . . .

Then what?

She couldn't remember.

"How?" she asked, accepting the truth and wishing for a pair of ruby slippers.

"I imagine you were abducted. The same way I was abducted close to six months ago."

Heart rampaging, Crystal met the other woman's eyes, realized she was just a girl. Young and pretty and dressed in what appeared to be ceremonial clothes. Her long-sleeved silver tunic was silk, finely stitched, intricately embroidered, as were the matching pajama-style pants. Her blue eyes were heavily made-up. A sheer scarf of the most delicate fabric and palest rose draped over her shoulders, front to back; the tails trailed to her hips.

"Abducted?" Crystal tore her gaze from the girl's

costume, which looked like a cross between something out of the *Arabian Nights* and a geisha house. "As in kidnapped?"

The girl nodded. She was petite. Peaches and cream complexion. Vibrant blond hair that curled around her face. A full, lush figure that even the tunic and baggy pants couldn't hide. She was beautiful—except for her eyes. Her eyes were flat. Lifeless.

Hopeless, she realized when the girl looked away.

Crystal reached out, covered her hand with hers. "Six months ago?"

The girl jerked her hand away; a sharp, cornered look filled her eyes before she composed herself. "Yeah. Six. Close as I can figure. The days . . . they kind of run into each other here, you know?"

No. Crystal didn't know. But she had a horrible, gut-wrenching feeling that she might find out.

"You're American, right?" Crystal sat up slowly, careful, this time, of the drums reverberating inside her skull.

The girl regarded her with a bemused look. "If I wasn't I wouldn't be here. His tastes run toward Westerners." She extended a paper cup. "You can drink it," she said with a nod. "It's bottled water. It won't make you sick."

Eyes burning, still fighting dizziness, Crystal carefully scooted back on what she'd just realized was a bed draped with a red silk duvet, and leaned against the headboard to help steady herself. She took a careful sip of the water. It felt so good going down, she drank some more. Tried to regroup.

She was in Jakarta.

Kidnapped.

It was too bizarre to process.

Too surreal to accept. She'd become a statistic. One of hundreds of thousands of women and children lost in the inhuman reality of human trafficking.

She turned back to the girl. Saw the weary acceptance of her horrible situation in her eyes and knew it reached clear to her soul. "Crystal Debrowski." She offered an encouraging smile although for the life of her she couldn't figure out what there was to be encouraged about.

"Dina Stornello," she said, watching Crystal as if she expected some reaction.

"I'd say I'm pleased to meet you but under the circumstances, I can't say I'm pleased about much of anything. What is this place?" She glanced around the garishly furnished room.

Instead of answering, Dina waited for Crystal's attention to return to her. "You don't know who I am, do you?"

Crystal searched the girl's face and for the first time saw something other than indifference. Disappointment, maybe? "Should I?"

"No," she said after a long moment. Her shoulders sagged; her expression transitioned back to an emotionless void. "Wouldn't matter at this point if you did."

"Look, Dina—" Crystal began but the girl cut her off.

"Okay . . . you can't call me that." She stopped abruptly and cast a glance toward the door. "Don't ever call me that."

"Don't call you by your name?"

Dina shook her head; worry had replaced the indifference in her eyes. Fear made them bright and wide and wary. "He doesn't like it when we use our Western names."

Crystal swallowed back a rolling nausea as her head continued to clear and the full gravity of her situation sank in.

"And you don't want him mad," Dina warned. "So don't do something stupid, like try to escape. You won't get away. And he'll punish us both because I couldn't control you."

Crystal's gaze sharpened on the girl. "He? Who is *he*?"

"The master," Dina said finally. "You'd just as well get used to calling him that, too."

Master. God. Could this get any more bizarre? Yeah, she realized as her drug-hazed mind cleared and she put it together. It could get a lot more bizarre. Jakarta. Abducted. Sex slave.

"Yao Long. He's your master, isn't he?"

"Mine and all the others he's bought and sold and stolen. And now he's yours," Dina said with a flat, weary acceptance.

Bought. Sold. Stolen. Yao Long wasn't just a warped dangerous man who plucked women off the streets for his own pleasure. He was a flesh merchant. A white slaver. Jesus. *Jesus.* Her head spun. She fought back another wave of nausea.

"There . . . there are others? Here?"

Dina shook her head. "Others, yes. Here? No. Around the city."

Crystal touched a hand to her forehead to keep it from reeling.

"He sent me to you," Dina went on. "To ensure that you have everything you need. And to help prepare you for the purification process."

Purification process? Oh God. She could hardly wait to hear this.

"Dina—"

The girl shook her head again, fear escalating in her eyes. "I am Cahya—Light, in Indonesian. You are now known as Bethari—Goddess."

Crystal couldn't help it. She laughed. Short of hysterical, but not very, because she was terrified. But she needed answers so she held it together.

"By order of Mr. Yao?"

"Yeah. Mr. Yao. Look. I know this is hard to take but you need to get something through your head. This is your new normal. You now exist only to please him. And if you don't, you'll end up someplace far worse than this."

The distressing hopelessness in her tone made Crystal's heart break. They existed to please their master because their master was a monster.

"Dina, listen to me. We've got to get out of here."

Defeated blue eyes slowly met hers. Slower still, she lifted the silvery silk tunic she wore, raised it until she'd bared herself from the shoulders down. She twisted at the waist and showed Crystal her back.

Crystal gasped when she saw the angry, puckered and very new scars; a series of long, deep gouges crisscrossed Dina's back.

"I tried to escape once." Dina lowered her tunic. "Only once."

"That bastard can't get away with this."

When Dina turned back to face her the sleeve of her tunic caught at her elbow, baring her lower arm. Crystal reached for Dina's hand, stared in horror. A Komodo dragon had been burned into the delicate skin on the inside of Dina's right wrist.

"His brand," Dina explained, following Crystal's gaze.

Crystal looked from Dina's eyes to the gauze dressing circling her own wrist. Suddenly frantic, she ripped off the bandage.

The same brand had been burned into her own skin. Skin that was still red and raw and weeping from the sting of the iron.

"He's marked you. You're his now," Dina said, her voice urging Crystal to accept her fate.

Seething with anger and hatred and defiance, Crystal met the younger woman's eyes. "Like hell I am."

4

He was little more than a boy. Fourteen, fifteen, maybe. He was thin. He was a native of Indonesia and he was one of Yao Long's houseboys. He was also scared spitless—just the way Johnny wanted him.

There was no time for idle threats or chitchat and the boy knew it. Johnny had been on the move for thirty-plus hours straight, tracking Yao Long from Vegas to Jakarta with a little help from his boss, Nate Black, and the BOIs and a lot of pent-up anger.

This kid didn't want to be messing with him or the Glock 19 Johnny pressed firmly against the kid's jaw. Savage and Green, both BOI operatives, had CIA contacts in Jakarta. They had arranged for someone to meet him at the airport with the Glock. It paid to have "friends" in low places.

Just like it paid to know a little bit about a lot of things—like the over two hundred languages spoken in the chain of seventeen-thousand-plus islands that constituted the nation of Indonesia. He opted for a butchered version of the colloquial form of Indonesian.

He'd picked up bits and pieces of the language near the end of his first tour with the marines when he'd spent a weekend of R & R in Jakarta. Seemed like a hundred years ago. Just like it seemed like it had been a hundred years since he'd burst into Crystal's apartment and found her gone.

It hadn't taken Sam but a couple of phone calls to learn that a Gulfstream G550, which just happened to be identical to Yao's private jet, had flown out of Vegas within an hour of the time Johnny had discovered Crystal missing. Neither had it taken a degree in chemical engineering to figure that she was on that flight. Or that she was in the worst kind of trouble.

Prostitution, human trafficking, illegal arms shipments, counterfeiting, drugs. The litany of Yao's sins had been playing through his mind like a broken record. Especially the human trafficking and prostitution part. Yao Long was definitely the cream of the crap. That's why, thirty-six hours later, Johnny had landed at the Soekarno-Hatta International Airport, jet-lagged, out of sorts, and bent on mass destruction.

A quick phone call from Sam on a cell phone equipped with a chip allowing international calls had given Johnny the address of Yao Long's upscale digs in a center city penthouse apartment where you had to be richer than God to live there and even the maids had maids but the houseboys didn't have the sense God gave a goat.

Johnny had maneuvered himself into the high-rise building with a smile and a fifty for the doorman, ridden the elevator to the penthouse suite, and knocked on the door. Damn if the kid hadn't just opened it—a small breach of judgment that he, no doubt, regretted now that he was backed up against a wall with Johnny's hand clutched tightly around his throat and the Glock locked and loaded and pressing against his jaw.

"*Di mana Yao Long?*" (Where is Yao Long?)

The kid's eyes grew wide. He swallowed, shook his head in short, panicked jerks.

"*Dia di sinikah?*" (Is he here?)

The boy shook his head again and remained stubbornly silent.

"You think *he'll* hurt you?" Johnny muttered, knowing the boy didn't understand him. "He's not going to have the chance if you don't tell me where he is."

He tightened his grip on the kid's throat. "*Cakap sekarang!*" (Tell me now!)

The boy caved. Lack of breath had that effect on a lot of people. He choked out an address. "*Dekat dermaga.*" (Near the wharfs.)

Made sense that Yao would have a hidey-hole near the coast. One of his legitimate business fronts was shipping. It was pretty much a given that he exported more than commodities. Johnny figured Yao also used his shipping business to cover up not only his counterfeit money shipments, but illegal weapons, drugs, and exports of the human kind. According to the information Mendoza had passed on to Sam, Yao shipped his illegal cargo to Europe, Asia, and points in between.

It also made sense that wherever Yao was Crystal

would be close by. At least he hoped to hell that line of thinking was on the money.

Johnny eased off on the pressure. *"Bagus."* (Good.)

He released the boy. Patted his cheek. *"Jangan memberitahu sesiapapun, faham, tak? Saya pun diam-diam."* (You don't tell. I don't tell.)

The boy nodded, stalled somewhere between terrified and relieved. Reed pressed a finger to his lips to reemphasize his meaning, then headed for the elevator. Crystal would soon be gone almost thirty-six hours. Every hour that passed lessened the chances of finding her.

Find Yao.

Find Crystal.

That was the theory.

So far, it was also the plan. The only plan.

There hadn't been time to round up any of the other BOI operators and with Sam's foot buggered up, it came down to him. Much as he'd like to, Johnny couldn't wait for the cavalry. He had to find Crystal and he had to find her now. Just like he had to hope like hell that now was soon enough.

Crystal stood at the wall of windows staring down at the lights of the huge, bustling city several stories below. At least ten stories below she'd decided, as she'd prowled her ridiculously appointed room searching for a way out.

Dina was right. There wasn't any way to escape. She was in a towering prison, the door to her room locked and bolted. The only other option was to break a window and plunge down ten stories. She might have a Tinkerbell tattoo on her shoulder but the wings were just for show. She was stuck here.

The desolate truth of that knowledge weighed on her like the brand burned into her wrist. *Bastard.* The bastard had branded her.

Less than an hour ago, Yao had arrived with his hired muscle. The perverts had stripped her. She'd fought, but four of them had held her down while Yao had "prepared" her.

Nausea rolled in her stomach when she thought about how he'd touched her. Shaved her. Made promises about what he had planned for her when he returned. Of what he would take away from her. Choice. Dignity. Joy.

It was dark now. Dina had left the room with Crystal's mostly uneaten dinner tray a few minutes ago.

"Master will be back later. You must bathe and purify yourself for his return. He'll expect cooperation," she added before she'd left. "Please, Bethari—"

"The name is Crystal," she'd insisted, interrupting her. After the degradation of his "preparation" ritual no way was she going to bow to another of Yao's edicts.

"You'll only make it hard for yourself if you fight him," Dina warned her; then she'd handed Crystal a small box covered in ornately patterned red floral silk before closing the door behind her and locking Crystal in.

Curiosity had her opening the box. Two round metal spheres lay nestled in red silk. Ben Wa balls.

"Yeah, that's gonna happen," she muttered, tossing the Oriental sex toy on the bed in disgust. She stared blankly around her, fighting a renewed wave of dizziness.

The sixteen-by-sixteen room—she'd paced it off—was a cross between a fishbowl, a birdcage, and a bordello. Everything from the picture frames to the fixtures in the tiny bathroom had been gilded, or was real gold or painted gold. An Oriental carpet patterned with koi fish and ferns and pagodas covered most of the wooden floor. Erotic Oriental art hung on the walls. Incense and a variety of perfumes, lotions, and oils sat in decorative decanters on a black lacquered dresser. Inside the dresser was every piece of risqué, see-through lingerie imaginable.

"Perverted bastard," she muttered as her head reeled. He'd tried to drug her again. She was sure of it. She felt just enough of a tug toward listlessness to realize it had been in her food. Thank God, she hadn't eaten all of it.

She glanced at the bed, shivered. It was a four-poster, covered in black satin sheets and that sleazy red duvet. Black roped tassels held back sheer champagne-colored netting that had been strung from the ceiling and draped over the bedposts.

Fabric matching the bed netting hung in panels from ceiling to floor at either side of the wall of windows. The sheers were pulled back, tied again with black roped tassels, leaving full access to a view that under other circumstances would have taken Crystal's breath away.

Beyond a few blocks of city rooflines was the harbor. Lights from hundreds of small watercraft moored to bobbing white buoys flickered in the distance. Large yachts nestled side by side in shallow-water berths, their running lights glimmering from stem to stern against gleaming white paint, teak, and chrome. Farther to the left in another harbor, hulking freighters and cargo ships lined a network of concrete and steel docks; overhead cranes yawned above them like lurking monsters while rows of pallets stacked high with shipping containers crowded the heavily trafficked wharfs.

Crystal observed it all from her glass prison, aware as she'd never been aware, of her insignificance in the vast expanse of the universe. If memory served her, Jakarta was a teeming city of over twenty million people packed into an enormous urban sprawl. She was one among millions. One lone American woman who did not speak the language. She had no money. No ID. No means of communicating with the outside world. With the exception of the items in the dresser, which included the green and gold silk tunic and loose-fitting trousers Dina had given her to wear, she had no clothes.

She was a prisoner.

A sex slave.

I'm his now.

She stared from the harbor lights to the brand on her wrist and finally gave in to the tears she'd fought since she'd come to.

No one knew where she was. No one would know how to find her. She sank down on the bed.

She thought of her parents and how horrified they would be when they returned from Italy and found out she was missing. She thought of Abbie and worried that her stress over her disappearance would jeopardize the baby. More tears threatened when she pictured the little stuffed lamb and the tiny yellow sleeper and matching booties she'd bought, anticipating Baby Lang's arrival. Her heart sank as she contemplated the very real possibility that she might never get to see that sweet little baby she'd already started to think of as her niece. Never get to have a sweet little baby of her own, and that brought a new threat of tears because she hadn't even known that deep down, deeper than she'd ever gone before, she wanted to be a mother someday.

Then she thought of Johnny Duane Reed and her spirits lifted marginally. Reed might come for her. Sure, their "nonrelationship" was based strictly on chemistry, but he didn't *not* like her. And fighting bad guys was his "thing," so he might sign on to rescue her on general principles.

"And find you, how?" Her voice rang in the silence and she rose and walked to the window again, pressed her forehead against the glass.

Sure, he would figure that Yao was behind her disappearance. Even if he came after her and even *if* he narrowed his search down to Jakarta, they were still talking over twenty million people. She was a needle in an Indonesian haystack. A grain of sand on the beach of the Java Sea.

Defeat set in like a heavy, smothering fog. No one, not even Reed, could find her here. Soon, Yao would be back to take even more from her. Realizing that, she felt herself hit rock bottom. She wallowed there for all of a minute.

"You pathetic, wimpy whiner," she berated herself, seeing her reflection in the glass and the tear trailing down her cheek. "So that's it? You're just going to curl up in a ball and let Yao win? That's your new MO?"

She squared her shoulders. Roughly swiped the tear from her face and fought the lingering effects of the drugs.

"Hell, no."

She'd been a fighter all of her life. She acted, not reacted. She solved problems, she didn't let them beat her.

Okay. So this wasn't a typical problem. Now as always, though, it was still up to her to solve it.

Adrenaline spiked with her new resolution. She could escape. She *would* escape. Somehow. Then somehow, she'd find her way to the U.S. embassy. If she made enough noise they'd have to take her in and if there was anything she knew how to do, it was make noise.

She turned back to the room, swept it with her gaze, searching for anything and everything that might help get her out of this place.

"You," she said, climbing up onto a chair and glaring at one of the offending pictures hanging on the wall, "are going down."

An hour later, she had assembled her arsenal. She'd ripped and torn the picture from its frame. Using a pillowcase to protect her hand, she'd broken the glass covering the print. Now she had two crude knives made of roughly eight-inch shards of razor-sharp glass. For her own safety, she carefully wrapped the blunt end of each of her makeshift daggers with torn fabric from another pillowcase.

"Look out, Yao, you warped little bastard. I'm taking you out." She laid the knives on the dresser alongside a piece of the thick picture frame. As clubs went, the length of frame was no baseball bat but it had heft and she figured if she put enough weight behind her swing, she could take down a five-foot-four Asian crime lord if she got the drop on him.

Refusing to think about how much muscle he might bring with him, she quickly untied the rope tassels from the bed and tossed them beside the club and the knives. Next, she uncapped and sniffed the bottles of lotions and perfumes and oils.

"This'll do," she decided, gagging as she unstoppered a bottle of strong perfume. She figured a good douse of it in Yao's eyes would blind him, at least temporarily. Temporary was all she needed.

She glanced around the room, then quickly shoved the remains of broken picture frame and torn print under the bed and carefully tidied up the glass. Satisfied that nothing looked terribly amiss, she emptied the contents of the perfume bottle into a decorative bowl and grabbed her club.

She was as ready as she'd ever be. Then a thought struck her and she sprinted for the bathroom. She quickly unscrewed the chrome showerhead, tested its weight. It was about the size and length of a handgun. Shove it into someone's ribs from behind and they'd have no way of knowing it wasn't a gun; she might be able to use it to convince someone to give up their weapon. Surprise the hell out of them when she showed them she knew how to use it.

She scrambled out of the tiny bathroom, flicked off the lights, and positioned herself behind the door.

Then she waited. What she lacked in size, she made up for in determination and pure, primal rage. It had been that way all her life. And all of her life, because of her diminutive stature, her dad had made certain that she could defend herself. While the other girls her age had taken tap and ballet, she'd been busting moves in karate class. She could still move like a dancer but her skills were a lot more effective on the self-defense front. Summers on the gun range had made her a crack marksman with long guns and pistols. So no, she was no pushover. And Yao Long was in for a big surprise if he thought she'd go down without a fight.

Dina had said Yao would be coming back later tonight. Crystal had a nice, passionate welcome planned for the dragon man—just not the kind of passionate welcome he had in mind.

* * *

Few elements of Western culture appealed to Yao Long. The music, for one, he thought as he stood motionless while Wong Li cleansed him in preparation for the evening ahead. Western music was boisterous, grating. He much preferred the sound of traditional Chinese instruments made of the eight natural elements: bamboo, reed, silk, wood, metal, stone, gourd, and hide.

Simplicity. Serenity. These were the things he longed for. These were the things he missed from his homeland. His business, however, profited from its location in Jakarta. His sexual appetite fared better as well. Many eyes turned blind to certain less acceptable aspects of his "ventures" in Indonesia.

He lifted his arms at Wong's subtle urging and slipped into an elegant silk robe—a gift from a business acquaintance. The robe was long and black and caressed his naked skin like cool water. An eagle perched in a pine tree was embroidered across the back in red and gold thread. The eagle symbolized strength, the pine tree longevity. When he was with a woman, he embodied both.

In the background a CD played the lyrical notes of a *gu zheng*, a Chinese zither. He breathed deep, absorbed the peace in preparation for the conquest ahead. He pictured Bethari, her lush body, siren's eyes, and flaming red hair. Anticipated their joining with the fervor of a blushing bridegroom.

That she would not be willing the first time was of

no consequence. He would break her. He always broke them. And if she proved to be more nuisance than pleasure, she would find herself on the auction block.

"It is time," he told Wong in their native tongue.

Wong dutifully stepped back, bowed out of respect as much as obedience, then turned and opened the door for his master.

5

Crystal didn't know how much time had passed. Thirty minutes, maybe more, as she leaned back in the corner behind the door, breathing deep, attempting to command control. Between the drugs still sluicing around in her bloodstream and her lack of food tugging her back toward unconsciousness—now was not the time to suffer from low blood sugar—she had to struggle to keep herself upright and lucid.

Over and over again, she mentally envisioned the door opening and Yao walking in, expecting to find her on the bed. She visualized getting the drop on him, quickly disabling him and his minions, then running like hell for the nearest exit.

She had it all planned out in her mind. Even if there was an elevator, she decided she'd take the stairs, rationalized they presented less of an opportunity to be trapped. Over and over, she played out her actions in her head, preparing herself for what was sure to be a violent confrontation. She talked tough, but the fact was, she'd never intentionally set out to hurt another living soul in her life. The guys who had jumped her in her apartment didn't count. That was self-defense. And as long as she thought about what was about to happen in the same context, she could get through it.

A bump outside the door jerked her right out of her Zen place and straight into attack mode.

"Adrenaline, don't fail me now," she uttered under her breath and grabbed the bowl full of perfume that she'd emptied out of the bottle. Gripping her picture-frame club in the other hand, she held her breath, heart rockin', and waited.

A scratching noise. A key in the lock, maybe. A snick of sound as the tumblers in the lock gave way.

The door creaked open and her heartbeat shot out of control.

Pale light spilled into the dark room from the hall-way. She assured herself that she had the advantage. Her eyes had adjusted to the darkness. Yao's pupils had to react as he was coming in from the light.

His shadow, backlit and distorted, fell across the bed that sat just inside the door. Because Yao was short, Crystal had calculated exactly where to aim the perfume so it would hit him in the eyes and temporarily blind him. Then she would go after him with the club and a few well-placed karate kicks. The knives were a last resort.

Heart pounding in her ears, she willed herself to wait, *wait, wait,* as the shadow loomed larger and Yao stepped across the threshold. As soon as she saw his foot hit the floor inside the room, she flew into action.

She jumped out from behind the door, hurled the perfume, and reared back with the club.

"What the—"

She swung with all her might, expecting to hit Yao's head—and encountered a wall of muscle instead.

"Jesus. What the—"

The door to the room closed, pitching it back into darkness.

She swung again.

Connected again.

"Stop it. Dammit, quit hitting me!"

Strong arms banded around her, immobilizing her, pressing her face against a muscled chest dosed with the gagging scent of gardenias and musk and God only knew what else.

"Crystal. Goddammit, stop. It's me. It's Reed."

The combo of residual drugs in her system and stark, virulent terror blocked her mind from accepting what she'd just heard. Fired on fury and fear for her life, she kicked and clawed and pummeled and bit, too overwhelmed by his size to use her karate.

"Ouch! Okay. That's it." Strong hands gripped her shoulders, set her away. "Listen to me, Tinkerbell. You've got to get it together."

Tinkerbell.

Oh God.

"Reed?"

"You were expecting maybe the tooth fairy?" he asked, sounding relieved.

He didn't know what relief was. "I was expecting the dragon master!"

She lunged for him and leapt into his arms. Then she wrapped her arms around his neck and her legs around his waist and dared God and all of his angels to even try to make her let go.

"Oh sure, *now* you're all over me . . . and with no handcuffs in sight."

That was Reed. He'd joke his way through a bomb blast.

"Hey, hey," he said gently, apparently realizing how shaken she was when she didn't give him any lip about his perpetual come-on mode. "It's okay. You're okay now. You are okay, right, Tink? Did he . . . did anyone . . ."

He held his breath until she spoke.

"No. No. No one—" She stopped. Swallowed. "They didn't hurt me. I'm okay. God . . . I thought you were Yao or one of his . . . ninja hit men."

He hugged her hard as she buried her face into the hollow of his neck. Relief and gratitude—his and hers—kicked into overdrive.

"How did you find me?"

"Tell you later. Right now we've got to beat feet before said ninja pricks get a clue."

A fresh surge of panic swamped her. "Yao's supposed to come anytime now."

"Let him come. You're not gonna be here. You sure you're okay?" he asked. "I mean . . . you can walk and everything?"

"Screw walking. I'm ready to run." She made herself climb down off him. Stepping away, she turned on the light and grabbed her homemade knives.

Reed glanced from her face to her outfit to the glass daggers. "Holy mother of God. Glad you didn't come after me with those bad boys."

"I was saving them for later."

"This is later, baby. Let's hope you don't have to use them." He pressed a finger to his lips. "Douse the lights."

As soon as she flicked the switch he cracked open the door and peered outside. Crystal scurried over to his side, hooked a finger in the belt loop of his cammo cargo pants, and hung on like he was a lifeline.

Who was she kidding? He *was* her lifeline. She'd never been so glad to see anyone in her life. She fought a sudden onslaught of dizziness, knew it was a combination of leftover sedation, terror, and low blood sugar.

"Stick with me, okay? Tight as a tick."

"If you think I'm letting you go, you're crazy," she whispered as they edged out into the hall and shut the door behind them.

"Wait a sec." He fished a short piece of metal out of a pocket, turned back to the door, and fiddled with the lock until it clicked. "Let's let him think you're still locked in there. Won't slow him down for long but we need every edge we can get."

He led her toward the stairwell door, cracked it open, checked inside, and pulled her in behind him.

They ran like hell, shooting down floor after floor. Crystal's legs were rubbery and her knees were weak by the time they hit the fifth-floor landing.

She stopped to catch her breath.

Above them a door opened. A man's voice shouted.

"They've got our number. Move," Reed said, as several sets of footsteps pounded down the stairs after them.

He grabbed her arm and they shot off at a dead run again. She was dizzy by the time they reached the ground floor. He tucked her tightly behind him as he quietly opened the stairwell door.

"What is this place?" She peered over his shoulder to see a cavernous and dark open area that looked like a garage or a warehouse, far too aware of the footsteps getting louder and closer behind them.

"Close as I can figure, floors two through nine are office space. You were locked up on the top floor. Ground floor is like a shipping and receiving station. Lot of pallets and forklifts. A few trucks."

"Are there guards?"

"Unless someone sent reinforcements, there's only one," he said. "But he's taking a little nap right now."

With Reed's help, Crystal figured. "They're getting closer," she whispered as the sound of rushing footsteps grew louder.

"It's clear," he said after a thorough look around. "Let's get the hell out of here."

Could it really be that easy? Crystal wondered as they stepped out of the stairwell and into the garage.

Reed spotted a piece of iron leaning against the wall. It was about the length and girth of a broom handle. He wedged it through the bar of the door handle and the frame.

"That won't slow them down for long."

They took off running across a cracked and broken concrete floor, stained with dirt and oil. The walls were rusted steel with exposed studs. The sliding door that led outside yawned at least twenty feet wide and fifteen feet tall. It was also a good thirty yards from where they were.

A few scattered ceiling lights—pale bare bulbs—hung from exposed wires and cast hulking shadows on the walls as Reed dragged her toward the door at a dead run.

Of course, it was locked when they reached it.

Behind them the stair door rattled as Yao's men put some muscle into working it open.

Reed dug into his pocket again and went to work on the padlock.

"Hurry," she whispered, shooting an urgent glance over her shoulder as the men trapped in the stairwell shouted and swore and kicked at the door. Reed's makeshift deadbolt couldn't hold much longer. "They're going to break through soon."

Reed continued to calmly work the lock. He popped it open just as the stairwell door slammed against the wall with an ominous, hollow crash that reverberated through the echoing space like a gunshot.

"Come on." He shoved the door open a crack and

slipped outside. Crystal was right on his heels. She chanced one last glance behind her to see two men lift sleek black rifles to their shoulders. "Oh God."

Reed tugged her the rest of the way through the exit door as a hail of gunfire tattooed the floor at her feet.

"Don't look back," he ordered as they hit a wall of city heat. They ran to the corner of the block, tucked around the building, and ducked into the first alley they came to.

They scurried through packing crates and a maze of bicycles and flattened cardboard boxes and rushed out into the busy street. A blur of shadows, lights, and scents whirled past her as they dodged foot traffic and vehicle traffic and wove their way at a sprint clip through a labyrinth of side streets and vendors whose shops were closed down for the night.

Pollution hung thick in the foul-smelling air. Garbage clogged the gutters; the humidity and heat, even this time of night, was cloying. The slight breeze that found its way in from the ocean did little to abate the stifling temperature.

And still they ran. They ran until her sides hurt. Until the soles of the thin silk slippers she wore were scuffed and filthy and the scent of the perfume she'd doused Reed with had faded to barely tolerable as opposed to obnoxiously oppressive.

Finally, when the stitch in her side grabbed so sharp it felt like a knife, she put on the skids. She collapsed back against the side of a building. Bent over, gasping for breath, she dropped her glass knives and held her screaming ribs, wishing she had about a gallon of water to quench her thirst.

"Nee . . . ed to c . . . catch my br . . . breath."

"Catch it fast," he said. "I think we lost them but I don't plan to hang around and find out."

After several deep, labored gulps of hot, sticky air, she finally looked up at Reed. Let the fact of his presence fully sink in.

He'd come for her. Damn, if he hadn't come for her . . .

She wanted to laugh. She wanted to cry. But more than anything, she wanted to launch herself into his arms again and kiss him until the cows came home.

"Thank you," she said, unable to hide her relief and gratitude.

"We'll figure out some way for you to show your gratitude later."

She pushed out a labored laugh. "One-track mind."

"I'm nothing if not predictable. Look. We can hash out the terms later but right now we've got to make tracks. You ready to rock?"

"Yeah. I think so." She pushed herself upright. A wave of acute weakness swamped her, then dizziness hit her like a truck and slammed her back against the building. Her low blood sugar combined with the residual drugs about the same time that her adrenaline crashed. Her head spun until all she heard were bells, all she felt was weak, and all she saw was black.

* * *

Johnny swore and lunged, catching Crystal just before she hit the filthy street. Out. She was good and out, he realized with alarm and shored her against his side.

"Crystal." He gently patted her cheek.

Nothing.

He patted again, with a little more persuasion this time. "Come on, darlin'. Let's get with the program."

Her head lolled on her shoulders like a doll's.

Tinkerbell's wings had definitely been clipped. Bastard had probably drugged her and starved her to boot.

He glanced up, looked around them. They were not on Prospect Boulevard. This part of the city was mired in poverty and decay. Most pedestrians out and about this time of night were either scavenging for food or drugs or sex for a price. What appeared to be a strung-out American didn't garner so much as a second glance from anyone.

Strike that. No one noticed except the knot of street thugs milling like moths beneath a light post on the far side of the street.

There were six of them and it was clear they were fast coming to the conclusion that he and Crystal would make easy marks.

"And me without my Uzi," he muttered.

If it had just been him, he'd have ignored them. If they were stupid enough to come at him, he would simply take them out. But it wasn't just him. It was him and a Western woman, and in Asia, on the streets of Jakarta, she meant money. Yao Long wasn't the only asshole profiting in the human trafficking market.

So yeah, these creeps saw money—lots of it—and they saw one man standing between it and them. He had to get her out of here. Fast. Before they called in reinforcements and it became a feeding frenzy.

He hefted Crystal into his arms and hauled her over his shoulder in a fireman's carry. Then he started walking, then sprinting, then flat-out hauled ass when he heard a pack of footsteps slapping cement behind him.

Something poked him in the shoulder. He reached up, shifted her weight, and dug into her pocket. He pulled out a showerhead. "What the hell?" He tossed it aside as he ducked around another corner at a run, flew down two blocks, then cut left.

"Fuck," he muttered, when he realized they were keeping pace with him. They knew this city. In particular, they knew this squalid district. He, however, knew something they didn't. If they so much as touched a hair on her head, they were dead men.

He preferred, however, that it didn't come to that. When he saw an opening to an alley ahead of them, he ducked into it.

Mistake number one. It was a dead end. Strike that. His first mistake had been signing up to play white knight for the pixie whose sweet breasts were currently pressed against his back and even sweeter ass that felt warm and firm beneath his palm.

6

Johnny spun around and headed back the way he'd come, hoping he could beat the street boys to the mouth of the alley. But his luck had just run out. He skidded to a stop as six lean, hungry males faced off in front of him, blocking his way, trapping him with the dead end at his back.

"Well, hell," he muttered, his gaze tracking from one hard face to the other. "Nothing's ever easy, is it?"

It got even harder when the gangbanger in the center of the pack produced a blade. Reed recognized the Butterfly because it was Gabe Jones's knife of choice. He'd seen his Black Ops, Inc. team member in action and knew how lethal the knife could be in the right hands. Just like he knew that these jokers were too close for him to draw his Glock. It wouldn't even matter if he had his Uzi. At this close range, if these guys knew what they were doing with their blades it would be all over but the bleeding before he ever got his hand on his gun.

Walking six abreast, they backed him deeper into

the alley. Step by menacing step, one guy led the way, showing off by flipping his Butterfly open, closed, open closed, giving Johnny a reason to like what he was seeing. An experienced knife fighter wouldn't let him see the blade and how he was holding it until he'd come in for the kill. Flashing it around this way was either the sign of an amateur or a monster ego. Either way, this dude was the clear leader of the pack.

There were two schools of thought on taking on a gang. Take the leader out or take anybody out. No matter who went down, it needed to be done in a very graphic, very visual way. And when they had murder on their minds like these nice gentlemen did, it had to be so brutal and quick and with such apparent ease that it would take the fight out of the hangers-on. Street gangs were essentially a collection of bullies, and one thing bullies realize is that when they are overmatched, the reward might not be as juicy as they'd thought.

Johnny decided to work on the theory that if you sliced off the head of the snake the body ceased to function. Nine times out of ten, it worked.

It was that tenth time that always gave him nightmares.

"You're gonna be the first to die," he told Butterfly Man, who didn't understand a word he said but couldn't mistake his intent. "That's right, I'm taking you out, dumbass."

The Indonesian smiled a "bring it on" smile. Smug and clueless and amused.

One by one the others followed suit as they closed in, backing him deeper into the alley.

First order of business. Protect Crystal. Without ever breaking eye contact with number one thug, he eased her off his shoulder. He knew they'd let him get her out of the line of fire. Damaged goods wouldn't bring as much money on the black market. The alley was packed dirt and decay and scattered with rotted garbage and broken glass and things he didn't want to think about laying her on. It couldn't be helped. Backing as close to the far wall as possible, he lowered her carefully to her side on the ground. Then he quickly stepped out in front of her, establishing himself as a human shield.

"Come to Papa, *si kecil*," he taunted, calling the ringleader a "little boy" just to piss him off and keep him thinking with his ego, not his head.

Worked like a charm. Butterfly Man spit at Johnny's feet and waved off the others. Perfect. He stepped in, flaunting his knife, high on adrenaline, testosterone, and who the hell knew what else he'd shot into his veins or snorted up his nose.

"Tough guy, huh?" Johnny grinned. "Gonna show the pack what a big macho man you are? How 'bout we show 'em how hard you fall instead, asshole?"

He waited for the perfect moment, letting the bastard come to him. When the guy finally worked up the courage to lunge, Johnny stepped into him at a right angle, grabbed the hand holding the knife, and snapped his wrist like a twig. At the same time, he punched down against the elbow joint with his other hand and broke it, too. Without losing his momentum, he twisted the guy's broken arm behind his back and popped his shoulder out of the joint.

The tough guy was screaming like a girl, trying to hunch in on himself as Johnny spun him around, stood him back up, and grabbing his forehead from behind, twisted. The bones in his neck made a popping, crunching sound, like a burst from a subgun. And then he wasn't screaming anymore—because he wasn't breathing.

As the body crumpled, Johnny snagged the Butterfly from the ground beside him. Stepping over the prostrate form, he mimicked their fallen gang member's taunt, flipping the knife open and closed, goading the remaining five with come-on motions of his other hand.

Five pairs of eyes widened in stunned shock as it sank in that he had annihilated their fearless leader in a sum total of twenty seconds. One of them puffed up his chest in outrage, feigned a lunge. Reed took one step toward him . . . and that was all she wrote.

He turned tail and hauled ass. The other four froze in various stages of hesitation before their brains engaged and they did a one-eighty and beat feet, too.

There was no time to celebrate. Johnny pocketed the Butterfly, hauled Crystal onto his shoulder again, and took off like a shot. He didn't want to be anywhere near here when the boys came back with fresh recruits or when the body was found. He much preferred home cooking to the fare in an Indonesian prison cell where they'd be happy as hell to lock him up for the rest of his life.

He burst out into the dark street, spotted an off-duty taxi at the corner, and made a beeline for it.

He jerked open the rear door, carefully shoved Crystal inside, and climbed in after her. *"Pergi!"* (Go!)

The driver grunted, pointed to the off-duty sign.

Johnny pulled out his Glock, shoved it behind the guy's ear. *"Pergi,"* he repeated softly, and let the gun do his shouting for him.

Hand shaking, the taxi driver shifted the car into gear. *"Ke mana?"* (Where?)

"Mana pun boleh. Panda sajalah!" (Anywhere. Just drive.)

"Wha . . . what's happening?"

Johnny sat back on the seat, studied Crystal's pale face as she struggled to sit up.

"Oh, nothing much," he said slipping an arm around her shoulder and tucking her up against his side as the driver pulled into traffic. While he'd never been a master at understatement, he figured this was a "what she didn't know wouldn't hurt her" moment. "Just had a nice chat with some locals. Welcome back to the land of the living."

But she was already passed out again.

For the first time since he'd landed in Jakarta and he'd started his search, Johnny took a breath that wasn't weighted with concern. True, they weren't out of the thick of it yet, but he planned to have her in the air on the way back to Vegas before Yao Long figured out how to pronounce her last name.

First things first. He gave the driver the address of

the parking ramp where he'd left his rental car with his go bag in it.

"*Makanan.*" (Food), he added.

The man nodded quickly, understanding what he wanted.

Tinkerbell needed protein. At least he hoped that was the worst of what was wrong with her. Yeah. He needed to feed her and he needed to get her gone from here.

Gone, however, ended up happening first.

Remembering became more important than breathing. Maybe, Dina told herself as she lay on the floor in the corner of the cell and fought the pain that consumed her, if she could just remember why she'd run away from home, it would make this bearable. If she could blame her dad for this, maybe she could work up enough anger to deflect the fear.

But she couldn't remember. She couldn't dig deep enough to find the reason she'd become so mad at her dad that she'd run away that day. That horrible, horrible day that had brought her to this end.

As she lay on the floor weeping from the last beating Wong Li had given her while her master had stood by and watched, all she could remember from home was a pink ruffled bedspread. Pretty lacy pillows on the bed. A poster of Daughtry on her wall.

Bits and pieces of memories. All that was left of who she had been. She'd been loved. She understood that now. Now that she was Yao Long's property and home was an alternate reality that brought more sorrow than joy.

"How did she escape?"

Wong Li's voice broke through the fog of pain. He wanted to know how Crystal had gotten away. She didn't know.

She didn't even know when Crystal had escaped. Had it been hours ago? Days?

She wanted to hate the American woman. Hate her for leaving her here to take these beatings. Hate her for the reminder that once she had been some*one*, not some*thing*.

"How did she escape?" Wong repeated. "Who helped her, Cahya?"

"I . . . don't . . . know."

"Your continued refusal to cooperate leaves your master with little choice." His voice softened, grew almost regretful. "You realize that?"

Dina closed her eyes. She knew what came next. Another form of death.

The noise was the first thing that registered as Crystal dragged herself out of a maze of cobwebby dreams. The noise—a *clatter-chug, clatter-chug*—she didn't recognize but seemed to rock and roll and give and sway with the rhythm of the car.

Car?

"'Bout time you're coming around again."

Reed.

She breathed deep—smelled curry and machine oil and perfume.

Perfume?

Gardenias?
Clatter-chug, clatter-chug.
Rock and roll. Give and sway.
She was too tired to figure it out.

"Oh, no you don't. Stick with me this time, darlin', or I'll be forced to take advantage of that hand that keeps wandering to my lap."

She sat up straight. Jerked her hand into her own lap. Immediately felt the absence of warm male heat and solid muscle.

She touched her fingers to her head where it pounded. Food. She needed food. "Don't suppose you've got anything to eat?"

"What do you take me for?" he asked with a smile in his voice. "A cheap date? Of course I've got food. Way past time you ate it, too."

Crystal forced herself to pull it together. She glanced at Reed. Lord, he looked like an outlaw. His blond hair curled at his nape. He hadn't shaved in, well, she didn't know how long but his stubble was almost thick enough to qualify as a beard.

He also looked very concerned. She must have been out for a while.

A series of buildings, lit by dim security lights, flew by in a blur outside the window, fleeting images in the night.

Window. A really, really huge window . . . of a train, she finally realized.

Clatter-chug, clatter-chug.
Rock and roll.

Give and sway.

They were on a train?

"What did I sleep through?" she asked, mystified that the last thing she remembered was running away from Yao.

He shot her a lascivious grin. She knew that grin. It was all about seduction and sex.

"Never mind. I don't want to know."

"Smart girl." He handed her a paper box that smelled like heaven. The scents wafting out were amazing and totally unidentifiable.

"Go ahead. It's satay. You'll like it. It's chunks of chicken on bamboo skewers. Kind of like the hot dog in NYC. There are vendors on every corner, grilling them over open coals. Dig deeper. Should be some peanut sauce and steamed rice wrapped in banana leaves in there, too."

She dug—and sweet merciful God, found chocolate. Warm and melting and necessary. She dove into it like a honeybee into a hive.

"Thank you, oh my God, thank you."

He chuckled as she licked the melting sweetness off the wrapper.

"Why are we on a train?"

"Because it was handy."

He was being deliberately obtuse.

"I meant, where are we going?"

"Bandung. It's inland from Jakarta. Should be there in around three hours. We'll book a flight home from there."

She licked her fingers. "We had to leave Jakarta to do that?"

"With Yao scouring the city for you? Oh, yeah. The airport will be crawling with his men about now. Wait. Look at you. You're a mess."

He leaned in to her, touched the tip of his tongue to the corner of her mouth, licked. "Umm. Sweet."

Well, *that* woke her up. A shock, hot, wild, and electric, shot from her lips straight to the center of her belly.

He laughed and sat back. "The look on your face is priceless."

"And the look on *yours* is getting old."

"Hey. What can I say? I'm a sucker for chocolate. Especially when it's on a woman. Particularly when it's on a woman's mouth."

"Have you ever seen a shrink about this obsession you have with sex?" she asked around a mouthful of something that tasted heavenly.

"No, but I'm writing my memoirs. I hear it's good therapy. I know *I* sure enjoy reliving the moments," he said with that slow, sexy grin that should have ticked her off but simply had her shaking her head.

"Now would you please eat the rest of that?" he asked, sexy transitioning to concern. "You need to shore yourself up."

He didn't have to tell her twice. She'd finished her first skewer of satay and was nibbling on the second when she stopped short, horrified when her synapses finally all fired in sync.

"Oh my God."

He grunted, and stretching his legs out in front of him, got more comfortable in the seat beside her. "Yeah, I had a few of those moments in the last couple of hours, too."

She shook her head, terror running a strong second to conviction. "We've got to get off this train. We have to go back to Jakarta."

Reed looked at her like she'd grown two heads. "Excuse me?"

"There's another girl. Damn Yao and his drugs. I can't believe I blanked out like that. Yao is keeping her captive in the same place you found me! Johnny, she's an American," she told him when he started to shake his head. "A kid. The bastard had her abducted from LA around six months ago."

He sat up straight. "You've actually seen her?"

She nodded. "I'd be surprised if she's even sixteen. She's defeated, scared. We have to go back. We can't leave her there."

He dragged a hand over his lower face, his expression grim and edging toward denial.

She understood in Technicolor. There was every possibility that not only she but Johnny could get killed if they returned to Jakarta. She'd just escaped a nightmare and if they went back—well, the thought of heading back into the dragon's nest had her pushing down a churning fear.

Dina's face, however, haunted her. She'd been so scared. So alone. So totally helpless.

"We. Can't. Leave. Her," she insisted, her voice rising as guilt won out over trepidation.

"Okay. Okay. Settle down. We won't leave her, okay? We'll get her out of there. As soon as we get to Bandung we'll call the U.S. embassy. They'll take care of it."

"Yeah—after months of waiting for red tape to unravel. She can't wait that long. He'll have moved her by then. Or worse."

He rubbed at the heavy growth of bristles on his jaw. "Getting you out was one thing, Tinkerbell. I had the element of surprise on my side. Yao wasn't looking for anyone to come after you. At least not this soon. He'll be ready if we go back. And he'll come after us with more than a couple of shooters with AK-47s. I'd need a team. That's just not going to happen."

What he said made sense. And yet how could they not at least try? Tears brimmed her eyes. "You're telling me that it's not worth the effort to save another human life?"

He exhaled a deep breath. "It's not a question of effort. It's a question of firepower and manpower. We don't have it. Look," he said after a quiet moment. "We're dealing with organized crime here. It's too big. There are thousands of girls in her situation."

"There's got to be something," she said, meeting his eyes.

He just shook his head.

Heartbroken, she stared at her hands, then absently pulled back her sleeve and gazed at the evidence of Yao's intentions.

Johnny grabbed her hand. "What the hell?" He glared at the brand and the red, inflamed flesh around it. She watched as shock transitioned to white-hot rage.

"He branded her, too," she told him. "Worse. Her . . . her back." She stopped, swallowed. "He had her whipped."

He stared from her wrist to her face. All traces of the sexy, playful flirt were gone. A stone-cold killer stared back at her.

"I'm going to kill that sick fuck with my bare hands."

7

The hotel in Bandung had once been a grand villa but was now like a woman who had seen hard times and neglect; age and the elements hadn't been kind. Instead of being classic, she was now merely old. Someone had recently applied a coat of yellow paint, but the flaws were still obvious and sadly emphasized a former opulence that had faded to shabby and no longer chic.

The upside was that the place was clean and it was cheap. It was also low profile, near the train station, and no eyebrows were raised or noses wrinkled when Johnny and Crystal walked in, in the middle of the night, smelling like gardenias and garbage with only his go bag for luggage. Another plus was that cash seemed to answer any questions the staff at the reception desk might have wanted to ask as he made quick work of registering Mr. and Mrs. John Brown. Unoriginal, but effective.

Bottom line, they'd needed a place to crash while Johnny worked on arrangements to get Crystal home. She was running on fumes. For that matter, so was he, which probably explained why he'd made a promise he couldn't keep.

His first order of business after he unlocked the door to their room was to get in touch with Nate Black, his boss and Black Ops, Inc.'s head honcho, and let him know he'd gotten Crystal out of Jakarta. He made the call, let it ring twice, then immediately hung up.

"You take the shower first," he said as Crystal stood in the middle of the room, looking like a bruised and battered doll that some child had thrown out with the trash. Her "slave girl" outfit—which might have made a fun fantasy if it hadn't been tragically real—was covered with grime, her flat silk slippers were frayed and filthy. Her face was bare of makeup, her hair lay flat on her head. She looked all of twelve, or would have, if not for the press of her breasts against the thin silk tunic and the curve of her ass that he had thought about way too much since hauling her on his shoulder through their fun-filled scenic tour of Jakarta.

"If you call Sam and Abbie, tell them not to contact my parents, okay? I don't want them worried."

"You got it," he said with a nod. "Now go take that shower," he urged again, and she finally walked on weary legs into the bathroom and shut the door.

A minute later his phone rang. He knew it was Nate, calling back on a secure line. "Yo."

"What's happening?"

Johnny pinched the bridge of his nose. "Not sure you really want to know."

He quickly filled his CO in on the situation with

Crystal, then told him about the abducted American girl who was still being held hostage. He didn't have to rehash what he knew about Yao Long. Before he'd left for Jakarta to find Crystal, Mendoza had put together a complete dossier on the Asian crime lord and e-mailed it to him at Sam and Abbie's. If Johnny had the info, so did Nate.

Yao was just the kind of scum the BOIs made a practice of putting out of business. It came as no surprise that Yao was near the top of Uncle's "who we'd most like to see take a long walk off a short pier" list. Any action the BOIs wanted to take against Yao would be met with the blind eye otherwise known as "sanctioned but disavowed." As always, the BOIs got a green light with the caveat that the U.S. government approved but could never publicly condone. It was a screwed-up system, but for the most part it worked.

This situation, however, wasn't that simple. They fought the fights they could win. At least they tried to. Organized crime and human trafficking flourished all over the world, but in this corner of it, the sex-slave trade was big business. Bigger than a few isolated cases of girls getting abducted.

The white-slave trade ran rampant, with Russia leading the way. Eastern Europe wasn't far behind, and even worse, the good old U.S. of A. was becoming a big player in the trade, with over eight hundred thousand abductions a year. Organized crime syndicates auctioned their "goods" to Middle East buyers, and many of their abductions took place in the United States where they preyed on runaways, kids who lived on the streets. And it wasn't just slavery for prostitution. Porn sites and peep shows on the Net gave a pretty good idea of what those poor kids—both boys and girls—were forced to do.

The U.S. government knew all about Yao's human trafficking operation. Hell, his was one of hundreds. It was a sad and sorry truth that of the thousands of Americans who disappeared every year, many of them ended up victimized by men like Yao. And while there was an ongoing effort to recover those people, these bastards knew how to make them disappear. Just like Crystal's lost girl. If he decided to, Yao could bury her so deep in the quagmire of his prostitution ring, she'd never be heard from again.

It made Johnny sick. It made him do crazy things like cave to a pair of sad green eyes. Yeah. She'd gotten to him. She'd begged him to at least ask his boss for help. So he was asking. And she was in the shower hoping.

"So you're wanting a team. In Jakarta. To try to find one girl."

Another deep breath. "That about sums it up, yeah."

"You know that's not going to happen," Nate said.

Yeah, Johnny knew. He'd known when he called. "I promised I'd see what I could do, okay? Now I've done it. I can deliver the bad news with a clear conscience."

"Get your ass back here, Reed."

"Roger that."

He disconnected, dragged his hands over his face, feeling as tired as if he'd just run a marathon. Then he

called Sam so he'd know they were okay and so Abbie
would quit worrying and he could relay Crystal's message about not contacting her parents.

After he hung up, he glanced toward the bathroom,
heard the sound of water running, and seriously considered stripping down to the skin and joining Crystal in
the shower. At least it would make them both feel better.

Guilt, however, won out over pleasure. He needed
to stay clear of her. She was beaten down if not beaten
up, and the news he had to deliver wasn't going to help
a damn bit. She'd been kidnapped, drugged, starved
and—well, God knew what else Yao had done to her.
She'd told him she was fine, that Yao hadn't touched
her. Didn't negate the fact that he would have if
Johnny hadn't gotten her out of there when he did. Or
that she'd thought she was going to die in Yao's vile little den of iniquity. The last thing she needed right now
was the likes of him coming on to her.

He walked to the bathroom door, cracked it open a
few inches, resisting the urge to peek inside. "Crystal?
I'm going out for a little bit. Don't open the door to
anyone but me, okay? I'll be right back."

She needed some clean clothes before she could go
out in public even if it was just to board the next flight
home. Hell, so did he, he thought, digging into his go bag
for a fresh T-shirt and a pair of pants. He was damn weary
of smelling like a flower. Eau de whorehouse just didn't
spell badass in his book and he seriously doubted he'd
convince any of Yao's thugs that he was a threat if he ran
into them again and they got a whiff of him.

He pocketed the Butterfly he'd taken off the gang-banger, slipped the Glock into his waistband at the small of his back, and covered it with his shirt. Then he headed out shopping.

For girly things.

Size sexy.

He found a small shop down the block from the hotel that was open twenty-four/seven and started pawing through a rack of lacy panties. God save him if Lang ever found out about this.

Half an hour later, carrying a sackful of "girl stuff," Johnny let himself back into the hotel room—and damn near tripped over his tongue when he saw Crystal.

A light burned by the bed. Dim, but enough to spotlight her there.

She was lying on her back. Sound asleep. Clean. Sweet smelling. But for the white bath towel strategically draped over some places he was particularly taken with, she was as naked as the day was long.

A ceiling fan spun lazily overhead, stirring tufts of short red silk around her face, permeating the air with her scent.

"Down, boy," he muttered as his hair-trigger dick rose to the occasion.

He rolled his tongue back into his mouth, sucked in a bracing breath, and headed straight for the shower where he seriously considered a little hand-to-dick combat to arrest the situation.

"What? Are you friggin' thirteen?" Disgusted with himself, he stepped into the shower.

He was and always would be all about control. While he loved some serious sack time with the right woman, it was the head on his shoulders, not the one in his pants that always led the charge.

Except when it came to Crystal. Then, apparently, all bets were off.

"Just worry about the way you smell, flower boy," he muttered, and shampooed and scrubbed until his chest felt raw.

He stayed in the shower until the water ran cold. Then he stood there a while longer. Hiding like a schoolboy who had a crush on the teacher and felt guilty about sneaking a peek down her dress.

"Get a damn grip," he growled, shutting off the faucet with a hard twist.

Still, he took his time toweling dry before stepping back into his cammo pants, commando. He lifted the shirt, stopped and sniffed. Hell. Flowers. He should have waited until after he showered to put on something clean. Too late to worry about that now.

He pulled the shirt over his head, wiped the steam from the vanity mirror with his towel, and did a double take. He looked like a damn hippie. Hair too long, five o'clock shadow times ten. Couldn't be helped. He finger-combed his hair away from his face and on a deep breath, stepped out of the steamy bathroom.

He lasted all of a second before he cut a glance to the bed. And, man oh man, he was totally and royally screwed.

She'd rolled over on her stomach and the towel

hadn't made the trip. He had a peeping Tom's eye view of her adorable little tush, all compact and kissable, with sexy twin dimples framing that silky, sensitive place at the small of her back, and that cute little Tinkerbell tattoo riding on her left shoulder.

She'd thrown her arms straight out to the side and the round of her breast plumped up full and delectable against the mattress. With only a little imagination and a pleasant memory, he could envision the tight peak of her nipple.

Then she stirred, shifted, hiked a knee up, and rolled to her side, facing him and he no longer needed his imagination.

Well, hell. Give a guy a break.

Or a condom, he thought, suppressing a groan as he stared at her and ole trigger-dick did its thing.

Instant hard-on.

He was lower than road tar.

But hell, show him a red-blooded heterosexual male who wouldn't react, he thought in self-defense. The first time he'd seen Crystal Debrowski, the words "sex kitten" had sprung to mind. Nothing about her had dispelled that assessment since.

She was hot in the sack, adventurous as hell, and the things she could do with her mouth had reduced him to begging, groaning, and on one occasion, unabashed weeping for joy.

For such a little person, she had the most amazing breasts. He'd initially figured them for fake, they were so round and lush and perfect. Wrong. The first time he'd held them in his hands, tasted them with his tongue, he'd known there wasn't an ounce of silicone or saline implanted beneath her creamy skin. Just like the neat thatch of curls between her thighs had confirmed that she was nature-made and a natural redhead. Talk about a turn-on.

Talk about bad timing.

She picked that moment—that *exact* moment—to roll completely over on her back and, *hello*, that way lay heaven.

Only he was going to hell if he so much as took a step toward the bed.

He should . . . go. He should march out into the hall, sit his ass down in front of the door, and lead himself not into temptation. But he was frozen in place. He'd be damned if he could look away. He knew what that lush body felt like beneath his. Knew her skin was as soft as silk, the downy curls between her thighs—whoa! Wait.

He squinted. Took a long look. There were no downy curls between her thighs.

His heart ramped up to about 200 mph.

The little imp had gone Brazilian.

Damn him for a sinner but the thoughts that zinged through his mind would make the roof of a church cave in on him.

Thoughts like: *She better have done that with me in mind because I'm not letting anyone with a set of balls near her ever again.*

Thoughts like: *Mine. Mine and mine.*

Which proved once and for all that he was sleep deprived and not firing on all cylinders. He didn't make claims on a woman. Not ever. Too complicated. Too messy.

Too . . . scary, but he wasn't going there now.

Now he had to reel himself back in and remember why he was here. He'd come here to save her, not seduce her, and while some might question his ethics, he lived by a set of ground rules when it came to scoring with women.

One, they had to be willing. Two, they had to know the score. And, oh yeah, three, they had to be conscious.

"You gonna stand there all night or are you going to come over here?"

He jerked his gaze to her face. She was awake. And smiling.

Well, hell. That took care of the ground rules. She was three for three. His for the taking. And while he'd damn himself for a fool later, he just couldn't do it. Not here. Not now, not after what she'd been through.

He forced a smile. "Let's um . . . let's just let cooler heads prevail, okay?"

A furrow formed between her brows. She hiked herself up on an elbow and Lord oh Lord, the sway of her breasts almost did him in. "Cooler heads?"

He swallowed. Hard. Dug deep for restraint. "You've been through a lot."

She actually smiled at that. "Aren't you just the master of understatement?"

"Yeah. Well. I'm just sayin'. You might be, um . . . I don't know. Looking for . . ." He held up a hand, searching for the right words, uncomfortable with the way she was looking at him. Like his sudden stab at decency was beyond her to comprehend and it tickled the hell out of her.

"Looking for love in all the wrong places?" she suggested finally.

Close enough. More likely she was looking for comfort. "Yeah. Sure. Whatever. Something like that."

Stupid. He felt so stupid. And inadequate and totally out of his element. Johnny Reed did not make a habit of trumping up reasons *not* to have sex. Apparently, that's why he was so bad at it.

"I'm just trying to be a little sensitive here," he said, willing his gaze to stay on her face instead of stray down that lush, curvy body that she, all of a sudden, wanted to serve him on a platter.

Brazilian.

God in heaven, help him.

"You *have* been through a lot. I don't want you to be sorry, you know . . . later."

She stared at him long and hard, like she couldn't decide what to make of him. Hell. He couldn't even figure it out, how the hell was she supposed to?

"Why, Johnny Duane." Her expression softened. "I may have misjudged you. There seems to actually be a trace of integrity beneath that glossy blond exterior."

He eyed her skeptically. "That was a dig, right?"

She smiled, soft and sexy and damn, really sweet. "I

didn't mean to be, no. You just surprised me, that's all. In a good way."

He wasn't used to surprising women in a good way. His usual kind of surprise was, "Sorry, gotta go now." Or, "Sure. I'll call." But, *surprise*—he rarely did.

It was different, this sensation of feeling good about doing the right thing where a woman was concerned. Not that he was one of those mean bastards who got a charge out of hurting a woman. He always left before it got to the point where he could hurt them. At least he tried to. Just like he was trying his damnedest to do the right thing now. That included putting off telling her about Nate's unqualified "No" to sending in a team to rescue Dina.

"Okay. Well, I guess I'll go take a walk or something." In the dark. In the rain, he realized as he heard the unmistakable patter of raindrops on the window. He turned toward the door.

"Stay," she said in a voice that could not be mistaken for anything but, *stay and come to bed with me*.

How much was a man supposed to take? He turned around slowly. Took one more stab at being decent. "You don't really want this."

She sat up, tucked her feet beneath her bare bottom, and he died a hundred deaths with the effort of staying exactly where he was.

"What I want," she said, her eyes somber and serious, suddenly, "is to feel the power in making my own choice. Yao took that away from me—at least he tried. What I want," she said, coming up on her knees and holding out her hands toward him, "is to have someone touch me, who I want to touch me.

"What I want," she continued, her fairy green eyes drawing him in like a tether, "is for you to make me forget that I almost had that taken away from me forever."

Heart rioting with feelings he couldn't identify and didn't understand, he gave it up. Threw in the towel. Stomped on the land mine.

He closed the gap between them, linked his fingers with hers.

"And what I need, right now, is you." Eyes locked on his, she leaned in toward him. Whispered against his lips. "Make me remember how it feels to forget about any moment but now. Right now."

It was all over for him then. The denial. The attempt to do the right thing.

The right thing was directly in front of him, inundating him with emotions that were as foreign to him as surrender. That's what this felt like. Surrender—only in a good way—to this small, strong woman who knew what she wanted, knew what she needed, and the name she gave both was, him.

She wanted *him*.

Needed *him*.

The responsibility humbled him.

He'd never been more to a woman than simple pleasure. Never been more than a good time and great sex. And yeah, he and Crystal had shared both. But this . . . this was bigger. Bigger than anything he'd ever taken on.

It scared the hell out of him. He knew he should leave, but he didn't want to go anywhere but closer to her.

The woman moved him. With her candor. With her trust.

As she leaned into him, pressed her warm, pliant breasts against his chest and sighed his name, he understood that this was exactly where he wanted to be, too.

She reached for the hem of his shirt, then lifted, shucking it up and over his head. "One of us," she whispered, moving back in to his mouth, "isn't nearly naked enough."

She set about rectifying that situation. He sucked in his breath, and his ab muscles contracted when her busy fingers went to work on the zipper of his pants.

"Um . . . careful, darlin', *one of us* has gotten a little too big for his britches. Gonna take a little finesse to dodge any serious injury."

She smiled against his mouth, then sat back on her pretty little bare feet again so she could see what she was doing.

Sweet heaven. Would you look at her?

Naked and lush, there on her knees, her thick lashes lowered as she watched her fingers slowly unbutton, then carefully unzip and finally free him. His fly fell open and she slowly pushed his pants down his hips.

"Better," she said with a smile that made his knees weak, then nearly buckle when she took his engorged cock in her hands and gently caressed. Then bold as brass, she leaned into him, flicked the tip of her tongue over the swollen head.

He sucked in his breath. Barely managed to remember his name let alone say hers. "Crystal. You don't need to—"

"I do," she whispered, pressing a whisper-soft kiss against his pulsing flesh. "I really, really need to."

8

Johnny lost the ability to speak altogether when she drew him into her mouth and enveloped him in wet, suctioning heat.

She was on her knees as he stood before her, her position submissive, his dominant, yet all the power in this act belonged to her. And she wielded that power ruthlessly.

He buried his hands in her hair and let her destroy him with sensation. Blind him with indescribable pleasure. And God oh God, she humbled him with her generosity even as she controlled him with her relentless assault. This wasn't just about sex, he realized, although, *damn*, it felt like it and *daaaamn*, it felt amazing.

This was about freedom. Hers. He felt it with every stroke of her tongue, with every throaty sound of possession as she dug her fingers into his buttocks and drew him closer, giving and taking and shooting him way beyond sanity and headlong into complete and ultimate capitulation.

Mine, he thought again, and driven by an unqualified need to possess, he hooked his hands under her arms, lifted her up, and dragged her hard against him. Then he devoured her mouth with his.

She became a wild thing in his arms. Squirming and clinging and desperately taking all and everything he was willing to give.

Their mouths clashed, teeth collided. Her nails dug into his back. Her hands demanded closer. He'd never seen her this way. He'd seen her petulant and playful, languid and sweet. But he'd never seen her desperate.

And desolate, he finally realized.

That's what this was *really* about. She was filled with despair. Yao had done this to her. He'd stolen her sense of security. Destroyed her sense of control.

She wanted it back. And she wanted *him* to give it back to her. *Demanded* that he give it back to her.

No problem. At this moment, more than anything in the world, that's exactly what he wanted to do.

He fell back with her onto the bed, twisted until he was flat on his back, supplicant, willing and ready to take anything she wanted to dish out.

She wanted plenty.

She straddled his hips, pressed her palms, against his shoulders and pinned him to the mattress.

"Tell me you've got protection in your go bag."

It took him a full five seconds to shift his focus from her magnificent breasts to the subject at hand. "Protection. Right. Protection."

He twisted at the hip, holding her in place with one

hand as he groped over the side of the bed toward the floor until he located his bag. A few seconds of fumbling around inside finally produced a strip of foil packets.

She snatched them out of his hand, ripped one open, and, holy mother of God, she suited him up and almost had him coming in her hand. But she was far from finished with him. She made it her mission then to tempt and torment and drive him flat-out frigging wild. She leaned over his mouth, offered up her breasts, cried out when he nipped greedily at a pebbled nipple and drew it hungrily into his mouth, suckling and soothing away the tiny pain.

She was wet and slick when she positioned herself over the head of his cock and slowly lowered herself down, inch by tantalizing inch.

Tight. She was so tight and hot and wet. And that surrender thing? Wasn't happening. Not now. Now was about taking, giving, celebrating the wonder of her body and the meshing of their desire.

He gripped her hips, lifted, brought her down against him with a sharp, hard plunge. Her breath caught, his exploded in harsh, labored puffs as he guided her up and down in a fast and frenzied race to complete the physical and emotional release that had driven them to this place. This place where rich and rare fell short of describing the sensations she evoked with her sighs. The electric friction she created with her body. The unexplainable sense of rightness the two of them made in this bed.

She fought release, fought it with everything in her,

but in the end it finally won. She came with a cry, and a long, delicious shudder that enveloped him in the power of her climax and triggered his own like a rifle blast. When she clenched around him, he shot into her in a mad, consuming arc of sensation that eclipsed anything he'd thought he could feel. It lasted forever, this extraordinary explosion of physical euphoria that only a woman could give to a man.

That only *this* woman could give to him.

Yeah, it lasted forever—and not nearly long enough.

When it was all over but the ragged, gasping breaths and the erratic heartbeats, and she'd collapsed, wringing wet on his chest, he wrapped his arms around her, held her tight.

She fell asleep that way. Sweat-drenched and languid. Hugging him tight, all trusting and wasted and sweet.

It took a while for his head to clear of the amazing physical sensations that had reduced him to a mass of rubber limbs and melted bones. But when the cobwebs finally parted, he stared long and hard at the ceiling, trying like hell to outdistance the feelings churning around in his chest.

New feelings he suspected he'd been running from his entire life. They were knee-jerk and powerful—and they scared him more than a hired assassin ever could. They were also more dangerous than an ambush.

A soft little purr puffed her lips where her cheek rested against his shoulder. And the feelings intensified.

He hugged her closer, his reaction involuntary. As necessary, in that moment, as breathing.

Mine, he thought again, then immediately felt a disturbing flicker of alarm.

Jesus, what the hell had he gone and done?

You're falling for her, dickweed.

Panic, flat-out, full-bore, and heart-thumping had his head spinning.

No chance. No way.

He was just tired. That's all.

He was riding the downside of edgy over getting her out of Yao's lair.

Falling for her? Hell, no. It was laughable, right? Johnny Reed didn't fall in love. Not for real. And he knew exactly why because he knew exactly what he had to offer a woman long-term. The same thing his old man had. Nothing. Nothing but grief because that's all the old man ever gave out, and for as long as Johnny remembered he'd been told he was the apple that hadn't fallen far from Les Reed's tree.

A no-good piece of shit. That's what the old man had called him. That's what everyone had called him. So that's what he'd set out to be.

He'd been damn good at it, too. Damn good at fooling people with his big cocky grins and don't-give-a-fuck attitude. He knew exactly what people had seen when they looked at him then, when they looked at him now. Eye candy. A pretty, petty boy with an ego the size of an Abrahams tank. It was an image he perpetuated. And it was an impression that always worked to his advantage—both professionally and personally—as most people tended to underestimate him because of it. And because hell, who would want to know the real him, anyway?

That's why he'd learned to be a chameleon at an early age—learned to hide his true feelings behind his cocksure grin and belligerent swagger. When you grew up with an old man who liked to knock you around and a mother too mired in her own self-destruction to notice that her child wore more bruises than she did, you learned to fake, you learned to cope. You learned real fast. A crack on the side of the head was a great educator. He'd had plenty of lessons.

But most of all, he'd learned to hide the pain. And to prove, at least to himself, that he was more than a punching bag and a source of disappointment for his old man.

That's where the marines had come in. It was either that or a stint in juvenile detention, so hell. It was in the marines that he'd proven the old man wrong. At least where it counted.

Yeah. He had fought for his country. He still fought. But be something good for a woman? He glanced at Crystal's sleeping face. Not a chance in hell.

Okay. Time to regroup. He gently pried her clinging little body off of his. Eased carefully off the bed so he wouldn't wake her.

When they got back to the States, he'd screw his head back on straight, because man, she had twisted it sidewise. He hadn't thought about his old man in years.

Hadn't felt that hollow fear in his gut, that self-loathing since, hell, he didn't know how long. It was all behind him. He'd worked through it. Until Crystal. Specifically, until Crystal had made him think about how he'd always felt like less back then and had been trying to prove he was more ever since.

Screw that. He didn't have anything to prove to anyone. And until he got her back to the States, he wasn't thinking about anything but keeping her safe. Starting now, it was back to business. No more messing around, he promised himself as he stepped into his pants. No more thinking he knew where her head or her heart was. Maybe she'd had a moment of confusion, too. She'd needed to let off a little steam, that was all. He'd been a handy release valve. That was the name of that tune and the end of the song.

He dug around in his bag for a tube of antibiotic salve he always carried, then carefully applied a liberal amount to the raw brand on her wrist. She flinched once but didn't wake up. Then he snagged a pillow off the bed and lay down on the floor beside it. He left the light on in case she woke up and was disoriented. And he didn't think about her naked, fragrant body curled up alone, without him in the middle of that big, spacious bed. He didn't think about that delicate little Tinkerbell tattoo on her bare shoulder that so exemplified who she was.

'Cause he wasn't going there again. Nowhere *near* there again. He was going to get her home safe and sound, then he was going to go on about his business. Game over.

She whimpered in her sleep.

He flew to his feet in a shot, saw a single tear track down her cheek. He stared for all of two seconds.

"Fuck it."

He turned off the light. Then he lay back down on the bed, pulled her into his arms, and absorbed her sigh of relief as she snuggled trustingly into him before drifting off into contented, blissful slumber.

He didn't blissfully do anything.

But he did quit fighting the one thing that seemed to be the ultimate truth in this untenable situation he'd gotten himself into.

Mine.

Yeah. Whether she liked it or not, she was his. And Lord help them both if when this was over, she didn't have the good sense to send him the hell away.

It was daylight when Crystal walked out of the bathroom, dressed, *thank you, God,* in the yellow tank top and khaki pants he'd bought her earlier. All things considered, he hadn't missed her size by much. The short tank was a little snug over her generous breasts but the pants were a tad baggy and a bit long—she'd rolled up the cuffs—so he figured one balanced out the other. He didn't want to know how the panties and bra fit. Just like he didn't want to remember that the bra was white and a little lacy and that the panties matched and that he'd bought them fighting thoughts about watching her take them off.

"Did you ever hear back from your boss?" she asked,

walking to the bed, then sitting cross-legged on the mattress where she applied another dose of salve to her wrist.

He'd been dreading this. Had put it off as long as he dared. "Yeah. About that. I'm sorry. It's a no-go."

Her finger stilled over her wrist. Her green eyes were somber and accusing as she looked at him.

He dragged a hand through his hair. "Look. I tried, okay? I'll make that call to the embassy. Right now they're her best hope."

"Dina. Her name is Dina, not *her*," she said, each word threaded with anger. "She's a real living person. Dina. Dina Stornello. She has a mom and a dad somewhere. Maybe a sister or a brother—"

"Whoa." He held up a hand, cut her off as a tight curl of apprehension merged with a memory of a briefing some, hell, five, six months ago. He struggled through the defrag process in his brain until his thoughts finally reassembled into something tangible. "Stornello? You said Dina Stornello?"

"Yeah." She sat up straight. "What? What is it? Do you know who she is?"

"Shit," he muttered. He reached for his phone and punched in Nate's number again. "Holy shit."

"Johnny—"

He cut her off again with a shake of his head, let the phone ring twice, then hung up.

"What's going on?" She eyed him with equal measures of confusion and expectation.

"What's going on is that Dina Stornello isn't just any

abducted girl. Man, oh man," he muttered. "I can't believe this. It's like winning the frickin' lottery of coincidence. Dina Stornello is the daughter of a three-star general, Crystal. Every alphabet agency on the Hill has been looking for her for the past six months. She and the general got in a big row one day and she took off. She's never been heard from since."

His phone rang before he could tell her any more. "Nate," he said by way of greeting. "You are not going to fuckin' believe this."

"Let me make some calls," Nate said several tense moments later following Johnny's sketchy account of Crystal's run-in with U.S. Army General Fitzgerald Stornello's daughter. "In the meantime, get her on a flight out of there, then get your ass back to Jakarta and lay low until you hear from me."

"So?" Crystal asked when he disconnected.

"He's workin' on it."

"On a way to get Dina," she concluded.

"Yeah. On that."

She looked at once relieved and sullen.

"You don't exactly look pleased. Isn't this what you wanted?"

She busied her hands by rerolling the cuff on her pants. "It's not right. I mean, yes, I'm glad someone is going to help Dina, but it's not right that it takes being the daughter of someone important to make it happen. What if she wasn't a general's daughter? She'd be as good as lost. That's wrong. That's just . . . wrong."

"Yeah," he agreed. "It's wrong. But the world's gone

'round for years on the old 'it's not what you know but who you know' axiom. And no. It doesn't make it right. Just makes it real."

Speaking of real, now that the excitement had settled to a dull roar, something else was eating at him. In the aftermath of the storm over Dina Stornello, not word one had been exchanged between them about their mind-blowing, life-altering, earth-moving session in that same bed not more than two hours ago.

He didn't know if he was relieved or disappointed about that. But it hadn't been too far from his mind that she hadn't said a word when she'd awakened. She'd simply stretched, all contented and catlike, smiled sleepily and grabbing her towel, headed for the bathroom. That had been about fifteen minutes ago.

"So what happens next?" she asked, perching on the edge of the bed and trying on the sandals he'd bought her. They were brown leather, flat soles, as close to hiking sandals as he could find.

He didn't kid himself into thinking she was asking about what happened next between them. She was asking about the Dina situation.

He shrugged. "Back to Jakarta."

"Great. When do we leave?"

"*We* don't. *You're* taking the next flight to the States."

9

Crystal's head jerked up. "What? Wait. No. I'm going with you."

Johnny started tossing things into his go bag. "Not gonna happen."

"You think I can't help?"

He could whitewash it but what was the point? This was an operation for the BOIs. Precision. Scalpel-sharp. No novices allowed. Besides, he didn't feel like whitewashing anything. His nose was about two cocks out of joint because she was still acting like nothing had happened between them but a hand-shake. "I *know* you can't help. These are bad people, Crystal."

"Yeah, I figured that out when they attacked me in my apartment."

He chose to ignore her sarcasm. "Then you should also be able to figure out that I just got you out from under Yao's thumb. I've got no intention of letting him get near you again."

"I can handle myself. I can *handle* a gun."

For some reason, that didn't surprise him. "Yay for you. You're still not going."

"I'm a black belt. I could drop you like a bag of dirt if I wanted to."

That made him smile. "When pigs fly."

She sprang off the bed, squared off in a defensive stance.

"Karate. Good for you. You're still not going."

"Give me your best shot." She made "come-on" motions with her fingers.

He grunted and turned back to his bag. "Yeah, that's not gonna happen either."

She moved in fast, clipped him behind the knees with a hard kick, and knocked him off balance before adding a series of chops, spins, and hacks that took him down. Stunned, he lay flat on his back, counting the cracks in the ceiling. She hadn't hurt him but she'd shocked the hell out of him.

"You were saying?"

He glared from the ceiling to her smug face as she stood over him, dusting her hands together like she'd just finished a dirty job. He didn't know what pissed him off more. The fact that he'd let her surprise him or the fact that she still hadn't said anything about their naked, horizontal tango and that her silence about it ticked him off.

"Don't make me hurt you," he said.

"I'm going to Jakarta," she insisted, ignoring his anger and recognizing his idle threat for what it was.

"Look," she continued, then jumped back when he rocked to his hips and sprang to his feet. "How are you going to get me out of the country anyway? Have you thought about that? No passport. No ID. And what if I did somehow manage to get back to Vegas? What's to stop Yao from coming after me again? Don't you get it? This isn't just about rescuing Dina. This is about stopping Yao from doing it again. It's about making that vile piece of crap pay for what he did to me. What he's doing to Dina and God knows how many other girls."

She had a point about the passport; it was a bridge he hadn't yet figured out how to cross. She also had a point about Yao. He would come after her again unless someone heavily impressed upon him the consequences of his lapse in judgment. It just so happened that part of Johnny's plan when he found the dirty bastard was to make sure Yao left Crystal alone.

"I want to be a part of taking him down," she continued, making her case. "I want to make certain he knows that if he ever comes after me again, it's going to be the last thing he ever does."

Jesus, she was something. Tinkerbell in Terminator mode. It had to defy some fairy code or something, didn't it?

"What are you grinning about?"

He held up his hands, penitent as hell. "I'm just trying to get a feel for this bloodthirsty side of your nature."

"Well, get used to it. I'm mad as hell."

"Yeah, I got that part." Just like he got the part that she was right. He couldn't send her home.

"So what part *didn't* you get?"

He clenched his jaw, angry, himself, suddenly. So he blurted out what had been bugging him way more than it should have. "The part about what happened between us in that bed."

She blinked. Glanced from him to the bed in question and back at him. "What . . . about it?" she asked, more wary than curious.

"That's what I'm asking." He jutted out his chin, not knowing exactly why he felt like an injured party but pretty much wallowing in a sense of righteous anger. "What about it?"

She shrugged, and wariness gave over to a pretty good scowl of annoyance. "It was what it always is. Sex. *Great* sex."

He glared at her. Fine. Guess he had his answer. He tossed the last of his gear into his bag.

"Did I . . . I don't know . . . did I miss something?" she asked, a frown furrowing her brow.

After a long, searching look that confirmed he was the only one with a problem, he finally shook his head. "Not a damn thing," he grumbled, not even knowing what he'd expected her to say—what he'd wanted her to say. What? Had he thought she was going to tell him she loved him or something? Get real.

He didn't want anywhere near that word. Should have felt relief that she didn't either. And yet, he was pissed.

"Grab your stuff, tough guy," he muttered, avoiding her searching look because he sure as hell didn't have an explanation for her. He couldn't even explain it to himself. "We've got a train to catch."

* * *

Crystal didn't have much "stuff" and what "stuff" she did have, Reed had bought for her. She handed him the plastic shopping bag that contained a change of underwear and an extra T-shirt and pair of pants, then watched, silent, as he tucked it into his bag. And she didn't think about him buying that underwear or about the reason he'd done such a good job on the size was because he knew her body as intimately as she did. She just couldn't go there. Just like she couldn't go past the "great sex" part of their relationship. That way lay ten kinds of trouble.

He was angry. She got it, chalked it up to her winning the argument about going back to Jakarta and possibly dropping him on his back. She wasn't about to say something stupid and get him all riled up again and risk a change of heart.

So she didn't say a word. She just fell into step behind him when he stomped out of the hotel room and followed along like an obedient underling, hoping to score some subservience points. Big bad male ego notwithstanding, she figured he'd get over it.

Two hours into their train ride back to Jakarta, however, he was still brooding like a bull that'd lost his favorite cow. It took her the same two hours to admit that while she was the cause of his foul mood, his anger wasn't focused solely on the Jakarta issue or the takedown.

. . . *what happened between us in that bed.*

Yeah. She'd been avoiding that part of their conversation big-time. She wanted to deal with the expression on his face when she'd summed it up as, "Sex. Great sex," about as badly as he wanted her going with him back to Yao's territory. But she couldn't avoid thinking about it any longer. She'd hurt him. She didn't get it, but she *had* hurt him. It had been written right there on his face. Raw and real and heart wrenching.

As illogical as it seemed, as *impossible* as it seemed, it appeared that he'd been looking for a different answer. An answer that proclaimed what they'd shared had been about more than sex. It didn't make any sense—not coming from Johnny Reed.

Baffled, she stared out the window at the passing countryside while he pretended to doze in the seat beside her. They were getting closer to Jakarta. The subtle beauty of the rolling green countryside had gradually transitioned to the steeper hills and deeper valleys that she remembered from yesterday. In the far distance a crumpled line of mountain peaks rimmed the horizon. She would have enjoyed the ride—in truth Java was quite beautiful—if she hadn't known what lay ahead of them in Jakarta.

Then of course there was the mystery of Johnny Reed that was both unsettling and confusing. His silence didn't compute. She knew men like Reed—hell, she knew Reed—and too many of these men to count had breezed in and right back out of her life. Like them, Reed was a good-time boy. Smooth with a come-on, quick with a good-bye. She had a network of self-defense mechanisms auto-programmed to protect herself from getting hurt by men like him.

And yet, *she'd* hurt *him.*

She turned to look at him where he sat beside her, eyes closed and feigning sleep as the train rumbled down the rails. She stared at the scruffy perfection of his stunning face, at several days of stubble that added interesting texture and substance to his bold jawline. At thick blond lashes that touched his sculpted cheekbones, at a mouth that knew too much about giving pleasure.

Sex. Yeah. They had great sex but he knew, just like she knew, that it stopped and ended right there. She made sure of it. She always made sure of it because damn and damn again she knew that if she ever let her guard down and fell for this man, she'd never recover when he left her.

And he would leave. History didn't lie. Men like Reed always left.

So yeah, she thought, tearing her gaze away from potentially the biggest heartbreak of her life, what happened in that bed had been about sex. It hadn't been about getting back her confidence. It hadn't been about needing him to be the one to help her. And it hadn't been about wanting his arms and only his arms holding her together so she wouldn't fall apart because, damn, she'd been as close to coming unglued as she'd ever been in her life.

No. It hadn't been any of that because she wouldn't let it be.

Just like she couldn't let herself believe what she thought she'd seen in his eyes, what she'd thought she'd heard in his voice. She hadn't hurt him. She'd just imagined it.

Just like when he held her, when he kissed her, when he made her feel like she was the only woman on earth for him, she'd let herself imagine—for one foolish moment in time—that it was true.

"Explain."

Wong Li stood before his master, head bowed in disgrace. It had been a full twenty-four hours after the Debrowski woman had escaped before he'd been summoned. Twenty-four hours in which he'd tried to find answers and had come up with no explanation.

"It would seem she had assistance from outside," he stated.

Yao Long sat behind a black lacquered desk in judgmental silence. "An army?" he asked finally.

Li swallowed, keeping his head bowed, accepting that his life was about to end. "Only one man." He had questioned the guard after extracting nothing useful from Cahya. That guard had since died by Wong Li's hand. As Li was prepared to die by his master's hand.

He waited as Mr. Yao rose and walked around his desk. He was resigned to the knowledge that he would soon join his ancestors. Expected to hear anything but what his master finally said.

"Find her."

"It ain't much, but for now, it's home." Johnny unlocked the door to a small, shabby hotel room on the north side of Jakarta and after checking it out, let Crystal step inside ahead of him.

She'd started to think they were never going to find something to suit him. He'd driven around looking for just the right place for over an hour in the rental car they'd picked up at the train station. "Just the right place" had the appearance of the worn, cut-rate "no-tell motels" dotting the streets far off the Vegas Strip.

Johnny had given her the requirements as they'd searched. One, the hotel had to be inconspicuous and off the main path and two, it had to have ground-floor rooms with off-street parking directly outside the door. The Hotel Anggrek—which meant orchid, Johnny told her—fit the bill although the bloom had long been off its flower.

Crystal looked on as he tossed his bag onto the nearest of the twin beds. *Twin* beds. She didn't think it was a co-incidence. Just like she didn't want to think about anything other than getting to Dina and making Yao Long sorry he ever heard her name. She especially didn't want to think about what had happened in that last bed.

Even if she did slip up and let this tension between them get to her, she'd never let Johnny know it. She considered herself a master when it came to masking her emotions. A quick smile. A catchy comeback. "The Debrowski Dodge" is how Abbie referred to it. Yep. Crystal had it perfected. During the train ride from Bandung to Jakarta, however, she'd learned that compared to Reed, she was a mere amateur when it came to avoidance. He'd been as distant as the Vegas Strip.

Except for a decided lack of flirting, he was at least talking to her now, even though he'd shifted into operative mode. That was probably a good thing all around. It kept her from thinking about what had happened in that bed. And it kept her from going into a panic mode, which would so not complement his mind-set.

She was scared. She'd never admit it to him, and she would not let it stop her, but the idea of being back in Jakarta, of going after Yao and looking for Dina scared her to death. Yeah, she talked big about shooting guns and her prowess at karate, and she was confident of her skills, but the thought of actually using them, for real, was terrifying.

All she had to do though, was think about Dina, about the horror she'd been through and would continue to go through, and a little case of cold feet seemed a small price to pay in comparison. She wanted to help Dina. She needed to help Dina, and she would not sit back like a wilted little flower and let the "boys" do all the heavy lifting.

"We'll set up base here," Johnny said, breaking into her thoughts. "Put some things in place while we're waiting for reinforcements to arrive."

He'd gotten a call from his boss when they'd stepped off the train. It had been a long conversation but he had yet to share the details with her. All she knew for certain was that more men were on the way and that those "things" he wanted to put in place had to do with cameras. She'd picked that up when they'd checked in as Mr. and Mrs. John Brown again and he'd asked the desk clerk, who wanted to practice his English, about the closest camera shop.

Because he was not happy about her being here, she'd been trying to keep a low profile. Curiosity, however, got the best of her. "So who are these reinforcements?"

"I'll fill you in as we go. Let's roll."

His game. His rules. She didn't ask him again as they got into their rental and headed off to the camera shop.

"We need eyes on the target area," Johnny said as they left the shop with two digital cameras equipped with zoom lenses: 80–400mm with 2× teleconverters which, he told her, doubled their strength.

She had to assume that the target was the building where Yao had kept her prisoner.

"How do we know Dina's still there?"

"We don't," he said, "but we've got no reason to think he moved her. It's Yao's playground, right?"

She shivered at the memory of her temporary prison, of Yao's total disregard for basic human rights. "Yeah. It's his playground."

"Then it stands to reason that he'd keep his toys close by—only under tighter security than he kept you. She's there, Crystal. He has no reason to move her."

Because Dina was nothing more than a toy to Yao, Crystal thought, revolted all over again by how close she had come to suffering the same fate.

"If we had the time and I could get my hands on

them, we'd position some wireless Web cams," he said
as they got back into the rental, "hook them up to a laptop, and watch who comes and who goes out of Yao's
warehouse. But we don't have the time, the equipment, or the manpower."

Since he was finally opening up a little, she decided
to try again. "Okay, I know you're being extra cautious
but why the big production? Why don't we just go in
and grab her like you grabbed me?"

"Because lightning doesn't generally strike twice. I
was damn lucky to get you out of there. That luck
won't hold again. The only reason it worked was because Yao wasn't expecting anyone would come after
you that soon—if he expected anyone to come at all.
Think about it. He set you up for a fall at the casino,
right? Got you arrested, then bailed you out. My guess
is he figured that since he snatched you right away, the
LVPD would peg you as a skip and if they looked for
you anywhere, it would be in the States, not halfway
across the globe. Yao also didn't figure on me," he
added.

That made two of us, Crystal thought.

"Now he knows different," he went on. "He
knows that whoever came after you isn't your aver-
age everyday accountant. And while he might not
figure we'll come back for Dina, he's going to beef
up security because he's pissed that someone took
his property."

It made sense. Just like it made sense that they spent
the rest of the hot, sultry day sweating and proving that

Johnny was right. Yao had brought in extra men to guard the building.

Varying their route, they drove by Yao's building with Johnny at the wheel and Crystal slumped down in the passenger seat, snapping photos from every angle and distance possible. They spotted guards all over the place. At one point they parked in an alley and sat there four hours watching trucks and men come and go, both of them taking photos. Twice during the day, they returned to the rental car agency and exchanged vehicles for different makes and models.

"A precaution," Johnny said. "I don't want anyone getting suspicious about the same car cruising the street."

With the city traffic bumper to bumper, Crystal couldn't imagine anyone picking them out from the crowd, but he was the expert so she didn't argue. Eighteen hours later, she had a real-time picture of what true surveillance was all about. Repetition, boredom, and exhaustion.

Just like she had a new appreciation for Johnny Reed. She'd seen him flirty, she'd seen him in warrior mode, she'd seen him sullen. This was a new side of him—all business, precise, focused—and she was impressed by his single-minded dedication and competence.

Didn't mean that a dozen times during that long day of surveillance, however, she hadn't thought about broaching the subject of what had happened in that bed. A dozen times, she'd cut herself off. Fear, she realized, stopped her. What if he said forget about it? What if he said she'd misunderstood the disappointment she'd thought she'd heard in his voice? Or what if he said something else? Something to the tune of wanting more than just sex from her? She didn't know which response would scare her most. And in the end, she opted to just let it go. Because of fear.

This was crazy. While she'd thought that a serious Johnny Duane Reed might be something she wanted to see, when actually faced with it, that idea scared her, too. If he got serious, then she might have to get serious, too, and man, she just wasn't ready to go there. Not with a man like him.

So when they finally made it back to their sweltering hotel room, not a single, serious word about what had happened between them in that bed had been spoken. Johnny headed straight for the shower, went to bed, and doused the lights.

What? she wondered. No "night-night, sleep tight, wanna fool around?" from the king of the sexual conquest? Fine. That was just fine with her. Sort of.

She washed off the sweat and grime of the day with her own shower, then punched her pillow and settled in. But as she lay there, alone in the dark, the night seemed horribly bleak and the man much farther distant than the three feet separating their beds. For all of a very long moment, she finally considered saying something. Something like, "Look. About what happened in Bandung. I lied. It was more than sex, okay? Maybe . . . maybe we should talk about it."

Before she could work up the nerve though, she realized he was asleep.

Saved by the snore.

She rolled over to her side, facing away from him, not knowing if she was relieved or vastly disappointed.

10

Holy sacred cow. Crystal leaned back against the headboard of her bed the next morning and steeled herself against the influx of testosterone that had just been injected into the small hotel room.

The reinforcements had arrived a few minutes ago and now she knew exactly who they were: Luke Colter, Wyatt Savage, Joe Green, and none other than Nathan Black, the head of the organization Johnny worked for, filled the small hotel room with broad shoulders, edgy expectancy, and that testosterone thing that was darn near overwhelming.

She still didn't know exactly what Black's organization was, but she did know one thing with absolute certainty: these guys weren't your run-of-the-mill security team. Her dad had always been her hero. He was strong, he was tough, he was the epitome of a good, honest cop. But these men brought an even bigger element to the playing field. They were Sam Lang caliber. Johnny Reed caliber. And if anyone could get Dina out of Yao's clutches, it would be them.

A slow-moving ceiling fan stirred air that, already this morning, was hot and humid and stagnant. The four men joined Johnny where they huddled around a laptop Black had brought with him, viewing the slide show of the digital surveillance photos she and Johnny had taken the day before. Pretty much all Crystal did was stare at them and think, wow, I would hate to tick one of them off.

The first time she'd met Sam Lang, she'd recognized a quiet intensity about him that made her aware of an underlying strength that separated him from other men. He hadn't said word one and yet it had been apparent from the get-go that Sam had integrity and purpose and an understated aura of danger about him. These guys were cut from the same bolt of cloth.

She and Johnny hadn't talked a lot during their day of surveillance, and when they had, he'd given her abbreviated bios of each of the men who were on their way to Jakarta so she'd have a feel for who they were when they arrived.

Luke Colter, aka Doc Holliday, was tall, lean, and she'd already discovered, quick with a grin. He was a former navy SEAL and the team medic. He arrived with the medical kit to prove it, and the buff, tough body of a man who knew his way around a gym—or a minefield.

Wyatt "Papa Bear" Savage was former CIA. He was big and bulky and while she'd never say it to his face, kind of cuddly-looking. He was also all business, clearly intelligent and, as was apparent by the solid set of his jaw, unyielding even though his soft Southern drawl undercut the effect somewhat.

Joe Green. *Mean* Joe Green, Johnny had added. Like Savage, Green was former CIA. Apparently both Savage and Green had spent a tour or two in Indonesia in a past life and knew the language and the lay of the land. Crystal hadn't yet gotten a read on Green, other than that he was stoic, silent, and built like an ad for home gym equipment.

Then there was Nathan Black—none other than the big boss—himself. Tall, slim, fit, he was a little older than the rest of them, and it was apparent by the deference they showed him, he commanded every measure of their respect. In addition to running the operation in Argentina where Johnny and the rest of the men were based, it seemed that Black also assisted a doctor down there—a Juliana Flores—in an underground railroad of sorts where they rescued abducted children. Helping rescue Dina was right up his alley.

Yeah. Like Johnny, these men were an impressive force. Other than the telltale stubble on their jaws that said they'd been traveling for hours and the hard intensity of their gazes as they digested the facts about Dina Stornello's captor, you'd never know the four of them had just flown in from Italy and Argentina and the States. They had to be jet-lagged and exhausted. Clearly, however, it wasn't going to slow any one of them down.

"You've been busy," Colter, whom the lot of them referred to as Doc, said as he reviewed the photos.

"Not as much intel as I'd like but it's the best we could do with the time and equipment we had."

"Oh, what I wouldn't give for a blueprint of the building," Savage said with a grim look.

Johnny nodded. "In a perfect world where we had time, we'd have it."

This world, Crystal realized, was far from perfect. This world was dark and dangerous, and she'd wondered more than once just how far in over her head she was. It didn't matter. Even if she could, even if she wanted to, it was too late to run home to Vegas now.

"These'll help." When Black dug into his bag and came up with a thin stack of paper, Crystal's curiosity got the best of her. She joined the men at the table where they'd plugged in the laptop. "Satellite imagery of the rooftops. I pulled them off the computer before we went wheels-up. This"—he paused, got out a pen, and circled something on the top page—"is Yao's building."

It took her a while to figure out that she was staring at the roofs of a row of connecting buildings running the length of a block.

"Looks like a fire escape scaling the back of this one." Black pointed out the building next to Yao's. "Possible access point. It's three buildings away but the rooflines look level. Just in case they're not, though, we'd better pick up a grappling hook."

Green, apparently, was the list maker because he started writing things down.

"Do we know what floor she's on?" Doc asked.

"I'm thinking tenth," Johnny said. "That's where they were keeping Crystal."

Black turned to her. "What do you remember about the inside of the building?"

She shook her head. "Other than the room where he kept me and the stairwell we escaped down, not a thing."

"He kept her drugged," Johnny explained.

They'd all noticed the brand on her wrist, had no doubt drawn their own conclusions about what had happened to her.

Savage looked at Johnny. "So tell us what *you* know."

"Main floor looks like warehousing space even though it was empty when I grabbed Crystal. We saw a lot of trucks moving in and out yesterday, though, when we did our recon. When I went in after Crystal, I accessed the building by walking in the front door." Johnny continued, "That simple. Here." He pointed to the wide double sliding doors.

"No resistance?" Black sounded surprised.

"One guard who didn't get too lathered up when I just walked in, no guard outside the building then, and the door wasn't locked. It was locked when we left though, probably by the same guys who chased us down the stairs when we beat feet. And there are at least four guards stationed outside the doors now. Gotta figure a lot more inside.

"Anyway, this guy wasn't too bright. I told him I was lost. When he offered directions, I took him down for a nice little nap and shot up the interior stairs to the left of the door," he explained, "to the tenth floor."

"How did you know I was on the tenth floor?" Crystal simply hadn't thought to ask before.

His gaze lifted to hers. His jaw clenched. "I saw you."

"Through the wall of windows," she surmised out loud.

His eyes held hers and something in those blue, blue depths told her it wouldn't have mattered if she'd been in a building with one hundred floors, he would have run to the top to get her out.

It stunned her, that look. And it touched her in the part of her heart that she'd walled up to defend herself from pretty blue-eyed men like Johnny Reed. And God, oh God, was he pretty. Rough, tumble, focused, and intent, he was a study in intellect, intensity, and competence. There was no "play" in his expression now, and the gradual transition she'd witnessed over the past several hours, from fun-and-games mode to take-no-prisoners warrior, was at once impressive and disconcerting.

"What about the girl?" Black asked. "You think they're keeping her on the same floor?"

"Best guess, yeah." Johnny tore his gaze back to the photos slowly scrawling across the laptop screen. "I say we start the search there and work our way down."

"What else are we going to run into on that floor?"

"Possibly Yao, which means Wong Li at the very least, most likely a few other guards. I didn't have much time to look around, but it was obvious some serious renovation and decorating had been done to the entire floor. I'm figuring he has living quarters of some sort there. Yao would want to have easy access to the party room."

"AKA the bordello," Crystal added, a shiver of disgust rippling through her as she remembered her prison.

"So," Doc said, looking around the room. "How do you guys see this going down?"

Green, silent until now, grunted. "Much as we'd all like to take out Yao, we've got one assignment this trip. Get the general's daughter out of there."

"Roger that," Black said, but the look he exchanged with his men told Crystal that if the opportunity arose, it wouldn't end there.

Good. She wanted Yao Long put out of commission. Green was right, though. Dina was the top priority.

"Any help from the boots on the ground?" Johnny asked.

He'd already mentioned to Crystal that since they were dealing with a three-star's daughter, it was possible that any CIA operatives—whom he referred to as spooks—who were currently undercover in Jakarta might prove to be valuable resources to them.

"We can reach out and put the touch on the CIA for weapons and gear but other than that, we're on our own."

Since Johnny had also shared that it was improbable the CIA could help in the manpower department, she'd been prepared for that answer.

"Why?" she'd asked him then. "Why can't they help?"

"Because just like us, they're not here," he'd said. Which was why, Crystal surmised, they called them spooks. Ghosts. Shadow warriors.

"And they can't risk blowing any ongoing op they're

already involved in," he'd continued. "The country—Jakarta in particular—has a heavy radical Muslim population. It's a hotbed for religious terrorists, very politically unstable at times, so they've got their hands full just monitoring the jihadists and all the splinter groups. And like every other alphabet agency, they're understaffed and overworked."

"Okay." Green's deep voice drew Crystal back into the current conversation. "Since we're it and considering we're practically going in blind, we're going to have to create some kind of diversion, draw whatever forces are in place away from the hostage."

Another thing Johnny had told Crystal yesterday was that normally when they planned a rescue—or snatch-and-grab, as he'd called it—they'd generally spend several days gathering intelligence ranging from the number of guards, what their schedule was, how they were armed and trained, to what kind of alarms were in play, whether the building was wired for sound, the type of building construction, and even more so they could determine the best way to breach it. Then, the team would find a similar building and practice, starting slowly and building up speed while working through all possible problems until they felt ready to roll.

"Police SWAT teams," he'd added, "don't have the time for that kind of planning, but then again, losing twenty percent of the hostages is considered acceptable 'breakage.' "

Crystal knew about SWAT teams. Johnny hadn't had to add that since they were dealing with "breakage" of only one person, twenty percent loss was far from acceptable.

"We need a truck." Green's deep voice brought her back to the moment. "We drive it through the front doors loaded for bear, keep the guards busy as a diversion while someone makes the snatch. How many guards are you thinking?"

"Figure on around fifteen." Johnny looked toward Crystal for confirmation.

"Yeah," she said, "that's what I figured, too."

"That's going to take all four of us on the diversion team," Doc said.

"Leaving you on your own to get the girl," Nate said, with a grim look at Johnny.

"He won't be alone," Crystal said. All eyes turned and met hers. "I'm going with him."

Johnny glared at her. "The hell you are."

She ignored him and turned to Black, hoping she'd find an ally in him. "Reed doesn't want to believe this but I can shoot the wings off a fly at twenty-five yards with my Glock."

Eyebrows rose around the room.

"Okay. So I can't," she admitted, because she'd accomplished what she'd wanted. She'd garnered their full attention. "But I *can* shoot half-inch groups at a hundred yards with my dad's old Remington 700." Anyone who knew anything about target shooting had to be impressed with that—didn't they?

"Look," she continued, still addressing Black because she knew he was the one she had to convince,

"I'm no sniper but I'm not inexperienced either. I trained to be a cop all my life—my bad luck I've got a slight hearing loss and couldn't pass the physical. Your good luck that I can lay down cover and I can do it without shooting off my foot or his head."

"Now *there's* a hard target to miss."

Hands on his hips, Johnny squared off in front of her, ignoring Doc's grinning jab. He looked mad and he looked mean. "There's a helluva difference between shooting paper targets and shooting at a man with an AK-47. *He's* gonna shoot back!"

"Dina knows me," she argued, holding her ground. "When she sees you she might panic and alert the entire floor and foul everything up. I can help. Accept it."

"When pigs fly."

"Yeah, well, seems to me they already did the day I dropped you on your ass."

Once again, all attention shifted to her. Johnny's eyes shot fire. The others regarded her with a newfound respect before looking to Johnny for confirmation.

When he didn't deny it, Doc broke into a grin. "A girl? An *itty-bitty* girl got the drop on you, macho boy? Hell, maybe you'd better sit out this op, Reed, 'cause you're obviously slippin'."

Johnny glared from Doc to Black. "Tell her she's not going."

Black rubbed his jaw. "In a perfect world," he said, restating what they'd already discussed, "she wouldn't. Fact is, we need the body and the extra gun."

"Jesus, Nate—"

Black held up a hand when Johnny wound up for another argument. "I can't spare anyone on the diversion team. You need an extra pair of eyes. And you need someone to provide cover in the very unlikely chance," he said pointedly, "that Yao's guards come looking your way. But if we do our job right, they'll all be occupied trying to take us out. Face it. The safest place for her to be is with you."

"The safest place is right here," Johnny insisted, jamming a finger toward the floor.

"Get real," she said, undeterred by his anger. "You honestly think I'd stay put like a fragile little wallflower? You leave me here, I'm going to follow. And who knows what kind of trouble I'll get into by myself?"

Johnny got right in her face, shook a finger at her. "I'm telling you for the last time, Tinkerbell—"

She batted his hand away. "I like a Glock 19 if you can get it. If not, a Ruger will do. And my shooter rifle is an AR-15 but I can handle an M-4 or M-16 or whatever you come up with."

"Damn." Doc beamed at her. "I like this woman."

"You like all women," Savage pointed out. "But I've got to agree with you on this one."

The room got very quiet then. Throats cleared all around. The men were waiting for Johnny to accept the inevitable. His scowl darkened but when he didn't stage another protest, Crystal knew she'd won.

11

"Okay." Black cleared the tense silence in the room. "Back to the truck and the diversion. We coordinate times and ram through the doors. That'll pull the guards from the rest of the building. Most likely the impact is going to trigger an alarm."

"Alarms," Crystal said with a frown. "Won't that draw a crowd?"

Nate smiled. "Bank on it. Last thing we need is to have a truckful of police pull up. It's not like we want to shoot the 'friendlies.'"

"Or create a major international incident," Doc added.

Black glanced at Savage and Green. "Cavanaugh still on board over here?"

"Last I knew," Savage said.

"Cavanaugh?" Doc broke into a grin. "He's one of your old spook buddies, right? Crazy bastard if the stories you told about him are true."

"Oh, they're true," Green said.

"Don't suppose he owes you any favors?" Black asked.

"Damn straight he owes us. We saved his sorry ass more times than we've saved Reed's."

That earned Green a glare from Johnny.

"What say you reach out and put the touch on him?" Black went on. "He can't help with manpower but he could help with a little distraction. We need to take the local law out of the picture."

Savage narrowed his eyes. "What? You thinkin' maybe we ask Cavanaugh to, say, drop a hint to the Indonesian intelligence community . . . maybe convince them that U.S. intel has picked up chatter about a terrorist plot?"

"Like a bombing at the airport?" Green suggested, fleshing out the plan.

"Yeah. Like a bombing. Have him time it so the call goes in right about the same time we hit Yao's warehouse," Savage finished with a nod.

Apparently, it was exactly what Black had in mind. "Ought to keep both the local PD and the military off our backs and give us room to move without their interference. Chances are Yao's got the locals in his pocket but national security trumps payola every time."

"Consider it done," Savage said.

"Okay." Johnny, who'd remained stubbornly quiet, finally rejoined the discussion. "The truck breaches the building. You four on board. Add a subgun and a few frag grenades to your list," he said, glancing at Green. "You're going to need 'em. At the same time, I'll—" He cut himself off, glared at Crystal. "*We'll* already be in place."

Her stomach dipped but she held his gaze and her ground.

"We'll climb the outside wall via the fire escape, then enter the building through the roof," he continued. "Do I see a skylight in this shot?"

They all leaned over the satellite maps for a second look.

"Looks like," Savage said. "Better take along some Semtex just in case."

"Semtex? Is that like C-4?"

Doc smiled at Crystal. "Yeah. They both go boom. It'll make a nice hole for you to shimmy through if we're reading the images wrong."

"Okay, this may be a stupid question, but, once we get in and find Dina, how do we get her out of there?"

Nate glanced up from the satellite imagery. "What kind of shape is she in?"

"I'm worried about that," Crystal admitted. "Yao had her badly whipped once. She's scared to death of him. Begged me not to fight him because he'd hold her responsible." For the first time since her escape she allowed herself to think of what might already have happened to Dina.

"Don't buy trouble," Black said, not unkindly. "We'll get her out. If she's hurt, Doc will take care of her until we can get her to a medical facility."

She nodded, surprised to feel Johnny's hand squeeze her shoulder before he quickly pulled it away.

"Take her out the same way we go in?" Johnny suggested, glancing at the other men.

"Unless she's hurt. If she's hurt, you've got a problem getting her back up on the roof and then down the fire escape," Doc pointed out.

"Same goes if you try to fight your way down ten stories with an incapacitated hostage. Major PITA," Savage added.

"PITA?" Crystal was lost. "How did animal rights activists get into this?"

"Pain in the ass," Savage clarified with a tight grin.

"I remember seeing an electrical breaker box at the base of the stairs on the first floor," Johnny said after thinking it through. "If you guys can hit it, take out the power to the building, then I could take her down the elevator shaft. We bypass any possible resistance on each floor that way. We hit the second floor, blow a hole in the wall, and rappel the short drop to the ground."

"It'll work," Black said with a slow nod. "You let us know when you're ready, we'll disengage, back the hell out of there, and hope we don't have to stop and scoop up any wounded on the way out the door. We pick you up on the street and make dust."

"In—out in what? Less than fifteen minutes?" Savage calculated.

"If we're lucky." Green glanced at Crystal.

"We're always lucky," Doc said.

Crystal noticed that he didn't say what kind of luck.

"Shopping." Crystal grinned when Green handed her a list. "Now this is something I definitely excel at."

"We'll rendezvous here," Nate said checking his watch, "at 1800 hours. I've got 1105," he added and the men all set their watches, which appeared, Crystal thought, to have more functions than an instrument panel in the cockpit of a jet.

He passed out wads of cash—her mouth dropped open when she saw it—and the men headed out the door. All but Johnny. He hung back, waiting until they were alone.

"Something happens to you," he grumbled, his face hard and angry and totally at odds with the concern in his voice, "I'm going to wring your little pixie neck."

Before she could assure him that she was too scared to let anything happen, he reached for her, dragged her against him, and kissed her. Kissed her like he wanted to punish and plead and devour her all at the same time. Kissed her hard and long and with a thoroughness that shouted possession and that scared her almost as much as the thought of getting shot at. Just as fast as he'd grabbed her, he released her, leveled her with one final, piercing look, and headed for the door.

Crystal staggered back, her head reeling from his hot, almost violent assault. Her heart slammed against her sternum, reckless and erratic and wild. And she just couldn't let him go.

"Reed."

He stopped in the open doorway, turned around. His blue eyes were sharp with something that was almost frightening.

"It wasn't just . . ." She paused, regrouped and tried

again because damn, this was difficult. "It wasn't just sex," she confessed, then waited for the fallout.

For a long moment, he just stood there. Silence and heat and hesitation were the only larger presences in the room.

Finally he nodded. Slow and steady and sure. "You got that right."

Dazed, mystified, and edging along the sharp side of panic, she watched him go.

Oh. Boy. What can of worms had she just opened?

The night was as black, hot, and tired as the beat of the overcrowded city. The adrenaline, however, flowed to the din of traffic noise that thickened the air like mud stew. Heart pounding, black from head to toe—even her face was covered with face-black—Crystal hugged the back wall of the row of buildings fortressing Yao's warehouse. Johnny stood beside her, a tall shadow in the dark, sizing up the precarious-looking ladder he was about to scale like Jack climbing a beanstalk.

It was a long way up. Her stomach rolled. Now was probably not the time to mention that she had this thing about heights. She didn't like them—a fact that was irrelevant. She was going up there. Mind would conquer matter. These men were here because of her. She would not let them or Dina down.

"It's not too late to back out." A big hand clamped down on each shoulder as Johnny turned her to face him.

"Yeah," she said, scared to death but determined to

meet his eyes in the dark with steady confidence. "It is."

The whites of his eyes seemed twice as bright in his blackened face. "This isn't a dress rehearsal, Crystal. This is the real thing. People could die here tonight. People probably will."

She nodded, very much aware of a stunning lack of exaggeration in his words.

"Just make sure you're not one of them," she told him, peripherally aware of the decay of the alley that smelled of old oil, dank earth, and a little of the sea. Far too aware of his gaze penetrating hers.

He touched a hand to her face and turned to go. No way could she let him.

She grabbed his arm, jerked him around toward her, and cupped the back of his neck. Then she dragged his head down for a deep, blistering kiss that rivaled the one he'd given her in the hotel room earlier.

"Stay alive," she whispered against his mouth, then reluctantly backed away.

The gruffness of his voice was at odds with the slow smile that spread across his face. "Count on it."

Then suddenly she was alone in the dark, heart and knees knocking as his black-clad figure scaled the rickety ladder toward the roofline, a length of rappelling rope and the equipment that went with it, coiled over his shoulder. His harness, like hers, was already in place and ready to tighten up when the time came. The safety factor of the ladder was tenuous at best. That's why he'd gone up ahead of her. He wanted to make certain it would hold their weight.

If there were stars, they were well hidden beneath a blanket of smog and a wash of light pollution. Crystal felt very small, very alone, and very vulnerable suddenly, even as she kept a tight grip on the M-4 rifle slung over her shoulder. She would have felt more comfortable with an AR-15, but Nate was quick to explain that the smaller, more compact M-4 was a lot easier to maneuver inside buildings and in what he'd referred to as CQB—close quarters battle.

Stay alive.

Yeah, she thought, as Johnny disappeared above her, his body blending in with the night shadows. Stay the hell alive. That went for all of them. Including Dina. God, Crystal hoped they weren't too late.

She couldn't think about that now. So instead, she ran and reran the plan in her mind as she waited, watching for the flash of Johnny's light that would be her signal to follow.

It would work. They were prepared. They'd all had busy afternoons. Like the others, Crystal's shopping list had been detailed and precise. Colter and Johnny had rounded up a truck and a van. The truck was for the diversion; the van they parked a few miles from the assault scene and planned to switch to it after they'd ditched the truck. Savage and Green had reached out to their CIA contacts to arrange the fake terrorist threat at the airport and for the arsenal they'd need to pull off the assault. All totaled they'd managed to obtain six Kevlar vests—one size extra small—five handguns ranging from Glocks to 1911As to a Sig, six rifles, an M-249 belt-fed machine gun, half a dozen frag grenades, and a cache of ammo large enough to jump-start a small coup.

She and Nathan Black had rounded up flashlights, the rappelling equipment, communication radios, and enough black shirts and scarves to outfit a cat burglary squad. The black do-rags the men wore made them look deadly. On her, it was merely a fashion disaster. As planned, they'd rendezvoused at the hotel a little before the target time and after going over the plan one last time, geared up.

Now here they were, fully engaged. If all went as designed, the local law enforcement and military presence were, at this moment, screaming their way to the airport and were well occupied miles from here. The diversion team of Black, Colter, Savage, and Green were idling a few blocks away, a belt-fed machine gun set up in the truck bed—Savage's specialty, she'd been told—waiting for the signal from Johnny that they were in place.

Finally, she saw the quick double flash of his Maglite and she knew he'd made it to the top. Without another moment's hesitation, she started her climb, fighting to outrun the butterflies launching into flight in her chest.

She would not let her acrophobia stop her. It was, however, going to make this the longest five minutes of her life. Her palms were damp, her thigh muscles trembling, and she was light-headed by the time she finally reached the last rung. Breathing hard, she hauled herself up and over the outside wall of the building where she rolled to her back on the roof that still held the heat of the tropical day.

After a short but heartfelt prayer to the gods of gravity for sparing her life, she allowed herself two deep breaths to fortify herself, then rolled to all fours.

"Don't look down," she whispered as, heart racing from both the exertion of the climb and her fear, she cautiously stood and scanned the rooftop for Johnny.

When she didn't see him, she pulled out her flashlight and flicked it twice as he'd instructed her to do. Waited. About fifty yards over came an answering blink.

Careful of the uneven surface of the roof, she picked her way from one building's roof to another, sent up another prayer of thanks that they were on the same level, and made it to his side. He was kneeling beside what had, indeed, proven to be a skylight, and was carefully extracting a pane of glass.

"Get a hold of the edge."

She dropped to her knees beside him, gripped the edge of the glass, and helped him lift and set it aside.

Without another word, he depressed the button on the radio clipped to his shoulder. "Pedal to the metal, boys," he said softly into the mike. "We're a definite go."

Though she knew she only imagined it, Crystal could swear she heard a truck engine roar to life ten stories down and three blocks away as Johnny disappeared inside the hole he'd made in the skylight.

"Come on down," he said, waiting for her inside.

Handing down her rifle first, she eased her lower body into the hole, never more grateful for his strength when he caught her around the hips and lowered her easily to the floor.

"Like a tick," he whispered, which summoned a ringing sense of déjà vu. It hadn't been that long since he'd given the same order as he'd led her out of Yao's lair instead of into it.

The floor was eerily quiet as they crept along the dimly lit hallway. Too quiet. And not nearly dark enough, Crystal thought. Any one of the many doors leading off the hallway could fly open at any second. They'd be exposed like ducks in a shooting gallery.

She held the M-4 to her shoulder, sweeping the open spaces, ready to fire if she had to. God, she prayed she didn't have to.

"How are we going to find her with all these doors?" she whispered as Johnny tried one door after another, encountering them all locked tight.

A distant rumble of gunfire, an earthquake rocking of the building answered her instead.

"My money says that's not Avon calling." Johnny snagged her arm and ducked into an alcove when bells started ringing like the fire-alarm drills she remembered from grade school.

They tucked deep into the shadows as doors flew open; men shouted in Chinese and Bahasa Indonesian and raced for the elevators.

The lights went out and the alarms fell silent just

then, which meant that Nate and the guys had taken out the electrical panel. With luck, they'd find the phone lines and disable the landlines as well, so no calls could be placed for reinforcements.

She heard the stairwell doors fly open with a hollow ring while they waited for the door to slam closed behind the last of Yao's men.

"Slick as snake oil," Johnny whispered and flicked on his flashlight. "Start knocking."

12

Crystal flicked on her flashlight and approached the closest door. "Dina?" she whispered, then listened for a response as Johnny did the same, working his way down a row of doors on the opposite side of the hall.

Sweat ran down her back and into her eyes as she made her way down the hall, praying for a response. Between the weight of her Kevlar vest, the tension, and the oppressive heat, she felt like she was slogging through a sauna.

"Over here!"

Crystal turned just as Johnny hauled back and planted his weight behind a hard kick. The door crashed open. She sprinted into the room, slanted her flashlight beam alongside his, and searched the darkness.

"Oh God. Oh Jesus," she whispered when twin beams illuminated a small cell. Inside, a huddled figure lay curled up on the floor with her back to them.

"Dina." She ran to the bars.

The girl moaned but made no other reaction.

"Stand back." Johnny dug something out of his pocket. The Semtex, she realized as he stuffed some into the lock of the cell door.

"Back," he repeated, dragging her with him out into the hall. "Cover your ears."

Then he wrapped himself around her and braced against the far wall just as a deafening *boom* shook the building.

He was gone before Crystal uncovered her ears. When she finally moved, she found the cell door blown wide open and Johnny on one knee by Dina, gently wrapping her in the rug that had served as her bed.

"Let's go," he said, rising. "Keep that rifle locked and loaded. The blast may have alerted the media. And give me some light."

Cradling Dina against his chest, he headed for the elevator at a sprint, following Crystal as she led the way with her flashlight.

It was all fast and furious and frantic then—at least on Crystal's part. Johnny remained as cool as ice. He laid Dina down on the hallway floor.

"Leave her be," he barked when Crystal would have attended to her. "I need you more than she does right now if we're going to get her out of here."

As hard as it was not to go to her, he was right. "Tell me what to do."

"I need light. And keep a lookout for company."

She held the M-4 in one hand and lit up the elevator doors with her flashlight as he pried them open with a crowbar he'd carried on his belt.

"Inside," he ordered, asking her to shine the light into the elevator shaft so he could see to rig his rope.

When he was satisfied, he clipped carabiners attached to the rope onto the harness he'd just tightened, then lifted Dina and hefted her over his shoulder. "I'll send the rope back up, okay?"

Crystal nodded. "Go."

Without another word, he gripped the rope and swung out into the deep, dark shaft and disappeared.

Time moved like a shadow cast by stone. Agonizingly slow. Almost undetectable. The only connection she had to Johnny was the sound of his feet hitting the walls of the shaft, which was almost drowned out by the thunder of her heartbeat as it pounded away inside her head.

She heard a noise behind her. Swung around, leaned on the trigger, and sprayed the hall with lead.

Silence echoed in the wake of her fire burst. Plaster dust drifted in the air as she shone her light toward her target . . . and saw that she'd just shot the hell out of thin air.

"Crystal!" Johnny's voice, frantic, echoed up the cavernous shaft.

"I'm okay," she shouted back, too scared to be embarrassed. "It's okay. Keep going."

Heart pounding, sweat trickling down her face, she ordered herself to calm down. She'd told him she was up to this. She'd just come very close to proving that she wasn't.

The sound of rope zipping over steel alerted her to the

fact that Johnny was sending the rigging back up to her.

"Got it," she yelled down the shaft, letting him know the rig had arrived. Then she tightened her own harness and hooked up her carabiners as he'd shown her earlier. On a deep breath, she secured her rifle over her shoulder, gripped the rope, and took the great leap.

"Jesus, Joseph, Mary, and Moses, please, don't fail me now," she muttered, clutching the rope with her gloved hands and lowering herself down, down, down into the dark, echoing shaft.

Another eternity passed as the blackness closed in and she descended deeper into the abyss. She felt like she hung suspended forever. It was so dark. She had no way of gauging her descent. The walls of the shaft smelled of dirt and must and oil and decay. The inside of her wrist burned where the leather of her gloves rubbed against the fresh brand. Above her, the beam holding the rope gave and groaned as she lowered herself down a little farther, her feet hitting the wall, her palms growing slippery inside her gloves.

With everything in her, she concentrated. Hand over hand. Inch by agonizing inch. She screamed when hard hands clasped her hips.

"Easy, Tink. It's a good guy."

"I knew that," she said quickly, trying to cover her embarrassment. "I just hadn't realized I'd made it all the way down."

"Right," he said. "So how come you didn't tell me you were afraid of heights?" he asked, as he directed her to shine her flashlight toward the exterior wall of the shaft.

"What makes you think I'm afraid of heights?" How the hell had he figured that out?

He was busy banging away at the wall with his crowbar. "Oh, maybe the fact that your face glows green under the Maglite."

"Yeah, so, fine. I don't like heights. Didn't stop me."

"No," he said with a huge grunt as he broke a small hole through the outer wall. "It sure as hell didn't."

Approval. She heard it loud and strong. Next, however, she heard the anger.

"You wanna play with the big boys, you don't keep secrets, got it? Secrets get people killed."

She nodded, properly chastised. "Got it. Sorry."

He grunted again, started tearing at old, smelly lath and plaster with his hands. "You did good, Tink. Now help me make a Reed-sized hole. With a little luck, we won't have to use the Semtex."

That was fine by her. Her ears were still ringing from the explosion that blasted the lock on Dina's cell. She moved in beside him, far too aware of Dina's still form on the top of the elevator at her feet. In a few minutes, working together, they had their hole.

"Almost home free," Johnny said. "This time, you go first."

She didn't argue. She reattached her carabiners to her harness and with Johnny's help, crawled outside the hole in the wall into the night.

"Send your harness up with the rope. I'll have to use it to lower her out."

Less than twenty seconds later, Crystal landed on the

ground, breathing air that wasn't clotted with plaster dust and explosives and the moldy smell of an old building saturated with sea air and pollution. Instead, she dragged the smell of the city into her lungs. If there'd been time and if the ground hadn't smelled like garbage and curry and exhaust, she'd have knelt down and kissed it.

She quickly loosened her harness, shrugged out of it, then tugged on the rope to signal Johnny to haul it up. The rifle firmly gripped in her hands, she stood with her back to the building, watched and waited.

"We're coming down," Johnny finally said from two stories above her.

Crystal watched as he eased out of the hole, with Dina's tragically lifeless form hooked to his. Carefully and slowly, he lowered them both to the ground.

Still supporting Dina against him, he quickly shrugged out of the harness and punched the button on his radio. "Goldilocks to Papa Bear. We've got the porridge. Do you copy?"

Johnny's radio erupted with the sound of distant gunfire. "You're a laugh riot, you know that, Reed?"

Crystal saw the relief on Johnny's face when he heard Savage's voice. His expression spelled out loud and clear that it didn't matter how many operations they made together, they all knew the risks of not coming back alive.

"Tell me you're ready to blow this shit hole," Savage yelled, sounds of the firefight thick and ominous in the background.

"Roger that. We'll be waiting."

"The hell you will. Meet us now. We're outta here."

Another barrage of gunfire accompanied his words, then the radio went dead.

"You heard the man." Hefting Dina into his arms, Johnny sprinted for the opening of the alley.

They hadn't any more than arrived when the truck came flying out of the warehouse bay. It screeched to a bouncing stop beside them with Savage in the back, riding the machine-gun trigger as he returned fire from inside the building.

Ducking behind the truck, Johnny handed Dina up to Green, then turned back and hauled Crystal up and into the truck bed. He jumped in after her, pushed her to the floor, and caught the M-4 Savage tossed him.

"Punch it!" he roared over his shoulder toward the cab of the truck and leaned on the trigger. Beside him, instinct took over and Crystal did the same, firing blind toward the muzzle flash of what felt and sounded like a hundred AK-47s set on full automatic.

With Nate behind the wheel, the diesel engine whined, laid rubber, and they peeled down the dirty street, exhaust smoke spewing in the wake of their re-turn fire as bullets caromed off the tailgate.

Five minutes later, they ditched the truck, quickly transferred their cargo to the van, and headed back to base. Thirty minutes after that, the adrenaline was still pumping like the pistons on the engine of the slow-cooling van.

"Lay her on the bed," Colter said, flipping on the lights as Johnny carried Dina into the hotel room.

"Jesus," Savage muttered when they unwrapped her. "She's just a kid."

Crystal crowded in close to the bed, able to see Dina clearly for the first time. She brushed the matted blond hair back away from Dina's face. Sucked in a breath. "Oh God."

"It's okay. She's alive. We'll take care of her," Doc said quickly as he dug into his kit.

Crystal shook her head, not wanting to believe what she was seeing. "No. I mean, yes. Take care of her, but . . ."

"But what?" Johnny asked, cuing in to her distress.

She lifted her gaze to his. "But this isn't Dina. My God, Johnny. Dina's still back there."

"No."

Crystal jerked her gaze to the girl on the bed, the girl with Dina's blond hair and fine features.

"Dina's . . . not there." She licked dry lips. "Please, please. Don't . . . don't give me back . . . to him."

"Oh, sweetie." Crystal leaned in toward her, covered her hands with hers. "Yao can't hurt you anymore. He's not going to get to you again."

A single tear trickled from her eye and ran into her temple.

"We need to get some fluids in you, okay?" Doc prepped the girl's arm for an IV. "Gonna be a little sting now."

"What's your name?" Crystal asked gently, wanting to distract her from the needle as much as she wanted information.

"Mary. Mary Conners."

"Mary," Crystal repeated, gripping her limp hand in hers. "I'm Crystal. And these guys . . . they're all here to help you, okay? But we need you to help us, too. Do you know where he took Dina?"

Mary nodded weakly. "He . . . he moved her into inventory. To the cribs."

"Jesus," Johnny swore.

Crystal jerked her gaze to his. She saw pure rage and experienced a fear so profound her body trembled. "What? What does that mean?"

The room grew ominously silent.

"The bastard sent her to a stable of prostitutes," Johnny said, his voice as hard as his eyes.

Wong Li watched in uneasy silence as his employer walked into the smoking aftermath of the assault on his primary warehouse. The acrid scent of gunpowder and sweat mingling with the stench of fear permeated the air.

Li hurried across the distance to meet him. He bowed in respect, then gave him the update he knew Mr. Yao would require.

"Three men are dead. Five more are wounded. The girl you had requested for the evening appeared to have been the primary purpose of the attack. She's gone."

She'd been a special favorite of Mr. Yao's. Li was certain he would not be alive to see another sunrise.

Yao's carefully restrained expression never altered but Li understood perfectly that a quiet fury simmered below the surface. His employer considered the girls his prime property. They had been hand-selected. Their education administered by Mr. Yao himself. He had gone to great lengths to acquire, abduct, or entice them for his personal stable. The loss of the Debrowski woman had been a staggering blow to Mr. Yao's ego. Relegating Cahya to the bordellos for her complicity in the other woman's escape had been necessary but still, another loss. And now the new girl was also gone.

No one stole Mr. Yao's personal property and lived to tell of it. No one.

Li waited, cautiously avoiding eye contact as his employer's gaze swept the warehouse.

"Who would dare to do this?" his employer asked in Chinese.

Li breathed deep, forced himself to bite back the ever-present fear that hung over his head like a black cloud of doom. It would do his cause no good to lose his employer's faith now. While Li could not have anticipated this second strike, Mr. Yao would consider him responsible.

"Americans," Li said, restating what the guards had told him. "Six of them."

"Did I not order additional security?"

"You did, yes. And your wishes were carried out. The Americans drove a truck through the warehouse doors, engaged the guards for several minutes with machine-gun and rifle fire."

Yao glared at a crater in the middle of the warehouse floor. "No rifle did this."

Li nodded. "They had grenades as well."

"You said six?"

Again, Li nodded. "Four breached the warehouse in a truck. Two more accessed the tenth floor through the roof, then escaped with the girl by way of the elevator shaft."

"Where were the police when the alarms sounded?"

A good question. The "donations" Mr. Yao generously bestowed on the local law enforcement were intended to ensure an event such as this would never happen. "I have a man checking into it. First accounts indicate they were otherwise engaged at the airport."

Yao walked deeper into the warehouse. Glared at the few men who weren't injured or dead. "Eliminate them."

Li understood. If they were alive and uninjured, Mr. Yao considered them inept at the least, cowardly at the most. Li nodded toward his lieutenant, then followed his employer as he turned and walked toward the door.

The screams of dying men accompanied the low-pitched *thunk, thunk, thunk* of an AK-47 as his man emptied a full thirty-round magazine into the unfortunate survivors.

"I will not tolerate another loss," Yao said in a tone that was as quiet as it was lethal. "Find them. Whoever they are, find them." While his voice never rose a decibel, the rage was apparent in every syllable. "I will not endure these Americans in my city. Find them all and bring them to me or it will be your head I will order severed and served to me on a platter."

13

As was the case in most equatorial regions, Johnny felt like he wore the air as well as breathed it—even at three in the frickin' morning. His shirt clung to his back, damp with sweat and humidity as he and Colter made the rounds at the edge of the red-light district. Back at the hotel, Black stood guard over Crystal and Mary. Three blocks away, Savage and Green searched their area of the quadrant, looking for Dina.

Cribs. The bastard Yao had sent her to the cribs. He swallowed back a roiling nausea, the same nausea that he'd been fighting since he'd walked into the first bordello and witnessed the absence of anything remotely immediate in the eyes of the women and girls the madam had paraded before him like used goods. Used and abused and many beyond hope.

None of them had been Dina. None of them had been easy to walk away from, and it would eat at him for the rest of his life that he'd had to do exactly that.

Crystal hadn't had to give them a description of Dina. Johnny had her photograph in his pocket, one of several Nate had brought with him from the States just in case . . . well, just in case they ended up doing exactly what they were doing. Searching the cribs that the deviant sonofabitch Yao supplied with abducted women and children.

Human trafficking was out of control in this part of the world. Everything Johnny had seen here supported that fact. It made him sick. Just as everything Mary had told them after Doc had checked her over, gotten her rehydrated and they'd fed her, made him want to kill Yao.

Mary Conners was all of fifteen. She'd grown up in London, one of six children in a lower-middle-class home where her mother managed a bakery and her father worked for the city sanitation department. A year or so ago, Mary had gotten caught up in the city's underground music culture and taken a few wrong turns in the judgment department. She started spending a little too much time on the street, and early one morning when she was headed home from a club, she was abducted between the South Kensington tube station and the Natural History Museum.

That had been three weeks ago. She'd been living Yao Long's nightmare ever since. Only by pure dumb luck had she known about Dina.

"I heard through the walls when Wong Li questioned her," she'd said, her big blue eyes recovering some life thanks to Crystal's gentle encouragement and Doc's medical attention. "They blamed her for another girl getting away."

"That girl would be me," Crystal had said, and

Johnny had ached for the guilt and pain he'd seen in Crystal's eyes.

"It was Dina we came back for," Crystal said. "I'm so glad we found you, Mary, but we need to find Dina now. Is there anything else you can tell us to help?"

What the girl had told them had led Johnny and the rest of the guys to canvass this area of the city. Their search had started three hours ago. To a man they understood the urgency of finding Dina before Yao took a notion to move her again or before some deviant did irreparable damage either physically or emotionally or both. And once Yao was told of Mary's rescue, he'd move fast if he decided to bring Dina back into his inner sanctum.

The red-light district made Johnny's skin crawl. Pain, despair, defeat. It was written on every face, young, old, female, male. It sickened him, prompted a residual sort of guilt for his gender in general. He wanted to personally cut off the balls of every man who'd ever paid for sex and contributed to the living hell that was the existence of these women and girls.

Just like the rest of the guys, he was running on little or no sleep. Didn't matter. It was all about speed now. That's why they'd been ducking in and out of bordellos and checking out peep shows at warp speed, playing the part of the sex-driven Americans out for some kinky fun. In his dirty clothes, unshaven, hair matted with sweat, Johnny didn't doubt he looked like a typical customer. Three hours in and he felt filthy inside as well as out from what he'd seen.

"*Gadis Amerika?*" (American girl?) he asked the house madam of a tawdry tarpaper and lath building. The sign outside boasted, "*Gadis—gadis!*" (Girls! Girls!)

"*Ya. Gadis molek. Gadis sexy,*" (Yes. Pretty girls. Sexy girls) she said with a wizened grin intended to entice but it left Johnny with an almost irresistible urge to shove his fist into her sweaty face. Apparently, business was good. In a country of small, slim people, the madam loomed as big as the Goodyear blimp. Piggy eyes squinted out at him from folds of sweating flesh. A tent-sized hot pink caftan draped over her gargantuan body like a bedspread. Jabba the Hut on estrogen.

He made himself smile, playing along, and touched his hair. "*Kuning.*" (Yellow.)

"*Ah, ya. Punya rambut. Kuning tu gadis barulah. Anda tentu sukalah!*" (Ah, yes. Yellow hair. New girl. You will like.)

For the first time since he'd hit the streets, Johnny felt a modicum of hope that they weren't chasing down another dead end. For show, he bartered for a price. When the madam was satisfied that she'd taken the foolish American for all she could get, she led him down a corridor lined with doors.

The building smelled of stale sex and the sickening sweet odor of cheap perfume, weed, and rotgut. She stopped by a door with the number 10 nailed over peeling green paint, rapped once, and shoved it open. "*Nah, buat'joli.*" (There you go, have a good time.)

Screw punching her. He wanted to choke her. Instead, he nodded his thanks and walked into the room, closing the door behind him.

A girl sat huddled on the bed, her back to him, covered only in a short, opaque robe. Her hair was blond. Her back was scarred and covered with fresh bruises.

"Dina?"

She stiffened. Slowly, she lifted her head and looked over her shoulder. Drugged, he realized as vacant and unfocused eyes attempted to meet his.

Jesus. This girl bore little resemblance to the vivacious teenage girl in the photos Nate had brought of the general's daughter.

"Are you Dina Stornello?" he asked, even though he was afraid he'd hit another dead end.

A spark of life fired in those dazed blue eyes.

"Who . . . who are you?"

She was American. His chest tightened. "Are you Dina?"

She watched him in a wary stupor, then slowly nodded.

He'd found her. Elation was trumped by the overpowering urge to kill Yao for reducing her to this shadow of the girl she had been.

"I'm a friend of Crystal Debrowski," he said gently, clenching down on his rage at the bastard who had done this to her.

His statement was met by a long moment of disbelief, then understanding thick with desperation. Huge tears pooled, then spilled down her cheeks. "Help me."

His heart fucking broke. He quickly dialed Doc's cell number.

"Colter," Doc answered.

"I've got her." He fired off the address. "Circle the wagons."

He was going to need reinforcements to get Dina past the nice gentlemen he'd noticed lounging in the shadows guarding the door.

"Can you walk?" he asked gently after he'd disconnected.

She stumbled to her feet. Johnny caught her before she went down, steadied her, and realized she wasn't going to make it out of here under her own steam.

"Are you with me, darlin'?"

He took the heavy wobble of her head as a no. He glanced around the room for clothes. Nothing. No sheets on the filthy mattress, no blankets. Swearing, he eased her back down to the bed, then stripped off his T-shirt and moving her arms like a rag doll, maneuvered it over her head.

He was a size XXL. She was a size XXS. The shirt fit her like a choir robe. All that mattered was that she was covered up and she was going home.

He lifted her carefully into his arms, apologized for hurting her when she winced. Then he opened the door and marched out into the corridor. He made it all the way to the front room before the madam figured out what was going on.

She met him at the exit door with a machete. Her beady eyes were almost lost in the fat folds on her face as her garish red lips spewed a string of curses. The two bouncers stood to attention and flanked her, Saturday night specials locked and loaded and pointed straight at his head.

He shifted Dina's weight, settled her over his shoulder and, eyes boring into the madam's, kept right on walking.

"*Ikut perintah atau mati.*" (Move or die.)

He'd have gladly killed her, too. She understood that and moved aside like a curtain, her caftan sweeping the filthy floor as folds of fat jiggled and rolled like inner tubes beneath the flowing cloth.

The bookends took a little more convincing, but not much. Savage, Green, and Doc walked in the door right then, and it didn't take an advanced degree in calculus for the hired goons to see that the good guys' guns were a lot bigger than the bad guys'.

With the BOIs covering his back, Johnny walked straight out the door, wishing with every molecule of life in him that he'd been personally responsible for someone dying today.

One girl. They'd saved one more girl. One who could have just as easily been Crystal.

His chest ached, his gut muscles clenched when he thought of how close he'd come to losing her in the rotten underbelly of a world that preyed on the innocent and profited from the weak.

Crystal wasn't weak. Not by a long shot. If Yao had had his way, though, he would have broken her. Like he'd broken Dina and Mary and God only knew how many others.

* * *

Crystal had waited until after the guys had showered and gone in search of Dina before she'd helped Mary clean up. Then she showered off her own face-black and grime and washed her hair. Now she sat on the bed with Dina, holding her while she cried. Johnny glanced at the men he called brothers as they all stood quietly by.

The small hotel room echoed with the sound of despair. Mary had grown silent. She sat alone on the floor in the corner of the room, huddled into herself, her eyes blank, her feelings walled up behind them with a haunting vacancy.

PTS. Post-traumatic stress. Johnny recognized it. He'd seen it. Experienced it in varying degrees and like most veterans of combat, struggled to keep it under control. Both Mary and Dina needed treatment— medical and psychiatric. Most of all, they needed to get home.

Without saying a word, Johnny also knew what each and every one of the team was thinking. They'd waged guerrilla warfare in jungles so dense day turned to night in the thick of the vegetation. They'd played hide-and-seek on the frigid, barren mountain slopes in Northern Afghanistan, survived bombings, coups, catastrophes, and the worst that terrorist cells had to throw at them.

Yeah. There was nothing the men of Black Ops, Inc. weren't trained for, prepared for, or weren't capable of doing.

Nothing except dealing with a woman's tears.

Feeling helpless and uncomfortable and chomping at the bit to make someone pay, Johnny turned to Nate. "We need to take this bastard out."

"Yao is not on the table," Black said.

His face, however, said something else entirely as he cast a glance around the room. Oh, yeah. They were going after Yao, all right. Nate just didn't want Crystal to know. Like Johnny, Nate had already figured out that if Crystal knew Yao was next on the agenda, she'd dig in her heels and insist on being a part of the assault.

Damn woman. She was as smart as a whip, brave as a storm trooper, but sometimes she didn't have the sense God gave a goat. And he didn't want her anywhere near Jakarta when the shit hit Yao's fan.

The sound of soft weeping from the bed haunted them all.

"So what's the plan?" Johnny nodded toward the women. "What do you figure is the best way to get them out of here? All three of them," he said pointedly when he glanced over Nate's shoulder and saw Crystal looking his way.

"I'm going to put in a call to Ann," Nate said. "See if she can expedite Dina's return to the States through her contacts in the U.S. embassy. She's probably got contacts in London, too, and can help speed up the process for Mary as well."

Ann was the mother of former Task Force Mercy team member Bryan Tompkins. Shortly after Bry was killed in Sierra Leone, Ann had given up both the prestige and the big bucks that came with her partnership in a high-profile law firm in Richmond to accept an appointment in the Justice Department as deputy attorney general.

She'd never said as much but Johnny had always figured she'd done it for the BOIs, who she insisted were hers and Robert's boys because their son had called them brothers. More than once since she'd joined the DOJ, Ann had proven vital to their missions. The latest case in point had been when she'd intervened and made a deal to keep Abbie's brother out of prison in exchange for intel on Fredrick Nader's operations.

Looked like she was going to provide critical assistance yet again.

Johnny broke away from the men to tell Crystal what was up. "Nate's going to make some calls. We want to get you all on the way home ASAP."

"What about the others?" Dina lifted her head. "You've got to get them out of there, too."

Johnny felt his chest tighten. The others. The hundreds of women and children trapped in the sex trade in Jakarta. He knew what Dina wanted, just like he knew he couldn't give her an answer that would give her peace. Or one that would make him feel like the hero she wanted him to be.

He glanced at Crystal. Her face said it all. She understood that his hands were tied.

"Let's just worry about you right now, okay?" Crystal said to Dina, tears filling her eyes as she took him off the hook. "Let's just get you home."

14

Three hours later, they were ready to move. Calls had
been placed, deals sealed, arrangements made. Dina
and Mary were settled into the rental car ready to leave
for the U.S. embassy. Doc was at the wheel of one car;
Nate rode shotgun. Green was the wheelman of the
second car with Savage up front beside him.

The only one absent was Crystal, who was determined not to go with them. Not more than fifteen minutes ago, Johnny'd had a knock-down, drag-out with
her on that very subject.

Looking frustrated and determined and more than a
little PO'd when he'd ordered her into the car with the
others, Crystal had pointed out what she'd thought was
obvious. "There's still no guarantee that once I get to
the embassy they'll be able to get me out of Jakarta.
Until I know it's a go, I'm staying put."

Unfortunately, she'd been right. Ann's pull extended
only so far, and she'd used up her quota making
arrangements for the general's daughter because her
case could be argued as a national security issue. The

protocol, however, didn't extend to Crystal. She had no ID and nothing to warrant a duplicate passport. Without a passport, she couldn't board a commercial aircraft headed for the States.

Still, Johnny wanted her behind the walls of the embassy compound and out of harm's way. "It'll only be a temporary delay," he'd pointed out. "So you have to spend the night at the embassy. Not a big deal. By this time tomorrow, Sam and Abbie will have tracked down your birth certificate and faxed a copy to the consulate's office and your passport will be in the works." He had spent an hour on the phone with Sam to make certain that happened.

"If I have to spend another night in Jakarta, it's not going to be at the embassy. I'll take my chances with you."

Belligerent times ten, she'd turned and walked into the bathroom, slamming the door behind her. Hands on hips, Johnny glared after her. Damned his big mouth for giving her an argument. Damned her for her stubborn streak.

"Reed," Nate prompted again from the car.

Johnny lifted a hand in surrender, waved him away. "Go," he said.

Nate gave him a long look.

"Go," he repeated with a shake of his head. "We'll take her tomorrow when we're sure her birth certificate arrived. Deliver the girls to the consulate as planned. I'll see you back here later. And bring food," he added when his stomach growled.

"Damn, woman," he muttered, then walked inside the room and shut the door. He dropped down on his back on the bed, angrily folded his hands behind his head. "Thinks she's James freaking Bond."

And she was determined to get herself hurt or killed.

He was pissed. He was concerned. He was . . . hell, he was proud of her. She didn't take any crap off of anyone, especially him. And she could handle herself. She'd impressed the hell out of him when they'd staged their snatch-and-grab and rescued Mary. The BOIs had been impressed, too.

But she wasn't one of the BOIs.

She wasn't one of the *boys*, either.

That truth was never more evident than when the shower went on in the bathroom and he pictured her naked and wet under the steaming spray.

He lay there for all of ten seconds before he bolted off the bed and found a condom. His clothes were still flying as he marched to the bathroom door.

He didn't bother to knock. He just wrenched the door open and stormed inside. Crystal peeked around the shower curtain, her eyes wide with surprise—until she lowered her gaze and understood exactly what was on his mind.

"Do I . . . um, take this to mean you're not mad at me anymore?" She pushed aside the shower curtain and made room for him to join her.

"I'm mad as hell," he growled, stepping under the spray and dragging her sweet, lush body flush against him. "You're a bull-headed, argumentative, irresponsible little fool and so help me God, if anything happens to you, I'm gonna freakin' kill you."

She looped her arms around his neck, went up on her tiptoes, and with a little help from him, clambered right up until her legs were locked around his waist. "Nothing is going to happen to me."

"Wrong," he snarled against her mouth. "Something is definitely about to happen."

"Only," she whispered as he reached between them and positioned his cock to her opening, "because I'm letting it happen."

She sucked in a sharp breath when he flexed his hips and plunged into her.

"Only—" She caught her breath on a gasp and pressed her forehead against his shoulder when he moved, burying himself deeper into her tight, wet heat. "Only . . . oh God, that feels soooo good . . . because I want it to happen."

"Wouldn't matter," he said, one hand spanning her ass and deepening the connection, the other knotted in her hair as the water sluiced down around them. "Nothing but this matters," he ground out, tipping her head back and plundering her throat with his mouth.

"Nothing but here." He dragged open-mouthed, biting kisses along her jaw. "Nothing but now. Nothing"—he whispered kisses across her face before claiming her mouth—"but this."

This, whatever it was, consumed him. Not just sex. Not merely compulsion. This was critical mass. This was heaven and hell and all parts in between.

He didn't just want to claim her. He wanted to possess and be possessed and damn if she wasn't doing a helluva job of making both happen. As little as she was, she dominated his mind and his senses as she gave and took and begged him to take her higher. She transported him away from the despair and misery of those eyes that would haunt him, and took him someplace clean and pristine and full of hope.

"Make me come," she pleaded, tightening her legs and her inner muscles and squeezing until what little blood was left in his head dove south.

He pumped into her like a piston, caught her gasps in his mouth, and clutched her hips with both hands as she rocked frantically against him, turning his entire body into one raw nerve shot through with electric sensation.

"Make . . . me . . . commmmmmm," she demanded, devouring his mouth, then stiffening on a low, keening moan when she convulsed around him.

Her wild and powerful orgasm was all it took to shoot him over the edge. He came right along with her, hot and thick and *motherofgod*, so strong it buckled his knees. He groped for and found the showerhead. Then he pressed her against the shower wall and hung on for the rest of the ride as she took him down the path to perdition.

Yeah. He was destroyed. Utterly. Irrevocably. Blissfully.

Tinkerbell had taken him down. And there wasn't a damn thing he could do or wanted to do about it.

* * *

Well. That had solved exactly nothing, Johnny thought as Crystal's wet, naked body lay sprawled across his on the twin bed closest to the bathroom. It was a wonder they'd managed to make it that far.

And it's a wonder she didn't try to knock the ever-loving crap out of him for the way he'd taken her. No mistake about it, he had taken her.

Or had she taken him?

Hell. He didn't know. One minute he'd been lying there, pissed at the world in general and her in particular and the next he'd been inside her. Ramming into her, slamming her up against the shower wall with all the finesse of a wounded bull. Needing her goodness and her life to remind him there was more than what he'd seen, more, even, than what he'd done in his life in the name of right that sometimes came from wrong.

She stirred slightly. Yawned. Her warm breath fanned his naked chest. "Did we just kiss and make up?"

He stroked his hand over her bare back. Silk. Her skin felt like silk. "Is that what you call it? Kissing?"

She lifted her head, crossed her arms on top of his chest, and rested her chin there. Her green eyes were all soft and sleepy when they met his. "Hi."

He grinned, though Lord only knew why. Because she made him want to, he guessed. "Hi."

She was quiet for a moment, her expression turning thoughtful. "Do you suppose they're at the embassy yet?"

He craned his head around to see the nightstand,

snagged his watch, and checked the time. "If not, they will be soon."

She uncurled a forefinger, touched it to his chin.

"They'll be okay," he assured her because she looked so sad.

She tried for a smile but didn't quite manage it. "I'm not a mother but I think I might know how a mom feels when faced with leaving her daughter behind."

It didn't matter that Crystal barely knew Dina or Mary. Johnny had watched as a bond had been forged between them. It was the one good thing that may have come out of their horrible experience.

"You're sure they're going to get out of here okay?"

"I'm sure." He lifted her hand, studied the inside of her wrist. Although it was red and raw and scabbed over, he was relieved to see that the brand showed no signs of infection. It pissed him off all over again that Yao had branded her. "Dina will be on a flight home before the day is over. Hopefully, the British authorities will react as efficiently for Mary's sake."

Again she was quiet before lowering her head and laying her cheek back down on his chest. "How does this happen? How, in this age, can human rights be so blatantly violated? I don't understand. I'll never understand."

Johnny touched a hand to her hair. Breathed deep. No. She didn't understand. He hoped to hell she never would. Hoped she would never find out about the things he'd seen, the things he'd had to do in the name of human rights—hell, in the name of *right*. And he prayed to God she would never know the worst of man's cruelty to man.

"It's going to be okay," he promised.

But she was already asleep.

"It's going to be okay," he whispered again, vowing then and there that when this was over he'd figure out a way to show her the best of him so she could forget about the worst of this.

Only one problem—he had to figure out what his best was.

Hell, maybe he didn't have a "best." He'd never thought about it before. Never seen the need. Now, well, now he wondered.

What if . . . what if this was as good as he got?

Was it enough? Could he possibly be enough for a woman like Crystal?

No-good piece of shit.

His old man's voice, never far out of earshot, echoed like the report of a rifle through a cavernous canyon.

He'd spent his adult life trying to outrun his father's words. Outrun, drown out, prove wrong.

But this was Crystal, not his old man. Proving his dad wrong had been an act of spite. Proving he was enough for *her*—hell. That was a whole new ball game.

Game. He tucked his head, looked down at the woman trusting him to be what she needed him to be.

No. No game. This was much more important than a game.

This was life altering. Course changing. Deal breaking. And he could not, *would not* fuck it up.

* * *

Crystal had learned over the years that men just didn't know how to handle it when Tinkerbell transformed into Mighty Mite and dug in her heels. Reed, it turned out, was the biggest pushover of them all. He could have physically forced her to go to the embassy this morning. And she had no illusions: even a locked bathroom door would have proven no deterrent if he'd decided he wanted inside. He'd proven that a little later. After the guys had gone.

Now they were back. She watched them refuel on the satay and curry puffs filled with chicken and potatoes and an assortment of fresh fruit they'd brought back to the hotel with them after delivering Dina and Mary to the embassy. All had gone well, Nate assured her, and she'd finally let herself feel relief.

"Do I want to know why these are called muddies?" she asked, picking up another delicious and spicy chili crab.

"That would be because they live in the mud of the canals in the harbor," Savage told her.

She stopped with one halfway to her mouth.

"No worries," Savage assured her with a grin. "As long as you don't make a steady diet of them, your heavy metal and mercury levels shouldn't set off any metal detectors."

"Live dangerously," Green suggested, handing her a bottle of water.

"Yeah, thanks to Yao, I think I've got that part down," she said. "Until the past few days, braving the subway system in New York one summer had been about as dangerous as my life had ever gotten."

"You handled that snatch-and-grab like a pro," Doc said with a salute of his water bottle.

The others nodded in agreement. All but Johnny, who polished off a curry puff, then stood. "We need to move out of here," he said abruptly.

Crystal thought that maybe it should concern her that she didn't have to ask why. Just like the rental cars they'd exchanged three times while they'd done surveillance, she figured he wanted to move as a precaution.

Probably, it should also concern her that it had felt like the most natural thing in the world to make room for him in the shower earlier and welcome him into her body.

No, she thought again, as she caught those blue eyes watching her. It wasn't just sex between them anymore. It was scarier than sex. It scared him, too, if the way he quickly averted his eyes when she caught him staring, told her anything. If the way he'd awakened her with a soft kiss and a whispered, "Better get dressed. The guys will be back soon," followed by another long, lingering kiss, told the tale.

"Make sure you put some more of that antibiotic salve that Doc gave you on your wrist, okay?"

Tenderness. He did it well. She wondered if he was even aware of the shift in dynamics between them. Wondered if it was a conscious decision on his part or if he was simply so concerned about her safety that he was mired in the logistics of keeping her alive.

Both were intriguing thoughts. Both ideas pleased her. As a rule, men pretty much matched their expectations to their actions. In her case, all most of them saw was a hot babe and a quick lay. None of them ever stuck around long enough to consider the protection angle because none of them thought beyond getting lucky with Chucky.

Once she'd figured that out, she'd gotten her heart broken a whole lot less because when she played—not that she played very often—she played it the same way they did. That's how it had started out with Reed, after all. Fun and games.

Now . . . well, the door to Heartbreak Hotel yawned wide open again.

She watched him move about the room, gathering his things, all buff and beautiful and capable and thought, *So help me God, if he lets me down, I'm going to slit my wrists—right after I cut off his dangly parts.*

15

"I spotted a hotel on the way back from the embassy that should work as a new base," Nate said when they were all packed up. "Ten blocks west, five blocks south of here."

A cell phone rang. All five men checked their pockets but it was Savage who answered.

"Yo," he said, then listened, nodded. "Roger that. Thanks for the heads-up."

He pocked his phone, scrubbed a palm over the stubble on his lower face. "Pays to have friends in Spooktown. That was Cavanaugh. They picked up some chatter. Seems our pal Yao's pouring a shitload of manpower into finding the 'Americans' who broke into his warehouse and stole a couple valuable pieces of inventory."

Nate grunted. "Pissed him off, did we?"

"Oh, yeah," Savage confirmed with a grim nod. "We've officially got a price on our heads."

"Perfect," Johnny grumbled with a glare at Crystal. "It's going to make it a helluva lot trickier getting you out of the country."

"Let's not borrow trouble," Nate said with a calm assurance. "Sam will come through with Crystal's birth certificate tomorrow, we'll get her to the embassy, get her on a plane, then we all blow this place. For now, grab what you want to take with you and let's book on out of here."

The second hotel was pretty much a carbon copy of the first one. Old, shabby, first-floor rooms that opened to the back lot where they parked yet a new pair of rental cars.

"So what happens now?" Crystal asked Johnny as he tossed his go bag on the floor beside a double bed. Looked like they were roommates again. Savage and Green shared a room on their left; Colter and Black flanked them on the right.

"Shut-eye."

She jerked around, surprised to see Nate looming in their open doorway.

"The guys need to catch a few hours. You'd best grab some while you can get it." He nodded pointedly at Johnny after checking his watch, making Crystal wonder if the boss man suspected what was going on between them. "Nothing we can do but lay low and wait out the rest of the day anyway."

Then he was gone. Johnny walked to the door and locked it.

"Kind of spooky how he just appears that way," Crystal said, collapsing on the bed. She'd caught an hour or so of sleep earlier but she could stand a few more. And the others—they had to be running on absolute empty.

"So . . . how badly does it complicate things that Yao's after us? I mean, no one's gotten a good look at you or the guys. I'm the only one any of them have seen."

The mattress dipped under his weight when he joined her on the bed. "Yeah, well, it's a complication we sure as hell didn't need, but trust me on this, okay? We're getting you out of here."

Once upon a time if Johnny Duane Reed had told her to trust him, she'd have not so politely informed him that would happen roughly at the same time that hot springs bubbled up on the polar cap. Yeah. Once upon a time before he'd given her little glimpses of who he really was. Once upon a time when he worked a lot harder at hiding who he was behind hey-baby smiles, blatant sexuality, and a damn fine act meant to convince her that what she saw was all she got.

She knew there was more. So much more. What she didn't know was why he chose to hide it.

She turned on her side to face him. "Why the act?" she asked bluntly.

His eyes were already closed as he lay on his back beside her. "What are you talking about?"

"I'm talking about the act you have perfected where you pretend you're so much less than what you are."

He was quiet for so long, she thought he'd fallen asleep. She'd almost dozed off herself before he answered.

"Keeps expectations low," he said on a weary breath. "Less disappointment all around that way."

His tone, as much as his words, made her heart break. She rose up on an elbow, searched his face. "Less disappointment for who?"

He turned his head, looked at her, his blue eyes clouded with something she thought she recognized. An old and long-suffered pain.

"Who set a standard you couldn't measure up to, Johnny?"

He lifted a hand, brushed the back of his knuckles over her cheek. "No one who matters anymore."

Or someone who mattered very much, she thought.

"Get some sleep, Tinkerbell." He hooked an arm around her shoulders and pulled her close. "While you've got the chance."

She snuggled against his chest. Absorbed the core solid strength of him and wondered if she would ever know. Wondered if he would ever give her access to those deep, dark secrets that had shaped him and made him both the man he was and the man he wasn't.

Most of all, she wondered, when this was over—if this was ever over—if Johnny Duane Reed in either persona would stick around to see what happened next between them. Then she tried to convince herself she wasn't scared by the very certain knowledge that she wanted him to.

The next time Crystal woke up it was night. A pale light from outside cast a dim glow into the room. The silence was overwhelming, until she really listened.

The low, humming drone of a small fan oscillated and whirred, moving the stale, warm air in the tiny hotel room.

A plastic window shade went *tap, tap, tap*, soft and rhythmic against the sill as the fan stirred the space around it.

Lying beside her, Johnny breathed in and out in a slow, steady cadence, proof of another life in the dark, a reminder of another heart beating.

The beat of her own heart quickened when she realized he was awake. That he was listening, too.

She reached out, laid her palm on his bare chest. Marveled at his heat, at his strength, at the way his heartbeat reacted to her slightest touch.

"Make love to me," she whispered, her voice caressed by the silence.

His response was immediate and profoundly moving. With only those soft, secret night sounds as witness, he moved over her, kissed her deeply, then slid home.

And new sounds filled the dark.

Sharp breaths of stunning urgency.

Long sighs of immeasurable pleasure.

Humming beats of awareness of an unbreakable bond being forged.

In the heat of the night, without a single word spoken, she felt everything change between them. Until this moment, they'd only played at love, danced cautiously around the prospect of commitment. But as he sank in and out of her body, immersing them in sensation and a profound stream of consciousness, he sought her gaze in the dark. What she saw in his eyes brought tears to hers as it became achingly, wonderfully clear. The biggest player of them all wasn't playing anymore.

He loved her. He couldn't touch her this way if he didn't. Couldn't move her this way if it were only a game.

Stunned, shaken, she clung to him as he murmured her name between deep, soulful kisses and took them beyond sex to something neither of them had been looking for and had never, in a million years, expected to find.

"We're good to go," Nate told Johnny from the open doorway to their room the next morning. "Got a call from Sam. He and Abbie located Crystal's BC and have already faxed it to the embassy. It should be there when we get there."

"Give us five minutes," Johnny said. "We'll meet you outside."

He drew a deep breath, shut the door, and turned back to the room—to see Crystal regarding him with a look that sent all of his warning bells clanging.

"I don't want to leave."

Fuck. He'd been afraid of this. Almost as afraid of facing her this morning. Last night. Whoa. Last night had been intense. Out of the box, uncharted territory, rocked-his-world intense.

There was no backing away from it now. There was no way to go back. He'd frickin' fallen in love with her.

Yeah, all the way back in Bandung, he'd thought that maybe it was possible. He knew it now. He didn't want to but he loved this woman. And he would do anything in his power to keep her safe and alive.

Even if it meant pissing her off. Even if it meant convincing her that his center of gravity hadn't been skewed beyond correction last night in this bed because everything he saw in her eyes told him she'd taken the big fall, too.

"You don't have a choice," he said while she stood there, searching his face, waiting, he suspected, for him to say something about what was happening between them.

Yeah. She felt it, too. Only like him, she had yet to say a word. Scary territory for her, too, he figured. He could alleviate that fear. He could flat-out shout it to the world—I love you!—and damn, he wanted to.

But he wasn't going to do it. Not now. Not here. Right now he was going to make her think she was dispensable when in fact he could no longer imagine his life without her in it.

Just sex, he told her with a look, because if she got to believing it had gone beyond sex to happily ever after, she'd dig in her heels and do what she was doing right now, which was insisting she wasn't going to leave him.

His reaction—distant and cool—hurt her. Hurt him too to see that confused, wounded look in her fairy green eyes. Couldn't be helped. She was going home and he was damn sure going to make it happen.

"What about Yao?" she asked, a brave little soldier,

tucking away the pain and carrying on, only with a new tactic.

He shrugged, resisting the urge to take her in his arms and confess that his big show of indifference was all an act. "He lives to fight another day."

"Bull. Shit."

Gawddamn, he thought, scrubbing a hand over his face. It was eight o'clock in the frickin' morning, they'd done more lovemaking than sleeping last night, and the pixie still had the energy and the moxie to wage war.

"Does your momma know you talk like that?"

"You're going after him, aren't you?" she pressed, refusing to let him sidetrack her. "I know you are. As soon as you ship me out, you're going after him."

He dropped his chin to his chest. Fought for patience. And lied through his teeth. "I already told you what happens next."

"Right. You'll catch a flight home, probably beat me back there. I heard. I want to know what you *really* have planned. All that talk about backing away from Yao? You actually think I bought it?"

This was why he'd always shied away from intelligent women. They were just too . . . *intelligent.* She'd seen through their little smoke screen with X-ray vision. Hell, yeah, they were going after Yao. They were all in agreement. Sanctioned or not, the entire team wanted to take Yao out of the mix and kill or at the very least cripple some of his lucrative enterprises while they were at it.

"It's gotta be clean and it can't lead back to Uncle," Nate had said when the guys had gotten together in Nate's room this morning while Crystal was in the shower.

In other words, SOP—standard operating procedure—provided they could get Tinkerbell back to never-never land.

"I want in on it," she stated with a look of determination that would have been cute if she weren't pissing him off so damn much.

"And I want peace on earth. That's not gonna happen either. You're not winning this argument."

For damn sure, she wasn't winning. Not, by God, this one. Her mouth was open, ready to lay into him when he marched across the room. She read his look for what it was and backed away, hands out in front of her like a shield.

"You're short on resources. *I'm* a resource," she reminded him, scrambling to get away. "You know I am. I proved that I am."

"What you are is in the way." He moved in fast. Before she knew what was happening, he picked her up, tossed her over his shoulder, and hauled her out of the room.

"Quiet," he barked when she swore a blue streak. "You'll wake up the neighbors. And goddammit, quit kicking!"

Because she deserved it, he swatted her rear before he shoved her into the backseat of the waiting car and crawled in after her. "Go," he told Green, who shifted

into gear and pulled out behind Doc, who was in the
lead car.

That, he told himself, was the end of that. She could
yell all she wanted. Or, fine, she could give him the
silent treatment—her method of choice at the moment.
He didn't care. He wanted her out of danger and since
he was bigger and badder than she was, he was going to
make it happen even if he had to haul her over his
shoulder again and carry her kicking and screaming
through the embassy doors.

And it *would* have happened, if all hell hadn't broken loose on the street when they neared the embassy
fifteen minutes later.

"Fuck," Green swore as he eased off the gas. Ahead
of them Doc had slowed to a crawl along with the rest
of the traffic.

"What's going on?" Crystal finally broke her silence
as the embassy grounds came into view on Jalan
Medan Merdeka Selatan.

To their right, a huge group of people marched in
front of the complex that made up the U.S. embassy
buildings.

"Looks like we got us a little demonstration," Savage
said.

Both foot and vehicle traffic crammed into several
lanes on both sides of the divided street. Several uniformed police officers carrying batons, rifles, and handguns and wearing dark gray pants, light gray shirts, and
white caps with black brims lined the streets. Dozens
more officers piled out of the open boxes of two dark

gray trucks with POLISI painted in yellow on the side.

Military personnel added to the numbers and were milling through the crowd, automatic weapons at the ready.

"This can't be good." Johnny reached for his phone just as it rang. He knew it would be Nate. "Yo."

"Not the kind of party we like to crash."

"No shit."

The chanting crowd moved like a huge, white wave angrily shaking signs and marching in protest of some U.S. policy.

"Check out the firepower, two o'clock about ten yards ahead," Nate said.

Johnny craned his neck so he could see out the window. A contingent of local police and a small squad of men wearing what he recognized as Indonesian military uniforms stood guard at the entrance of the building that housed the consulate.

Green's phone rang then. He answered, listened, and hung up.

"That was Cavanaugh," Green told them. "Passing along another piece of intel they just picked up over the wires. It seems that what we've got here, ladies and gents, is a bona fide goatfuck. That little welcoming committee with the artillery?" He nodded toward the show of military force. "It's most likely for us. Yao's kicked the hunt into high gear. He called in his chips and spread a net over the whole city. The entire police force and military are now on the lookout for us—and the story's changed a bit. We're now a rogue band of

American mercenaries who attacked his business and killed his 'innocent' employees."

Johnny relayed the info to Nate, who was still on the line.

"He must have figured we'd try to reach the embassy with the girls," Nate concluded.

"And what do you want to bet the train stations, both airports, and the seaports are swarming with Yao's flunkies just waiting for us to make a break for it?"

"We'd better make tracks. Look sharp, now. This is bound to get dicey," Nate said, then hung up. They all knew what they had to do. Vacate the premises. ASAP.

"Guess that confirms that Yao has bed partners in high places," Savage said with a grunt. Keeping his pistol low and out of sight, he double-checked his magazine.

A small crack opened up in the traffic and Doc nosed through. Green stuck on his bumper like a license plate. Together, the two vehicles inched their way toward the next intersection.

"Where is he headed?" Crystal asked after what felt like hours. Doc had managed to gradually work his way into a lane of traffic that moved a degree or two faster than a decrepit snail.

"Anywhere but here," Savage said from the front seat. "Yesterday, if possible."

Tomorrow didn't even look likely as another small eternity passed and they moved all of three yards.

"Possible threat right." Savage slumped a little lower in the passenger seat as a patrol of soldiers worked their way toward them.

Johnny pulled a Ruger out from under the front seat. *Goatfuck*, he thought again. With a capital F-U-C-K.

"Stay low." He checked the magazine and slid a round into the chamber. When he looked up at the patrol, all of them carrying AK-47s, they had closed the gap between them and the crowd to around twenty yards. Clearly, they were searching for anyone who looked out of place. It didn't get much more out of place than six westerners driving two cars with rental plates.

"Shit," Johnny swore. "I think they made us."

16

All eyes turned right. The foot patrol of half a dozen uniformed men had a bead on them. They were sitting ducks. Their cars were locked in a sea of traffic moving at a pace that made a tortoise look like a sprinter.

"Time to scatter." Savage jammed the vehicle in park and shouldered open the passenger-side door.

Johnny already had his hand on the door handle. Nate and Doc were also bailing as the soldiers, less than ten yards away now, picked up their pace, shoving through the crowd, shouting at everyone in their path to get out of the way.

"Go," Johnny said with a nod to Savage and Green. "We'll reconnect later."

He grabbed Crystal by the arm and took off running into the clot of milling protesters jamming the streets and sidewalks and interchanges surrounding the embassy grounds. A quick look back into the loud and boisterous crowd told him what he wanted to know. The divide-and-run tactic had thrown the patrol off task. The few seconds it had taken for the military detail to decide to split up and follow Nate and Doc, who had taken off in one direction, and Savage and Green, who sprinted in the other, had provided the edge they'd all needed to make their escape.

"Blend!" Johnny shouted, ducking low to keep from being spotted above the crowd.

"Always the comedian!" Crystal shouted back as she struggled to follow him through the mass of bodies streaming in the opposite direction.

Yeah, he was a laugh a minute. The truth was, it was a tough trick to blend in when the bulk of the population topped out at around five-six or -seven and most of them wore white shirts and black hair and the mood was fast edging toward riot mode. A regular magic act for a six-foot-plus blond American in a black T-shirt and cammo pants and a petite redhead wearing a flowered tank and a Tinkerbell tattoo riding on the curve of her bare shoulder.

Behind him, he felt the tug of Crystal's slight weight when she stumbled and almost went down.

He reeled her in close beside him. "We've got to get out of this mob!" He had to yell to be heard above the chanting.

"*Matilah Amerika! Matilah kapitalisme!*" (Death to America! Death to capitalism!)

The entire radical Muslim contingent seemed to have picked today, of all days, to show up in force to advocate the demise of America. Like they didn't have enough trouble.

This wasn't working. The crowd was fast getting out

of control. The only reason their focus wasn't on him and Crystal was because they hadn't yet discovered the two Americans in their midst. As soon as they did, it would all be over but the beheadings and the burning in effigy.

No sooner had he drawn that conclusion than a man reached out and grabbed at Crystal.

"Back off!" Johnny shoved him away. He tucked Crystal under his arm, held her snug against his side, and made it clear by the look on his face that the next person to touch her was dead.

"*Orang Amerika!*" (Americans!) the man shouted, drawing the attention of the mob.

That soaked it. Johnny drew out the Ruger and pointed it dead center at the chest of the closest merry-maker. Several people screamed but the crowd shrank back, separating for him the way the Red Sea had parted for Moses. Eyes alert, Johnny marched straight ahead, using the Ruger to clear their path as they crossed the eastbound lanes of Jalan Medan Merdeka Selatan, then sprinted through a median strip filled with low shrubs and scratchy flowering trees.

"Stay with me," he shouted as they gradually eased out of the nucleus of the mob and dodged westbound lanes jammed with bumper-to-bumper traffic. Finally clear of the street, he ran into a wooded area where he finally pulled her behind a stout tree.

"What is this? A park?" Crystal leaned against the tree trunk, panting in the heat.

"National monument." He chanced a glance behind them to see if they were still being followed. "At least that's what I remember. Shit," he swore, when he spotted two soldiers about thirty yards back, systematically sweeping the grounds. "Time to make like a tree and leaf."

He thought he heard a breathless "har, har," as he latched on to her hand and shot off at a run again, dodging and ducking behind one tree after another, putting as much distance as he could between them and the nice men with the big guns.

Nothing like a race for your life to roust a girl out of a snit, Crystal thought, gasping for breath as Johnny ducked into the overhang of a shop of some sort and dragged her in behind him.

Sucking air, she leaned against the building, staring at his back as he scanned the street for threats. Thank God he'd finally stopped for a breather when they'd broken out of the park and reached this little business district. And all this running was painful.

Where oh where was a sports bra when a girl needed one?

She made herself focus. Knew she had to get back into the very real game of life and death if they were going to get out of this alive and intact.

Pedestrian traffic buzzed by like a swarm of bees. She'd never seen so many people. Walking. Talking. Bartering. On almost every corner merchants hawked spices or hats or flowers or food. Shoppers clogged the walkways haggling for deals. An old, wrinkled woman sold bread and pastries not three feet from where they stood while a young woman displayed tablecloths and bed linens made of the most beautiful batik. And how weird was that? Crystal recognized the batik because she'd taken a textiles class in college. Knew that the design on the cloth was made by melting hot wax into the fabric, then dyeing it prior to removing the wax, but this was like no tie-dye she'd ever seen. For a mindless moment, she wanted to take the time to examine the exquisite designs.

Johnny tossed some cash at the startled woman, then snagged an ivory and cream tablecloth. "Wear this over your head and shoulders like a shawl," he ordered and started walking again.

As a disguise, what it lacked in originality, it more than made up in the "blend" department. Jakarta appeared to be a city straddling the line between Western and traditional dress. While many of the women bared their faces and heads, just as many wore shawls and veils.

"We need to hitch a ride." He ducked under yet another doorsill while on their right a little boy—he couldn't have been more than eight or ten—sold intricately carved ebony figurines. "Get the hell out of this part of Dodge."

Hitch a ride, how? she wondered. The street traffic, like the foot traffic, was horrific. Bumper to bumper, exhaust fumes thicker than soup. Millions of motorcycles wove in and out of multiple lanes of cars and vans that alternately stopped, started, stalled, and roared between intersections.

"This way." Head ducked low, his arm clutched tightly around her shoulders, Johnny took off again—at a fast walk this time—then broke into a run. When she saw the bus ahead, she realized why. They jumped on board and squeezed through the doors just before they closed.

"Where are we going?" She had to tip her face up to his to be heard above the roar and grind of the diesel motor and the jumble of conversations as he hung on to an overhead strap and she hung on to him.

"Away," he said simply, then quickly crouched down so his head and face were hidden behind the man in front of him.

She whipped her head around so she could see what he'd seen. There on the street corner just outside the bus, two armed soldiers scoured the crowd. Knowing who they were looking for, Crystal pulled the table-cloth more fully over her face.

Certain the soldiers would stop the bus and search it, she waited, too afraid to breathe. The bus coughed to a lurching start. The driver shifted gears and they jerked forward again, finally leaving the soldiers behind. She exhaled in relief, only then realizing she'd been holding her breath—and that Johnny was still trying to make himself invisible.

She looked down at the top of his head. Damned if she knew why, but seeing him attempt to hide his broad shoulders, blond hair, and six-foot-plus frame behind a man half his size shot her straight out of fear mode. "So, how's that blending thing working for you?"

He finally stood, met her grin with a glare. "About as well as my plans to get you out of this fucking city."

Yeah, she thought, as the bus continued on its jolting, jerking way, *there was that*.

Crystal soon learned that besides being scary, overcrowded, and hot, Jakarta was a monstrous, dirty, sprawling megalopolis made up of many Dutch colonial structures as well as unusual buildings heavily influenced by Chinese and Arab cultures, some old, some new, and some reduced to slums. A lot reduced to slums. Busy pockets of commerce cropped up everywhere, all swirling around traffic circles that were flooded with motorcycles, buses, and little tin cans on wheels Johnny referred to as "bajajs." And there were bicycles everywhere.

She also learned that the city was filled not only with locals but also with a few expats from dozens of countries, although for the life of her she couldn't figure out why anyone would want to live here. She supposed it was a lot like any big city. It had its bad elements but there were certain to be good elements, too.

Of course, she thought, as they exited one bus and jumped on another, her impressions of Jakarta might be a tad colored by the fact that she hadn't exactly been on a luxury vacation. She'd been abducted, drugged, branded, shot at, hung on a rope over an elevator shaft, and in general, been on the run the entire time she was in the city. And now, after several hours of switching buses, breathing exhaust, curry, and sweaty bodies, she was hungry, exhausted, and she had to pee.

They finally stopped at the Senen bus terminal so she could use the facilities.

And, oh my God.

"There was a snake in there," she ground out between clenched jaws, still trying to regulate her heartbeat when she met Johnny outside the public restroom where he waited for her.

"As long as he paid his six cents, I guess he's as entitled as anyone else."

She didn't like him very much right about then. Truth be told, she hadn't liked him very much since she'd awakened this morning and found the new, unreadable Johnny Duane Reed waiting for her, instead of the sensitive lover who'd made her feel cherished in the night.

Gone was that "love" connection she'd thought they'd made. She'd wanted to talk to him about what had happened between them, but this morning, everything seemed to have changed.

For God's sake, she thought in disgust. She had bigger problems at the moment than trying to figure out what made Johnny Reed tick. Men with guns were hunting them like dogs. Yao wanted them dead. They were running for their lives, yet here she was, staring at Reed's broad back, following him to yet another bus, more worried about their relationship than staying alive.

It was just that whatever had happened between them

seemed to have been reduced to only another round of hot, sweaty sex. Amazing, intimate sex, she amended, still unable to concentrate on anything but him.

His beard was beyond redemption, his shirt was stained with sweat now, but this morning, the man had been cucumber cool. Instead of soulful and sweet, he'd been cold and distant when she'd faced him in the morning light. All business. He'd closed whatever door he'd unlocked on his emotions . . . emotions that he'd shared last night in that bed.

What had happened in that bed had been . . . profound.

Oh my God. Just listen to you, she thought in disgust. In the immortal words of legendary baseball player Yogi Berra, it was déjà vu all over again. Only in reverse. *She* was the one wondering what had happened in that bed, not Johnny. That, she assured herself, was because Johnny knew how to pick his priorities, and at this moment in time, priority number one was staying alive.

That fact didn't, however, keep her from hitting the proverbial wall when he grabbed her elbow and hustled her through the waiting lines. "Step it up."

Step it up? She'd been stepping it up, down, inside out, and sideways all the fricking day long. And she had had it with his drill sergeant edicts.

She put on the skids. Glared at him when he spun around to see what was holding her up.

"You know, I'm about this far from the end of my rope." She pinched her thumb and forefinger together and shoved it under his nose. "So don't be ordering me to *step it up*."

He batted her hand away, leaned down, and got right in her face. "Why don't you shriek a little bit louder? I don't think the nice policeman over by the exit with the automatic rifle heard the waspish American shrew throw her fit. Come on. I know you can draw more attention because, hey, that's what we've been trying to do all fricking day."

Caught somewhere between chastised and ticked, she glared right back.

He swore under his breath, then grabbed her elbow and started dragging her to yet another bus platform and away from the new threat before they were spotted.

Okay. So he'd made his point. And yeah, he was tired, too. It didn't mean she wasn't still PO'd. "This is your plan?" she ground out in a strained whisper. "To ride the bus for the next, oh, month or so?"

"If that's what it takes to keep you alive, yeah, that would be the plan. But just for you, we're going to head for a safe house."

She stopped short again when he would have dragged her on yet one more bus. "There's a safe house?"

"There is now," he said, lifted her off her feet, and stuffed her through the bus's open door.

"And you couldn't have told me that before now?"

"What? And miss your little hissy fit?"

"I did not—"

"Cool your jets, Tinkerbell. I just found out myself.

Nate called while you and the snake were making friends. Cavanaugh came through for Green. This bus should take us within a few blocks of where we want to be."

She almost wept with relief.

"Hang in there, Tink." His voice gentled then, along with his expression, and with it, her sour mood took a hike.

"I'm sorry I got bitchy."

"I'm sorry you did, too."

Since he grinned when he said it, she just rolled her eyes and grudgingly grinned back.

"So this is what you do for a living," she said with a shake of her head.

"Sometimes we get to be the cha*sers* instead of the cha*sees*. It's a lot more fun that way."

"Fun. I have a vague recollection of that concept."

Miraculously, a seat opened up next to them. Johnny eased into it and pulled her down onto his lap. She sagged against him with a sigh.

"Just a little while longer. You're doing fine," he whispered, wrapping a strong arm around her waist and lowering his cheek to the top of her head.

"We *were* doing fine," she said, weary enough, defenses low enough, that she decided to broach the subject that had been bugging her all day. "Last night. We were doing *great* last night."

He was silent for a long moment. "Not the time. Not the place."

Yeah. She knew that. Knowing, however, didn't make things any easier. "Will it ever be?"

Another prolonged silence passed before he hugged her hard against him. "Let's tackle one thing at a time, okay?"

No. It wasn't okay.

But she wasn't calling the shots here. He was, so for now it would have to be.

17

Green was making lists again. Crystal was still struggling to process her current surroundings. Talk about your one-hundred-eighty-degree turnaround. She'd seen every low-rent slum district in the city along with some truly spectacular temples and urban skyscrapers on their un-planned "scenic" bus tour. Now, however, after finally getting off their last bus and making their way on foot to the address Nate had given Johnny, the six of them were reunited and basking in the lap of luxury.

An amah—a woman house servant—anticipated their every need in the formal dining room of a man-sion that, with its steeply pitched gables, large airy win-dows, and soaring finials could have come straight out of a historical movie set about the Dutch East Indies.

The interior, like the exterior, was cool, spacious, and regal. The service and food, straight out of a five-star hotel. Think you might want a beer? An ice-cold bottle and frosty glass magically appeared before you. Have a yen for fresh fruit? Watermelon, pineapple, grapes—you name it—appeared on the table in huge, ornate bowls to join a heavenly array of spicy dishes laid out before them in a sumptuous banquet. After the duck-and-run day they'd all had dodging Yao's men, no one was shy about digging in, either. Or about taking advantage of the hot showers and cool air-conditioning.

"Who did you say lives here?" Crystal had asked Joe Green when she and Johnny had finally made their way to the compound and met him at the gates around five p.m.

"An expatriate by the name of Windle. Apparently Cavanaugh is tight with him. And since Windle thinks Cavanaugh holds an upper-tier position in the U.S. embassy, Windle is always open to scoring points. You never know when a good back scratching will net a big favor."

So this is how an expat lived in Indonesia, Crystal thought, not for the first time since they'd arrived. If they all lived at this level of luxury, she could understand why they might find Jakarta appealing. Just like she understood why Cavanaugh would consider them safe here. A high cement wall surrounded the compound. On the way through the guarded gates she'd caught a glimpse of jagged pieces of glass embedded along the top of the twelve-inch-thick concrete wall—a convincing deterrent for anyone even thinking about climbing over. Of course they'd have to get past the dogs and the *jagas*—night guards—first.

"I would think it would be risky for Windle to offer this place up to us," Crystal said, still absorbing the silk damask upholstering the beautifully carved dining-room chairs, the richly paneled walls, and the strikingly vibrant art adorning them.

"It is a risk, yes."

All eyes turned to the double-arched dining-room doors and the stunningly gorgeous man with the deep, cultured voice who stood in the open doorway.

"But some risks are worth taking. Gentlemen," he said with a nod to each of them before he directed his attention to Crystal. "Lovely lady. You have my sympathies," he told her with a soft smile and a nod toward the men.

"They're my cross to bear," she said, seeing the spark of amusement in his dark eyes. "Thank you so much for helping us."

"My absolute pleasure." Never breaking eye contact, he walked over to her, lifted her hand to his mouth, and kissed it, earning a snort from Johnny. "Who is this charming creature?"

If his BS factor hadn't been so thick, Crystal might have bought into his flirtation. Clearly, the guy was a player, a charming one, but a player nonetheless. She could have kissed him, however, over Johnny's reaction. His carefully blank stare had slowly transitioned to the glare of a green-eyed monster.

It made her little heart go pitty-pat.

In the meantime, an expectant silence engulfed the room. It was apparent that everyone had questions but was holding back.

"You may go now, Dira," the man said to the amah, then walked her to the dining-room entrance and closed the doors behind her, allowing them complete privacy.

No sooner had he turned back to the room at large than Green grabbed his hand in a hard shake and clapped him affectionately on the back. "What in the hell are you doing here, Cavanaugh?"

"Cavanaugh?" Nate glanced at Savage and Green for confirmation that this was the Cavanaugh they'd both worked with during their hitch in the CIA. When they both nodded he turned back to the dark-haired man in the designer slacks and tailored shirt. "So *you're* the infamous Cavanaugh that Savage and Green seem to love to keep secrets about?"

"Infamous? Apparently my reputation has preceded me."

Crystal didn't know what she'd expected Cavanaugh to look like but it wasn't this dashing, GQ-quality man with the sparkling brown eyes and perfectly styled hair.

"Which would mean that you and Windle—" Savage prompted.

"Are one and the same, yes," Cavanaugh said with a shrug. "Sorry for the subterfuge but—"

"You didn't want to take any chances having your cover blown," Savage finished for him. "Christ, Cav. Nice digs. You've come up in the world since we worked undercover as lowly U.S. embassy staffers and shared a fifth-floor walk-up."

"Have to be some perks after this many years, don't you think?"

Despite their dangerous situation Crystal was fascinated by the turn of events. "So . . . there really isn't a Windle? It's just a cover?"

"Ridiculously dramatic, isn't it?" Cavanaugh's throwaway smile had no doubt won any number of women over to the dark side. "Speaking of dramatic, you all have managed to piss off the wrong man in this part of the world."

He dug into the breast pocket of his silver-gray silk shirt and pulled out a folded sheet of paper, holding it out to Savage.

Savage let out a low whistle after unfolding and studying it. "It would seem Yao's surveillance is a bit more sophisticated than I'd have figured."

Crystal joined the rest of them at the table. "Oh God."

It was a wanted poster, complete with headshots of everyone but Nate Black.

"How did they get these photographs?" she wanted to know.

"The brothel," Johnny said after thinking about it. "Had to be there, where we found Dina. Must have had security cameras in the lobby."

The individual photos were grainy but very recognizable headshots of Johnny, Doc, Savage, and Green. Crystal's photo was also included, which was kind of spooky because she didn't remember when it had been taken. The drugged look in her eyes explained why.

"What does it say?" she asked, referring to the captions.

Cavanaugh translated. "Cliff Notes version: American mercenaries, wanted dead or alive."

"Just like the wild, wild West," she said, still stunned by the implications.

"Complete with frontier justice," Cavanaugh agreed. "Yao couldn't have done a better job on distribution if he'd flown a fleet of Cobras over the city and let loose a paper rain. As of midday today, there's not a street corner, place of business, or public or private transpo depot that isn't papered with these things. The whole city is on the lookout for you. Major reward on the line for anyone providing a lead."

"I'm not up on my conversion rates from rupiah to dollars but anytime I see that many zeros I feel a swell of pride," Doc said. "How much are we worth American?"

"One hundred K per head," Cavanaugh said.

"Even Reed?" Doc asked with a grin. "Hell, I wouldn't have thought he'd have brought much more than a five-spot."

Used to Colter's trash talk, Johnny flipped him the bird. Crystal merely shook her head. It hadn't taken long for her to realize that the more trouble these guys were in, the more joking they did. Black humor. Release valve. Whatever. They had the routine down pat.

"Over here, one hundred thousand dollars buys a lifetime of living in high style," Cavanaugh continued, impervious to the good-natured ribbing.

"So why are you sticking your neck out like this, Cav?" Green asked.

"Beats the hell out of me. Guess I'm just a sucker for an ugly face," he added with a smile at Savage. "Had I known you had the good taste to keep such exceptional company, however"—this he addressed to Crystal— "I'd have signed on sooner. And don't you think it's time one of you Neanderthals summoned up the manners to introduce us properly?"

"Reed. Johnny Reed," Johnny said, moving to Crystal's side. "And Miss Debrowski is with me."

Crystal didn't know who was more shocked by his blatant show of possessiveness, her or the guys.

"Crystal," she said. "Please call me Crystal. And I'm afraid I'm the reason everyone is in so much danger."

"Sweet lady," Cavanaugh said, smiling brilliantly, "any man worth his salt would gladly follow you into the fire. I seriously doubt a single one of them would be here if they did not wish to be. So don't heap guilt on those pretty shoulders."

Was this guy for real? she wondered, glancing up at Johnny, who was staring at Cavanaugh with a "give it a rest, asshole" glare on his face.

"Luke Colter." Luke stepped up and extended his hand. Crystal suspected he was also running a little interference to diffuse the tension. "Call me Doc."

Cavanaugh returned Doc's handshake, then turned to Nate. "You would be the leader of this motley crew?"

"Guilty as charged. Nate Black," Nate said. "Appreciate the help."

"About that," Cavanaugh said soberly, "nothing's changed as far as the Company is concerned. We've got our hands full with the radical Islam element in Jakarta. Even if we weren't otherwise occupied, though, you all are way too hot a target. We can't afford any link."

Nate nodded. "Understood."

Crystal understood, too, but only because she had asked Johnny earlier why Green's and Savage's CIA connections couldn't be more help. He'd explained that the reason why the CIA—or the Company, as Cavanaugh referred to them—wasn't doing something about Yao was the same reason Nate and the boys were routinely dispatched to do the deed. It was in the interest of national security to ensure the US of A didn't leave any kind of footprint in this part of the world. Johnny and the guys worked exclusively for Uncle Sam, he'd told her, but they weren't on the payroll. From that she'd surmised that physical distance was the reason they were based out of Argentina.

"But, because I'm just a big softie," Cavanaugh continued with a straight face to which both Green and Savage reacted with a snort, "I'll do what I can to help you out. Totally off the books. You've got to make tracks though, and soon. Within the next twenty-four if possible. I'm out on a limb the size of a small twig even having you here. But like my boys keep reminding me"—he glanced at Savage and Green, who had both crossed their arms over their chests and were looking at him like they wondered what kind of a line he was going to come up with next—"it's back-scratching time.

"And then, there's the lady." He flashed a set of perfect pearly whites Crystal's way. "Anything to help the lady."

"We'll be happy as hell to get out of your hair," Johnny said stiffly, "as soon as we figure out how to get a line on a back door out of Jakarta."

Cavanaugh looked more amused than insulted by Johnny's brusque attitude. "You'll never make it past Yao's men at the airport or train depots. Highway travel is also out. He's got roadblocks set up on every off-ramp, back road, and highway out of the city."

"Short of teleporting us out, that kind of narrows down the options," Savage said with a grunt as Cavanaugh walked to an ornately carved buffet. He fished a key out of his trouser pocket and opened a drawer, then felt around until he removed a false bottom, opened it, and drew out a manila folder.

"These shots were recently taken in the harbor district," he said after clearing a space on the dining-room table and spreading out the photos. "Short geography lesson for the first-timers. There are actually two distinct harbors. Here and here." He pointed them out on the aerial shots. "The first is Ancol. The other is Tanjung Priok. Ancol is for private boats. The shoreline is clogged with yachts, clubs, and resorts, lots of money floating around—pardon the pun—with the jet set. Tanjung Priok is industrial. All the cargo ships moor there. Also the large fishing fleets.

"These larger sailboats with the long pointed bow?" He dug out a close-up shot, tapped it with his finger. "They're called boogies—spelled: b-u-g-i-s. The shots are black and white but every boat is a different color.

"Special little tidbit for you, Crystal. Once upon a

time, the pirates that sailed around the South China Seas and in this general area launched their attacks from these boats—that's where the term 'boogeyman' came from."

"Can we stay on task here?" Johnny asked irritably.

Cavanaugh grinned and pulled pen and paper out of the drawer. "I'm going to give you a number." He wrote while he talked, then handed the slip of paper to Nate. "I've got a man—Garuda—he's waiting for your call."

Nate ran his thumb over the paper, looked up at Cavanaugh. "Company man?"

Cavanaugh shook his head. "Longtime informant. He can be trusted—he's grown accustomed to the relative life of luxury that payment for his services has provided over the years."

"Payment that can compete with Yao's reward?" Johnny asked, skepticism coloring each word.

Frankly, Crystal was also distrustful of anyone whose loyalty was available to the deepest pockets, especially in this part of the world where human lives were bought and sold and bartered for with impunity.

Cavanaugh leveled Johnny a look. "I would trust Garuda with my life. I am trusting him with it at this moment by simply having you here and giving you access to him."

Nate glanced from Cavanaugh to Savage, then Green. Both men gave slight nods, confirmation that if Cavanaugh trusted this Garuda guy, they trusted him, too.

Seeing this, Cavanaugh continued. "Garuda is, as we speak, seeking transport to get you out of here by boat. He's got a line on a freighter, the *Bima Raya V.* She made port at Tanjung Priok this morning and has been taking on cargo all day. She's scheduled to sail for Manila before daylight. If you can get on her, the captain will take you to Manila. You can catch a flight back to the States from there."

"So our first problem is getting to the harbor without being spotted," Nate said, thinking out loud.

"There are three vehicles parked on the street three blocks south." Cavanaugh dug into his pants pockets and fished out three keys. "You're welcome to any one or all of them."

"So that leaves boarding the freighter," Nate said with a nod of thanks. "Do we know exactly when she sails for Manila?"

Cavanaugh shook his head. "Garuda will know soon. You need to be ready."

Cavanaugh produced yet one more key, which he also handed to Nate. "To the basement storeroom. I think you'll find any number of items that might be of assistance. Oh, and you *will* need these even if you've got cell phones now. Sorry I have only three." He reached into the buffet drawer again and this time came up with three cell phones. "Garuda will expect a call from this number," he said, handing a phone to Nate after checking the number. The other two he tossed on the table.

"Who's footing the bill for this?" Savage asked abruptly.

Cavanaugh dug around in the same buffet drawer. He came up with a city map and tossed it onto the table with the photos. "Let's just say Windle has a tidy little petty cash fund and leave it at that." He flashed a quick smile.

"Is this what I think it is?" Johnny asked, picking up one of the photos and inspecting it closely.

Cavanaugh stepped in to get a closer look. "If you're thinking it's Yao's yacht, then you're right on the money."

Crystal looked too and saw a sleek white vessel, complete with a teak deck and gleaming chrome fittings. It stood out for two reasons. One, it was the largest of several moored at the marina at Ancol. Two, a Komodo dragon emblem was painted on the bow.

"Asshole loves his dragons," Doc sputtered.

Crystal wasn't aware that she'd touched the brand on her wrist until the pain reminded her it was still healing.

"Unfortunately, I have to leave you to your own devices now. I'm due in Bali." He checked his watch. "An hour ago. Good luck," he added as he headed for the door. "In the meantime my house is your house—as long as you're out by morning.

"Crystal." He turned to her with a soft and very interested smile. "Another time, perhaps."

After brief nods to Savage and Green—silent acknowledgment that the score had been substantially evened in the favors department—he left. Crystal got the very distinct feeling that Johnny was more than happy to see him go. And despite the deadly and precarious position they were in, she smiled for the first time that day.

18

Within minutes of Cavanaugh's departure, Nate called the number on the cell phone Cavanaugh had given him. After a long conversation, he hung up and turned back to the group with a hard look. Johnny recognized that look. It was Nate Black in problem-solving mode.

"Okay, I'm guessing you're going to give us the bad news first because there is no good news?" Doc speculated because he knew what every one of them had already surmised.

"Yao's seek-and-destroy mission has intensified," Nate reported grimly. "According to Garuda, he's mobilized twenty more companies of infantry."

Doc made a sound of disbelief. "Twenty *more*? How the hell many were already on the hunt?"

"Upwards of thirty," Nate said.

"Fuck." Johnny couldn't believe what he was hearing. "Five-thousand-odd soldiers on our ass."

"Don't forget the police force," Savage said. "Last I knew, it was about two hundred thousand strong."

Yao Long not only had his own army at his beck and

call, he also had the Jakarta police department tucked in his hip pocket, starting at the top and going down.

"How does he make this happen?" Crystal asked.

"Men like Yao—meaning men with money and no scruples—can break laws with impunity because police and military corruption is commonplace here," Nate told her.

"Okay, so there's a shitload of guys with guns after us. They can't cover the entire city," Green pointed out.

"They don't have to," Nate reminded them with a nod toward the wanted poster, "because the entire city is on the lookout for us. According to Garuda, every television station in the country is now flashing those pictures at fifteen-minute intervals. Oh, and the reward has been doubled. Plus, per Garuda, the TV bulletins are now billing us as terrorists."

"Nice upgrade from thief," Doc said conversationally.

Nate cut him a look. "Anyway, the boys with the guns just have to come in and play cleanup when someone spots us."

"Then we'll just have to make sure they don't spot us," Johnny said, good and pissed now that Yao was leaning so hard and with so much pressure. "I think I know how we can stay way out of the path of Yao's radar."

"Were you planning on sharing this brilliant plan anytime tonight?" Doc asked, checking his watch. "We've got a bit of a deadline crunch goin' here, in case you forgot."

"In a minute." Johnny needed some information first. "Did Garuda have an ETD on the freighter?"

"An hour after daybreak, which is around 0600 hours. She'll continue to take on cargo until 0400, then she pulls out again bound for Manila."

"So we need to stow away before daylight," Savage said, thinking aloud.

Nate shook his head. "Actually, no. According to Garuda, the skipper is willing to take us on but we're going to have to catch up with her after they leave port. While he doesn't know it's Yao after us, he's only willing to risk so much and wants to make sure he's clear of the harbor and in international waters if things get dicey."

"Is nothing ever easy?" Doc grumbled.

"Actually, this is perfect," Johnny said as his ideas began to jell.

"In your warped world, maybe," Savage said.

"You're going to like this idea," he said. "Gather 'round, boys. Prepare to be dazzled."

"Last time that word came out of your mouth," Doc said, eyes narrowed, "it involved a stripper by the name of Penny Sillan."

Crystal didn't say anything, but the look she gave him could have peeled paint.

"Thanks for the memory," Johnny muttered, glaring at Doc.

"That's what friends are for."

"Your idea, Reed?" Nate prompted, interrupting their little joke-a-thon.

"Okay. So Yao's got his fingers in a lot of dirty pies, right?"

Nate nodded. "Besides his sex slave business, his network is hovering on the verge of becoming a major player in arms shipments into Pakistan and Iran. His drug pipeline into Mexico is growing stronger. And then there's his counterfeiting op. Those twenties he spread around in Vegas to frame Crystal may be just the tip of the iceberg."

"And we've got intel on the locations of his little ventures, correct?"

Again, Nate nodded. "Most of them. Mendoza touched base with his contact in the State Department before we left. We didn't know what we were up against, so we briefed on everything the guys sent. We've got locations and general specs on Yao's warehousing system, his ships, and his munitions facilities. Nothing on his funny money base though."

"Okay," Johnny said. "We go with what we've got. We've been wanting to take the bastard out from the get-go. I say we do it. Stage a little aggressive hampering of those lucrative little enterprises, hit him where it hurts the most."

They stared at him—hard—when they realized what he intended.

"You want to go on the attack." Savage's look of disbelief pretty much matched the expressions on all the guys' faces.

"Hell, yeah."

"You're forgetting one little thing, Reed. There are five

of us. Thousands of them." Doc looked at once amused and bemused. "All of them ready, willing, and eager to do their damnedest to blow us off the face of the earth."

"You say that like you think it's a problem," Johnny said with a smile.

"Actually"—Colter grinned back—"I'm kind of liking the odds."

"There you go. We use surprise as a force multiplier. Think about it," Johnny went on. "Where's the last place Yao would expect us to show up? I mean, we're on the run, right? Running *away* from him and trying to get out of the city. No one's going to be looking for us to go straight into the belly of the beast."

"We're a little hamstrung by time and resources, here," Green reasoned. "Even if we can breach his defenses, we can't do much more than throw a few hornets into his nests."

"A few hornets can create a world of havoc," Johnny assured them.

"And draw some of Yao's forces out of the hunt and back to protect the trouble spots," Nate said with a slow nod, which Johnny took to mean he was coming around.

"By which time, we'll be long gone," Johnny said. "And we'll have bought ourselves a little breathing room and opened a window to get to the freighter."

He could see that the guys were starting to appreciate the possibilities in his idea.

"With Yao busy scouring the city for us, I'm thinking he won't have much use of that yacht anytime soon."

"Whoa."

Johnny turned toward Crystal, who had been quiet up until now.

"You're suggesting that we pirate Yao's yacht?"

"We've got to get to the freighter somehow. Might as well go in style."

She looked to the other guys, waiting for them to join her in her argument. The only thing she got was silence. And smiles. "Oh my God. You're all liking this idea."

"Gotta admit," Doc said, "even though Reed came up with it, it pretty much rocks."

Crystal looked like the wind had been knocked out of her. "Amazing," she muttered.

"Let's go check out the basement," Nate said, moving on. "See exactly what Cavanaugh has tucked away that he thought might be of help to us."

"Jesus H. Christ," Doc muttered when Nate unlocked the storeroom door and they all got a gander at the contents of the room. "Third world war, anyone?"

Green grinned. "Fuckin' A."

Johnny laughed out loud as they mentally cataloged the astonishing arsenal of weapons, ammo, and gear neatly arranged in the sixteen-by-twenty-foot room.

He picked up an M-4 fitted with an M-203 40mm grenade launcher. "Like I always say, go big or go home."

"Gentlemen." Nate smiled from one man to the other. "Looks like we're in business."

* * *

Yao Long stood statue-still in the ceremonial dress of a warrior as Wong Li prepared for the ritual.

Lined up before him were the symbolic essential elements of warfare.

Wood. Fire. Water. Air. Earth.

He stood before each one in turn, paid homage to its power.

Wood destroys Earth, by covering it.
Fire destroys Wood, by burning it.
Water destroys Fire, by quenching it.
Air destroys water, by burning it.
Earth destroys air, by smothering it.

He would destroy his enemies by using any means. He would not bring shame to his family name of Yao. He would live up to his given name of Long, which meant dragon.

He was a dragon. A creature without conscience. Without remorse. And if the opportunity arose, without haste. These Americans had become an embarrassment, a stain on his honor.

In the background, Wong Li chanted from the Shambhala teachings of warriorship. It was the Shambhala view that every human being had a fundamental nature of goodness, warmth, and intelligence. That this nature could be cultivated through meditation, following ancient principles, and could be further developed in daily life, so that it radiated out to family, friends, community, and society.

It was Yao Long's view, however, that no matter how long the Shambhala teachings had been imposed upon him as a child, at the very heart of him was a different kind of warrior, and that warrior's heart fought against any goodness that might have once been salvaged.

This he understood. This he accepted. So it was not a question of fighting the Shambhala teachings, but gleaning those essential elements that gave him the strength and power he possessed today. His Chinese lineage gave him intelligence. His devotion to the existence of a cycle of creation, consumption, and opposition might, however, have helped him amass his fortune.

That, and his prowess as a fierce and potent warrior.

A warrior who destroyed all who would threaten his power.

Tonight, he would take up the blade himself—and he would bask in the triumph of personally drawing his enemy's blood.

They were certifiable, of course. If Crystal hadn't figured that out when they all got on board with Johnny's plan, she knew it for certain after everyone had gathered back in the dining room three hours and two pots of coffee ago, and laid out the assault plan.

She was on board now, too, but only with the "alarm" part of the equation after hearing details of what they had in mind. "You're really going to blow up a ship?"

"Maybe two." Colter studied the photos of the harbor.

"Okay, now you're just showing off." Savage turned to Crystal. "These SEAL types have a little problem with ego."

"That just earned you a spot on the snorkel detail, Savage," Colter said. "Papa Bear, you're with me."

Savage took it in stride. "Guess someone has to be there to haul your scrawny ass out of the drink when you botch the job. Might as well be me."

Yeah, Crystal thought. They were hide-the-scissors-and-call-for-a-shrink *in*sane. Not only were they going to blow Yao's cargo ship—or ships—they were going to set fire to or blow up the warehouse where he'd held her captive and where the guys had decided Yao based his counterfeiting operation, and they figured on taking out his weapons and ammo facility. Oh yeah, also steal his private yacht for their getaway to the freighter that would take them to Manila.

"I should have keyed in sooner on the funny money, but at the time I was a little preoccupied dodging bullets and keeping Yao's goons pinned down," Green had said.

"What are you talking about?" Nate asked.

"When we ran diversion for Reed and Crystal to grab the girl," Green explained, "I saw something but it just now clicked. Lots of boxes were stacked in that warehouse. Boxes with ink and paper. I know, because I blasted a couple in the process of laying down fire. Paper the size of U.S. currency flew all the hell over the place. Just like ink ran out of some of the other boxes and pooled all over the floor."

"Makes sense," Savage said. "The warehouse is near the docks, easy off-loading of materials, easy getting the bogus bills out of there."

"Sometimes, ya just get lucky," Doc said. "Let's see who can make the bigger boom, okay?"

Since he and Green were on ship detail and Savage and Nate were handling the warehouse, that left her and Johnny to, as he put it, "light up Jakarta with a major cook-off at Yao's weapons and ammo dump."

To that she'd said, "Yikes."

She was scared, sure. She'd be foolish not to be. But she was a little excited, too. Big surprise, the guys were enjoying this, looking forward to the risk. For the last three hours Crystal had watched and listened and learned as they strategized, planned, and fine-tuned their attack on Yao's enterprises.

They were thorough, professional, and serious, despite the jokes and trash talk. And as she'd observed them going through their paces, it was glaringly apparent that they worked together well, had worked together often, and had complete trust in each other's abilities.

"Is this actually going to work?" she asked Johnny when they took a quick break to stretch muscles that had grown stiff from poring over photos and reports and hashing and rehashing their plan until they'd pummeled it to grit.

He shrugged as she followed him to a chef's dream of a kitchen in search for something other than coffee to drink. "A team would normally spend upwards of six months planning a takeout of an operation this size. We don't have six months. That doesn't mean we can't still do some serious damage with the toys Cavanaugh has stacked in his basement playroom."

Toys like the M-249 belt-fed machine gun, a boatload of Semtex, the explosive they'd used to blow the door to Mary's cell and what Colter planned to use to, as he'd put it "blow a hole the size of a capital S—for SUNK—in the bellies of Yao's cargo ships."

"Hell," Johnny said as she poured them each a glass of pineapple juice, "if this plays out the way we think, we can sting him until he hurts big time."

"We rub enough salt into the wound," Nate said as they returned to the room, "it might really wind him up, get him a little desperate. Desperation leads to carelessness. He'll start getting sloppy. He's not going to care as much about finding us anymore as keeping the rest of his investments safe when he thinks his entire empire is crumbling down around his head."

Yeah, Crystal thought. If his boats were blowing up and warehouses were demolished, Yao was bound to get a little ticked off. And while it saddened her to know they weren't going after his prostitution business, she understood why. Collateral damage. Too big a risk of innocents getting hurt or killed.

But it wasn't over for those women. She promised herself it wouldn't be over for them. She was going to help. She was going to do something . . . but only if they accomplished their second goal: get to the freighter alive.

19

"Cavanaugh is an intriguing man."

Johnny looked up, grunted as Crystal walked out of the in-suite bathroom in the bedroom they were sharing for the night. It was close to ten p.m. The plan was to catch a few hours' sleep while they could before they set things in motion at exactly 3:00 in the morning—the magic hour. Enemy biorhythms were out of sync; alert levels were on the downslide. And the night was the blackest.

"If you like the God-complex type," he grumbled from the bed where he was lying naked on his back, hands crossed behind his head.

Wrapped in a bath towel, she walked to the bed and pressed a knee onto the mattress. It dipped beneath her slight weight; his skin warmed where her thigh touched his ribs. "Well, he *is* a bit of a god," she said, sounding impressed.

Johnny snorted, wishing he was immune to both her touch and the fist of jealousy knotting in his chest. "In his own mind. Jesus. I can't believe you bought into all that hand-kissing, smooth-operator bunk."

"Never had my hand kissed before."

He clenched his jaw, wondering if she knew just how slippery the slope was on the hill she'd chosen to climb.

"Never knew you wanted it kissed," he muttered, finally looking at her.

That's when he realized she was messing with him. Tinkerbell, he decided, was about to get her wings clipped.

He snagged her arm, dragged her down on top of him. "You know what they say about playing with fire, don't you, Tink?"

"No," she said, laughing when he rolled her beneath him and quickly dispensed with her towel. "What do they say?"

"You're gonna get burned, baby."

Then he set about lighting a fire.

She sucked in her breath on a gasp when he lowered his head to her breast, drew her hot and hard into his mouth—and kindled a spark that he knew would lead to a bonfire if he kept it up.

And oh, he kept it up, lavishing attention on her beautiful nipples, then tracking his way slowly down her sweet, sexy body with hot, wet, open-mouth kisses until he had her writhing beneath him and every bit as hot as he was. Every bit as needy and greedy and damn, this woman did things to him— things he'd never wanted and now couldn't imagine living without.

"Open up, darlin'," he coaxed in a gruff murmur as

he slid down between her thighs. Whispering kisses against her pubis, he parted her sensitive flesh with his fingers, then delved into the heart of her with his tongue.

Long strokes, delicious licks, relentless suction. He loved the heat of her. Craved the taste of her and the wanton stretch and flow, reach and yearn of her body as she pressed herself urgently against his mouth in an effort to experience every nuance of pleasure he willingly gave.

Her body stiffened on a long, low moan, blazing shock waves of sensation hot and low in his groin as her lush sounds turned the heat higher and higher between them.

She came with a cry as he wrung out every sip of her release, every keening sound, then waited with her until her world stopped spinning.

Spent, shattered, she lay limp and wasted as he pressed tender, settling kisses along the inside of a silken thigh, the quivering flesh of her belly, working his way leisurely up her body to the tender round of a breast until he met her mouth for a long, eating kiss.

Mine, he thought, unable to fight the notion, and slipped into her like silk. Let himself come after a series of slow, savoring strokes, then collapsed on top of her to ride out the aftermath of the inferno.

Several long moments passed before he felt her hand stroke his hair and her breath settle.

So this was bliss. So this was contentment. He could get used to it. He could come to require it.

"Nice," she said on a dreamy sigh.

Yeah, nice. "Next time, we'll make do with the hand kissing if you'd rather."

Her soft chuckle reverberated beneath him as she wrapped him in her arms and held on. "After that? Just try to get by with kissing my hand . . . see where it gets you."

They lay that way for a long while. Just him. Just her. Just them in the moment. And for that moment he thought she'd fallen asleep—until her quiet question came out of the dark.

"We're going to get out of this, right?"

The tremulous quality of her voice told him she wasn't nearly as detached from the danger as she'd like him to think she was. That like him, she'd needed this little pocket of time and space and detachment from the reality that would hit in less than five hours.

"Yeah," he promised, rolling to his side and bringing her with him. "We're going to get out of this."

Then he lay there in the dark and held her, hoping to hell he could deliver on that promise and finally get her home.

The night was still. The room was dark. And the sheets beside him were empty and cool when Johnny woke up. He stretched, yawned, and realized a damp night breeze drifted across his bare torso, competing with the air-conditioning in Cavanaugh's house.

He sat up slowly, scrubbed the sleep out of his eyes, then punched the glow light on his watch. It was pushing one a.m. He glanced across the dark room. One of the double doors to the balcony off the bedroom was open. The same damp breeze that cooled him lifted the sheer white curtain panels draped over the long panes of glass. A slice of moonlight peeked into the bedroom.

He pushed off the bed, dragged on his boxers and, bare feet soundlessly hitting the cool tile floor, walked to the open door. He knew what he'd find before he got there.

Crystal.

Restless.

Edgy.

Scared.

His heart did that sinking thing it sometimes did when he thought of her. Of what she'd been through the past few days. Of how tough and strong and brave she'd been.

He stood back in the shadows until his pupils acclimated to the dark. She was little more than a shadow herself as she leaned a hip against the low concrete balcony rail.

Jesus, would you look at her. This was a woman he'd rarely seen. This woman was no tough-as-nails commando who'd survived a war to get to this point. This woman was no hot Vegas chick who wore her skirts short, her heels high, and an attitude as big as the MGM Grand Hotel. No, this woman didn't look so tough right now. She didn't look so strong.

What she looked was vulnerable, beautiful, and so damn breakable, he was afraid that if he touched her she might shatter. She wouldn't want him to see her this way. Made it a point to not let anyone see her this way. So he stood. And he waited. And he watched.

She'd found a robe somewhere. Cavanaugh, it seemed, took care of his houseguests like the staff of a five-star hotel. Gourmet food. Scented soaps and shampoos. Plush towels. Delicate silk robes.

This one was blue. Like a sunset sea. Short, like the woman who wore it. Sexy, like the body the thin fabric hugged.

The deep, fractured breath lifted her shoulders as she stared, unaware of his presence, beyond the night to something only she could see, and broke his heart. He'd been alone a lot in his life. Knew what it felt like. Knew about lonely. But he'd never witnessed anyone so bleak with the weight of her solitude.

"Couldn't sleep?" He no longer cared that she would be embarrassed. He just wanted to . . . to what? Touch her. Help her. Be with her because yeah, he knew a lot about lonely.

She glanced over her shoulder at the sound of his voice. Moonlight lined her pretty, fairy features. His body reacted with a hard clutch of his abdominal muscles. A quick intake of breath.

"I didn't mean to wake you," she said, then turned back to her silent vigil.

"You didn't," he assured her and joined her on a balcony that was just big enough to accommodate two lacy white wrought-iron chairs, a small table, and the two of them.

Her continued silence didn't say "leave me alone," exactly, but she didn't invite him into her space, either. Not that he let it stop him. He moved up close behind her, hooked his forearm across her chest just above her breasts, and drew her gently back against him.

"Penny for your thoughts." He rested his chin on the top of her head and wrapped his other arm around her waist, enveloping her in what he hoped she translated as support.

The sound she made passed for a soft, ironic laugh. "Trust me. A penny doesn't come anywhere near covering what I'm thinking."

"Whatever they cost, I've got it covered. Talk to me, Crystal," he urged gently.

She swallowed hard and he could tell she was fighting tears.

"Babe," he whispered, instinctively knowing what this was all about. "Don't think you're the only one under this roof who's worried about tomorrow."

"*Worried?*" Her breath caught on a sob; she reached up and gripped his forearm with her small fingers. "Worried doesn't even come close. Worried doesn't come within a continent of covering how I feel."

He held her tight, then turned her in his arms and pressed her cheek into his chest. And then he just held her while she clung to him. She smelled of lemon soap and midnight breeze and the lingering scent of the love they'd made. She was tiny and soft and dammit, he didn't want to be in love with her.

"How did this happen?" Her breath felt hot against his

bare skin. "How . . . God. Never, in a million years would I have *ever* seen something like this happening to me."

No, Johnny thought. No one ever sees themselves kidnapped, then hunted like an animal.

"And the worst part? The very worst part?" A warm tear dampened his chest. "I should be feeling like the luckiest woman alive. Because I *am* alive. Because I got away from Yao. Because you . . . and . . . and Nate and Doc . . . all of you . . . you are probably the only men on the planet who could possibly get me out of this. But those . . . those girls."

Her anguish ripped a hole in his heart. She tried to push away from him. He held her fast as hot tears poured down her cheeks.

"Those girls . . . God, Johnny. What will become of them? How much hell will they go through? No one's going to save them."

And I'm not entitled to be saved, either. She didn't have to say the words for him to know what she was thinking.

Survivor's guilt. He'd witnessed it before and often. He would witness it again. In his line of work, there was always guilt. But this was Crystal. This was Crystal struggling with a pain far beyond her own comprehension. This woman, who liked to make everyone think she was hard as nails and as deep as the top layer of skin, was dying a little inside over something she couldn't control.

"It's not your guilt to own, Tink. It's not your cross to bear, either. You don't let go of it? It's going to eat you alive."

"I've got to help them. Somehow, I've got to help them."

She was in a place in her head where nothing he could say was going to help her. He tried anyway.

"Then help them by helping yourself. Don't zone out now, Crystal. You've got to stay strong if we're going to get out of here."

"And leave them all behind."

"And go back to the States and do something," he countered, giving her a little shake. "Raise awareness. Lobby for human rights."

She made a derisive sound. "A Band-Aid on a sucking wound."

"Yeah," he agreed. "It's a Band-Aid. But it's also a start. You can't do it all. But you can do some. The thing is, you've got to be alive to do it."

She blinked up at him, her green eyes tortured in the moonlight. No, there was nothing he could say. Not this night.

"Come on." He wrapped an arm around her shoulders, guided her back inside. "You need to catch some sleep."

And he needed to hold her. So that's what he did. He held her the rest of the night because *that* was something he could do. Something he had to do, more, he suspected, for himself than for her.

"I'm ready."

When Crystal turned to Johnny three hours later, her eyes were wide and white in the midst of the face-black covering her skin. The black do-rag, black shirt and pants, and a pair of black socks beneath the brown sandals would have to do. There wasn't a pair of black boots to be had in Cavanaugh's stash that would fit those tiny feet.

It killed him to see her beautiful face smeared with black again. Killed him that her eyes were as haunted now as they had been when he'd coaxed her back to bed and that once again, she was firmly in the mix of what could be the biggest goatfuck he'd ever been a part of.

Yeah. It was his plan. And yeah, in theory it ought to work. But damn, they were figuring on taking some mighty big bites out of Yao's operations—bigger, maybe, than they could chew. Bigger bites than anyone should expect Crystal to swallow.

Just like his strategy to rout the street thugs who had cornered him and Crystal, Johnny meant to chop off the snake's head so the body couldn't function. Yeah, as far as he was concerned, the goal was to kill the snake.

A gust of wind rattled the shutters on the bedroom window. On its heels came a splat of rain.

"Seems we're in for some weather."

"Is that a good thing or a bad thing?" Crystal asked, making Johnny proud of her. She was back in the mix. She was carrying on.

"Could be either. Guess we'll see how it plays out. You ready?"

"I will be . . . just as soon as we take care of one little thing."

She moved in to him, turned her face up to his, and kissed him. No rough and desperate claim this time. No demand. No possession. Instead, she gave him something richer. Something sweeter. A soft, tender expression of faith that could have brought him to his knees if he'd let it.

"It's going to be fine," he promised, pressing his forehead to hers and feeling the tension strung taut in her body.

She nodded. "I know."

He held her close, wanted to stay like this, knowing he could keep her safe right here for just a little while longer. But that was as much of a pipe dream as thinking Yao was going to let them walk away without a fight.

Jesus, he didn't want to lose her.

On a deep breath, he forced himself to let her go. "We've got to move."

She tipped her head back, smiled. "Reed, so you know, I'm pretty sure I'm falling in love with you."

Once, those words would have thrown him into a flat-out, backpedaling panic. Hearing them now, well, the panic was still there. Only for entirely different reasons.

He touched a hand to her face, made himself toe the line. "At the risk of repeating myself, not the time, Tink. Not the place. Adrenaline. It's an aphrodisiac. It muddles the mind."

"Okay. So I had a bad moment last night. I'm fine now. And it doesn't mean that my mind is muddled."

"Yeah, well, it's revved up to warp speed right along with your heartbeat. Trust me. I've been here before."

"Been here? As in been in love?"

Damn, she was persistent and deliberately misunderstanding him.

"In battle mode. It skews perspective, okay?"

"Muddled and skewed. Hum. I must be a mess."

Dammit, he didn't want to smile.

"Can we have this discussion when we get back to Vegas?" Because, by God, he was getting her back there. He'd face another kind of fear then. The fear that came with her waking up, remembering who she was dealing with, and doing a little backpedaling of her own.

She hid her disappointment behind a smile. "Yeah. Let's do that."

Johnny took Crystal's elbow and they walked into Cavanaugh's dining room together just as the hall clock chimed 0300 hours. Nate and the guys were waiting for them there.

"I've got 0300 on the dot," Nate said and they all checked their watches.

"We squared away?" Nate searched each face in turn. Satisfied with their affirmative nods, he moved on. "And we're clear on when and where to meet?"

Another round of nods.

"All right, then. Good luck, people. Let's go stir up those hornets."

"We sure this is the place?" Crystal asked as Johnny peered through night-vision binoculars at the gated complex across the street from where he'd parked the older model SUV Cavanaugh had provided.

They were a good ten miles from the warehouse where Yao had held Crystal and where Nate and Green were currently setting things up to blow the place. Johnny and Crystal had arrived here five minutes ago. He'd parked along the curb, cut the lights, left the engine on idle, and had been trying to get a solid line on breaching the facility ever since. The rain came down in a steady stream now and kept fogging up the lenses.

"Yeah. It's his weapons stash. At least it's one of them. And a big one too by the looks of it." He lowered the binocs, slumped down a little deeper in the seat, and checked his watch. It was coming up on 0400 hours, an hour since they'd parted ways with the BOIs. Alpha team (Nate and Green) and Bravo team (Colter and Savage) ought to be getting their ducks in a huddle by now.

"Lotta trucks," Crystal said.

Yeah. A least a dozen transport trucks were parked in the fenced area near what appeared to be a storage facility. "Judging by the way they're sitting low in the back, I'd say they're fully loaded."

He reached into the backseat and snagged the pack he'd preloaded with enough C-4 and thermite grenades to make an impressive fireworks display. "Those full trucks just made my job a helluva lot easier. It also means he's getting ready to transport a big shipment. Some poor little terrorist is gonna cry great big crocodile tears come Jihadmas morning and there won't be any presents under the tree."

He turned back to Crystal; only the whites of her eyes showed in the dark interior of the SUV. "You're clear on what you need to do, right?"

She nodded. "Fire on your signal."

"No hesitation." Last night he'd had her dry-fire the M-4 with the grenade launcher over and over and over again until he was satisfied she was fluid and comfortable with the action and the reload.

"Sucker's going to kick like hell," he said, knowing she was going to have a badly bruised shoulder no matter how careful she was. Better bruised than dead is what he kept telling himself to justify putting her in charge of the grenades. "So brace yourself for the recoil."

"I know. I've got it covered."

Yeah, he thought. *She did.* "You're one tough, cool cookie, you know that, Tink?"

"You wouldn't say that if you knew how bad my knees are knocking."

He smiled because she wanted him to smile. "If you weren't scared, I'd be worried."

"Well, then. You can definitely relax because I'm scared spitless."

"That's my girl." He cupped her jaw in his hand, leaned in, and kissed her. "For luck," he said.

"For luck," she repeated. "Don't do anything stupid."

They both smiled because they both knew that what he was about to do fell far short of a smart move.

Them's the risks, he thought. "You know where to go and what to do if anything goes wrong."

"We're the good guys," she said adamantly. "Nothing's going wrong."

"Wish somebody had told me about that rule before. I'd have slept a lot better last night." He touched his hand to her cheek and shoved open the door.

He'd already unscrewed the interior lightbulbs so he slipped out of the driver's seat and shut the door without making a sound. Traffic in this part of the city this time of night was basically nonexistent, which was just the way he liked it. He sprinted across the wet street, then went down on one knee to minimize his profile, and pulled out his wire cutters. The six-foot-tall fence was chain link and, as he'd hoped, not wired to any security alarm system.

The dragon man might be shrewd but he was also too confident. That was what happened when you were king of the dung heap. You started taking things for granted. You started figuring you were above not only the law but impervious to any outside elements because, hell, everyone was scared shitless of crossing you.

Everyone but an American whose day had just been made when he cut his way through the fence, sprinted over to the closest truck, and lifted the tarp covering the cargo bed. It was packed full of rifles and ammo.

"Bingo."

Oblivious to the steady downpour, he shrugged his pack off his shoulders and got to work, hoping to hell that Alpha and Bravo teams were on schedule.

* * *

"The gods are smilin', buddy," Doc said as Savage shoved his snorkel mask onto his forehead and trod water beside him. "We'll be out of here in no time."

The water was as black as the night, calm and quiet as they worked their way along the barnacled hull of Yao's aging cargo ship. Fat raindrops pebbled the shallows of the harbor.

Couldn't happen fast enough for Savage. He did water but he didn't like it. He liked even less that Doc was setting limpet mines that were detonated by time fuses. Time fuses spelled precision and you didn't do precision without practice, practice, and a little more practice. They'd pulled this op together in a few hours, held it together with Elmer's glue, and hadn't so much as managed a dry run.

"You'd have thought with an operation the size of Yao's," Doc continued as if he were conversing about the weather, "he'd have one of those modern super-cargo ships. Suckers have double-hull construction. They're also twice the size of this old tramp steamer-type cargo vessel."

"So he cuts corners for the sake of the profit margin."

"Mistake. It's gonna cost him big time." Doc's teeth shone white in the dark as they continued to work their way to the aft end of the ship, where Savage helped him shift his pack off his back and pull out the first limpet.

"When this grandma blows, she's gonna lay a little collateral damage on her sister ship berthed beside

WHISPER NO LIES 239

her." Doc flashed his trademark gambler's grin. "Be right back. Ten to one I'll wrap this up in less than twenty minutes."

Savage snorted. "Like I'm stupid enough to take those odds."

"Where's your sense of adventure?"

"Left it in my pants along with my wallet. Now what can I help you do?"

They went to work arming and setting the times of each of the four limpets Doc had brought with him.

"Insurance," Doc said when Savage asked why so many. "Murphy's Rules of Combat tell me one of the mines might not go off. Then there's my rule: anything worth blowing up, is worth blowing up real well."

Savage trod water and waited as Doc disappeared and reappeared to suck in air over and over again. He broke the surface one last time with a gasp for air and a grinning thumbs-up. "Done deal."

Savage lifted his wrist, depressed the light button on his watch. 0415 hours. They were right on schedule.

"Swim for your life, little fishie," Doc suggested. "We've got exactly fifteen minutes to haul ass out of here or we'll end up as a five-thousand-piece jigsaw puzzle."

20

"Clear," Nate whispered into a shoulder mike as he crept through the rain along the alley behind Yao's warehouse.

Green passed him in silence, then held up when he reached the corner of the lot. "Clear," he repeated after looking around, then waited for Nate to catch up.

They both carried M-4s fitted with sound suppressors. In the small pack on Nate's back were a couple of timers and a roll of det cord. The night they'd stormed the building looking for Dina, Green had spotted a welding setup. And where there was welding there was all the material Green needed to blow this place sky-high.

First, they had to get inside. Rifles raised, they flanked the back door. Nate went to work with a pick kit. The steady downpour covered the *snick* of sound when he pushed open the old wooden door, then stood aside and covered Green, who went in fast and silently took out the guard inside the back door.

Nate followed, crept behind a stack of shipping cartons. He counted fifteen guards—most of them nodding off at their posts.

He glanced at his watch. "What's keeping the—"

Boom!

Their preset decoy blast went off in the empty warehouse across the street, rocking the building.

Green raised a brow. "You had a question?"

"Guess not." As planned, the explosion sent the guards scattering and grabbing for their guns. The confusion lasted all of thirty seconds before the lead man ordered the bulk of the team out the front door to check out the explosion. That left two guards inside— both standing in the warehouse's front doors, which had been slid open to allow the other guards out.

As soon as the remaining guards had the doors closed behind them, Nate and Green took them out, locked the doors, and went to work.

"Four canisters ought to do it." Green headed for the rear of the warehouse where he'd spotted the acetylene and oxygen tanks the other night. In the right hands, used for the right purpose, they were harmless. In the wrong hands, however—wrong for Yao—the welding materials were about to create an explosion big enough to blast this building and everything in it to smithereens.

They were both dripping with sweat by the time they'd dragged the acetylene and oxygen canisters into the middle of the warehouse and cracked open the valves. Taking a page from the Iraqi insurgent's IED handbook, Green rigged his cell phone to a blasting

242

cap, which he tied to the det cord he'd wrapped around the canisters.

"Dial-a-boom," Green said with a tight smile.

"They're going to shoot their way back in any second now," Nate informed Green when the guards started pounding on the door.

"Go." Green started cracking the valves on the tanks. "Once the oxygen and acetylene leak out, it'll displace the air and we'll be deader than a Saturday night at a church camp."

Nate sprinted for the back door. Green detoured with a quick jog to the far corner of the building and shredded a box with his M-4. Then he reached inside and pulled out a handful of riddled counterfeit bills.

"Souvenir," he said, joining Nate at the door where they let themselves out and ran like hell.

"Hope to Christ that's worth the ringing I'm going to hear in my ears for the next millennium," Nate grumbled as they sprinted down the alley and away from what would soon be a dress rehearsal for Armageddon.

Crystal was glad she didn't have a watch. She didn't want to know how long Johnny had been out there in the rain, hiding from bad guys and setting his explosive charges. Just like she didn't want to think about how she'd fallen apart in front of him last night on the balcony.

She wasn't used to laying herself bare. Not to anyone. Especially not to a blue-eyed *boy*-man she had sized up, judged, and filed away under "loser" several months ago after he'd flashed her one of his hey-baby grins.

She'd been fighting misconceptions about herself her entire life. Because of her size, because of her style, because most people got a look at her breasts and immediately tagged her "bimbo," she'd developed her own brand of defense. She perpetuated the image. She let them think anything they wanted, let them see exactly what they wanted to see. People constantly underestimated her because of it. The looks on their faces when they finally realized how short they had sold her, was worth the price of the respect she eventually earned.

Yeah, she thought, as rain ran down the windshield, she let them see what they wanted. So, why hadn't she recognized that Johnny Reed played the exact same game?

There was more, so much more to the man than hot looks and flirty smiles. Last night . . . well, last night she'd been falling apart. He'd put her back together with tenderness and compassion and a strength of character that she suspected surpassed that of any man she'd ever known.

"Keep him safe," she whispered skyward. She wanted the chance to tell him what a good, good man he was. She wanted the opportunity to show him that he didn't fool her, that he didn't scare her, that he didn't have to pretend to be someone he wasn't. He was safe with her. Above all else, she wanted him to know that he was safe to be who he was.

* * *

The rain had started dropping like bullets as Johnny ran to the last truck and set his last blasting cap.

He fucking hated working with explosives. C-4 on its own was harmless. You could shoot it, bake it, cook with it, run it over, beat it on your head if you wanted to. Look cross-eyed at a blasting cap, though, and the sucker would take your hand off.

That's why he'd given a big thumbs-down to Green's suggestion to prep the C-4 with the caps ahead of time.

"So I can end up missing some of my fingers like one of your old demo pals? That's a big pass," had been his response to that stellar idea.

He'd take his chances setting the charges on the spot. As he'd done with each of the previous eleven transport trucks, he went down on one knee behind it and crimped his fuse into the blasting cap with a pair of pliers. Ducking his shoulder and protecting the material from the rain and the wind that had started to pick up, he carefully stuck the last blasting cap into the C-4. On a deep, steadying breath, he placed the loaded charge securely under the tarp in the back of the truck and hung the tail of the fuse outside.

He stood slowly, looked around to make sure he hadn't been made. Now came the hard part. He had to light all twelve fuses, then run like hell. Oh yeah, first he had to ram one of the trucks into the storage facility with the equivalent of a ticking time bomb cooking off in the back.

He closed his eyes and visualized what had to happen next. If he'd gauged the length of each fuse correctly, he could systematically light each fuse in turn, light the fuse in the lead truck last, haul ass into the driver's seat, fire up the truck, shove it into gear, steer it toward the storage facility, put pedal to metal once the truck was on the right trajectory, then bail.

Piece of cake. Provided he was still able to run to the SUV after he'd hit the pavement.

He fished around in his bag for a chem light, snapped it in half, then hurled it in the general direction of the SUV where Crystal waited for his signal. One Mississippi, two Mississippi, three Mississippi—

Boom!

"That's my girl." He smiled into the dark, lit a punk, then set it to his first and the longest fuse.

Not more than three seconds and two more lit fuses later, Crystal fired a second grenade.

Damn, the girl could shoot. She'd laid both grenades on the far side of the storage facility. Since the M-203 grenade launcher had a kill zone of around ten meters and the SUV was parked about forty yards away from the building, he wasn't expecting catastrophic damage. What he wanted was diversion. What he hadn't wanted was Crystal any closer to the action than she absolutely had to be.

By now, anyone who might be inside guarding that facility would be racing to the end opposite of the one he planned to ram—less chance of them seeing him coming that way.

He quickly worked his way down the fuses with his lit punk. Eight down. Ten. Eleven.

Now for the big number twelve. He'd already checked and the keys were in the ignition. Like he said, Yao was way too confident. He set the punk to the fuse, excruciatingly aware that because of the rain he'd had to cut the fuses shorter than he'd have liked.

Boom!

Shit. Too short, evidently, because the first truck blew about the time he'd managed to climb up into the cab of his rolling bomb, turn the key, and swear a blue streak while he waited out the whine and the grind of a pre-fuel-injection engine that had spark plugs in bad need of cleaning.

Finally, thank you, God, the engine caught as the second truck lit up the sky in Technicolor and shook the ground for several miles around. Trying not to think about the very real possibility that any second now the concussion from the other blasts could set off the C-4 in this truck, he jammed it into gear, put pedal to metal, and headed straight for a closed bay that was big enough to drive a truck through.

When the speedometer hit ten kilometers per hour, which was approximately sixteen and change miles per hour if his math was correct, he shouldered open the driver's-side door. With his right foot still on the accelerator, he slid left until his left foot hit the running-board. He goosed the gas one last time, then unassed the truck.

He hit the pavement feetfirst, folded his knees, and rolled to his shoulder . . . and rolled and rolled until the momentum propelled him to his feet. Then he did his damnedest to break the Olympic record in the fifty-yard dash as he flew across the open asphalt while the C-4 blasted each weapons truck in succession and the ammo started cooking off like M-80s on the Fourth of July.

Crystal marked the opening he'd made in the chain-link fence with the beam of her Maglite. He felt his shirt rip as he ducked under and ran for the SUV. She'd already shoved the door open. He dove behind the wheel and made like an Indy 500 pack leader on race day.

"Sonofabitch." He laughed when the blast from what had to have been the rolling truck shook the earth, lit up the sky, and sucked all the air from a mile-square radius in every direction.

"My God." Crystal peeked back over her shoulder as they sped on down the street. "You set the whole block on fire."

"Yep," he said, shooting a whole lotta cocky into his grin. "I'm *that* good."

He checked his watch. "So are the other guys. Right about now, if all went as planned, there ought to be one or two less cargo ships and one less funny-money operation on Yao Long's inventory."

"Uh-oh. Flashing lights ahead."

Sure enough, the red-white-and-blue strobes appeared through the rain in the distance. It was time to boogie.

He stepped on the gas, made a hard turn right and found himself face-to-face with an oncoming police car.

"Now what?" Crystal buckled her seat belt.

"Now we bet on the odds and odds are, Mr. Policeman is a lot more worried about getting to the arms facility than he is about a beat-up SUV cruising the streets this time of the morning."

He slowed down to a crawl, drove straight for the oncoming cruiser, making himself poke on down the street like he had all the time in the world. If he raised any suspicion at all, he'd end up with a hundred cruisers bearing down like locusts.

It worked. The cruiser roared past, siren blaring, lights flashing and whirling.

As soon as they were well clear, he put pedal to metal again and, keeping off the main streets, headed for Ancol harbor.

"Close call," Crystal said, breathing deep.

He laughed. "Wish it was the last one."

Yeah, they'd stirred up those hornets, got them good and riled. The trick now was flying under the radar long enough to catch their ride home.

Control was intrinsic to Wong Li's life. He practiced control with the same reverence he practiced obedience. That his hand was shaking when he hung up the phone was an insult to his principles. An indication of failure. Yet his reasons for this loss of composure were many.

He glanced at the clock. Four forty-five a.m. The sun would be rising over the Java Sea in less than an hour. Would that he had time to embrace what might be his very last sunrise.

His master was a demanding man. And a savage one. The fact that Li was yet alive remained a mystery. He'd been living on borrowed time since the Debrowski woman had made her escape. The subsequent losses of yet two more prizes from Yao Long's select stable of girls should have resulted in a killing blow.

And yet he lived. This latest news, however, would seal his fate.

He was head of security. He alone was responsible for any breaches in his master's vast and lucrative enterprises. Mere minutes ago, three of those enterprises had been destroyed. The loss of revenue would be staggering.

The loss of face for Mr. Yao, however, would be unforgivable. Li drew breath from deep in his lungs and collected himself. Then he walked down the hallway and knocked on the door to his master's bedchamber.

Only moments passed.

"Enter."

Li stepped inside, keeping his eyes lowered out of respect—not for the young girl lying naked in his master's bed, but in deference to his subservient position.

"Apologies for the intrusion."

"One must assume that only bad news could compel you to enter my bedchamber at this hour of the morning."

Li nodded, swallowed back the shame.

"Speak."

"We have lost three properties."

Silence permeated the room, hung there in thick, deadly layers.

"Leave us."

The rustle of silk, the sound of small feet hitting the floor, the slight stirring of air was all Li registered as the girl left the master's bed and scrambled out of the room.

"Explain."

As precisely and concisely as he could manage, Li related the news of the destruction of the Base 1 weapons facility, the counterfeiting operation at the warehouse, and the two cargo vessels.

The news was met by stunned silence. It transitioned to a visceral rage that radiated through the predawn stillness in palpable waves.

"Five thousand military personnel. All of the city's police force. A legion of men all under your control. All of them searching for this handful of Americans who would destroy me. How does this happen?"

Li swallowed. "Perhaps . . . perhaps they have assistance."

"Assistance?" Yao bellowed, his voice shaking with rage. "In *my* city?"

Li closed his eyes. Waited.

"Reassign details to protect my other interests."

"I have already done that, sir."

"Call for my car. I wish to see the damage. We will begin at the harbor."

"Yes, sir." Li turned to leave.

Yao's steel-cold voice stopped him. "I regret that I will have no further use for your services."

Li felt a chill as cold and thick as ice freeze his blood.

"As you wish, sir."

"Do not disappoint me again."

Li nodded, then walked out of the room and closed the door softly behind him. He returned to his office, picked up the phone, and called for his master's car.

Then he sat behind his desk for a moment contemplating what had brought him to this place where once his life had been all promise. Now, it was merely over.

He opened his middle drawer and drew out the jewel-encrusted dagger. Yao Long had presented the ritual blade to him on the first day of his employment many years ago. "It is my greatest hope that you will never have cause to use this."

It had been Li's greatest hope as well.

All hope, however, had long since vanished.

He considered the Japanese ritual suicide barbaric. Remembered precisely the description he had read and carried with him in his head and his heart for years: *Sepuka, hari-kari, the act of self-inflicting two slices to one's own abdomen with a sword, that which is within shall fall out into one's lap, and soon after one's head is sliced off by one's friend in order to end one's suffering.*

Honorable? Perhaps. In Li's mind, however, if he were to die by his own hand, it would be swift and done.

He closed his eyes. Breathed his last earthly breath. Thought his last conscious thought.

Then he drew the dagger across his throat, slicing from ear to ear.

21

What had started out as a steady rain had whipped itself into a low-level tropical storm by the time Johnny and Crystal reached the Ancol harbor district. Wind, rain, and thrashing sea met them as he double-parked the SUV on a side street a block from the central marina.

"Not what you'd call a stellar morning for a boat ride."

Beside him, Crystal unfastened her seat belt. "But it's a great day to get out of Jakarta."

"God willing and the creek don't rise," he agreed with a quick, tight grin and a loose drawl as he twisted around in the seat and started gathering the weaponry he could fit in his go bag.

Outside, rain pummeled. A gust of wind rocked them.

Crystal grabbed the M-4 tricked out with the grenade launcher. "I see a really bad hair day coming on."

Johnny met those big green eyes of hers. They stood out like jewels in the midst of all the face-black. All she

needed was a bandolier criss-crossing her chest and a
K-bar and she was a mercenary's wet dream. He tugged
down her do-rag so it covered an exposed strip of skin
on her forehead. "You ready to do this, Rambo darlin'?"

She gave him a look. "That's Rambo-ette to you,
dude."

He pushed out a laugh. God, she was something.

"Tick tight," he reminded her and shouldered open
the driver's-side door.

They were both soaked to the skin by the time he
grabbed her hand and sprinted toward the marina
where the air smelled of diesel fuel, fish, and suntan lo-
tion. While Tanjung Priok harbor was strictly relegated
to industrial and commercial shipping, Ancol harbor's
commerce and the chaos that surrounded it leaned
more toward pleasurable pursuits. Small boutique ho-
tels battled with the larger chains and lined the long expanse of beach.

At the crack of dawn and with the storm slamming
in, however, the seashore that generally rocked and
rolled twenty-four/seven with the party crowd had been
reduced to a smattering of umbrella girls, as the locals
called the working girls, who had tucked into doorways
apparently abandoning ideas of stirring up any business
until the squall rolled back out to sea or blew itself out.

Squeezed in among the resorts, the yacht club's slips
were stacked full of gleaming white-and-teak luxury
vessels.

"It's like a frickin' armada of the rich and famous,"
Johnny grumbled, bucking the wind and wiping the

rain out of his eyes. "Heads-up." He had to yell to be heard above the beat of the rain pelting the dock, the surf slamming the wooden pilings, and the wind howling in off the water. "If the guys aren't here yet, they soon will be."

Yachts were stacked side by side like eggs in crates, tugging against their bow and stern lines and bobbing like very pricey corks in the rolling swells.

"Is that smoke?" Crystal caught his attention and he followed her gaze along the distant shoreline.

Dawn hadn't yet broken but there was enough light to see that, sure enough, smoke billowed and rolled skyward, thick and gray and voluminous, combating the rain and wind and making its presence known.

He leaned in close so she could hear him. "That would be Doc and Savage's handiwork. Score another point for the good guys."

He led her at a fast clip down the series of slippery, sturdy docks. "We've got a date with a dragon boat."

"Over here!" Savage popped his head out from behind a sleek white schooner. "What the hell took you so long?" he barked against the wind as Johnny and Crystal jogged over.

"Stopped at IHOP for pancakes," Johnny said with a nod toward Doc, who motioned them to follow him.

Head down, shoulders hunched against the downpour, Johnny kept a tight grip on Crystal's hand. Hell, as small as she was, this wind could pick her up and send her airborne.

"Bad news," Nate said when they reached him and

Green, who'd arrived ahead of them. They all huddled behind the bow of the yacht, using it as a windbreak. "Can't pilot this monster out in this wind. Too many ships, channel's too tight and too shallow. We'd either run her into another boat or run her aground."

"What about one of those?" A pair of sleek, twin-engine speedboats were tied off the stern of Yao's yacht.

Nate scowled. "I don't know. Big waves. Little boats. What do you think, Doc?"

The former Navy SEAL squinted against the wind and rain. "What I think is that we may not have any options. We've got company."

All heads turned to see half a dozen men about seventy-five yards away and bearing down fast. The *thunk-thunk-thunk* of automatic weapons fire and the ricochet of bullets sent them scrambling for the smaller boats.

"I knew this was going too well," Savage grumbled.

Doc was the first to pile into the open speedboat. Savage followed, whacking the lines securing the twenty-one-foot inboard to the side of Yao's yacht with his K-bar.

Johnny lifted Crystal off her feet and handed her down to Nate, who quickly tossed her a life vest. Johnny jumped in last and helped Green shove the boat clear of the dock as Doc revved up the engine and shifted into reverse.

"Down." Johnny pressed on Crystal's head as the AKs let go with another barrage of gunfire.

"My God, it's Yao himself!" Crystal shouted above

the roar of the motors as she peered up over the side of the boat. The velocity of the powerful engine as Doc backed out of the slip toward the open waters of the Java Sea knocked Johnny to his ass as he leaned over to grab the M-4, which he'd preloaded with a grenade. On his feet again, he steadied the barrel on the top of the windshield.

"Cut the motor," he yelled.

They stopped abruptly, the sudden shift of momentum jarring them. Johnny waited out a deep swell and when they popped back up over its foamy crest, he fired at the boat that Yao and his men had piled into.

The rolling water skewed his aim; the grenade hit a glancing blow off the stern of the yacht, missing Yao's boat altogether.

"I don't suppose that discouraged them." Johnny dropped down on his knees between the two front seats as Doc shifted into forward gear, cut the wheel sharp right, and whipped the bow around toward open water.

"That would be a no." Nate lifted his chin back toward the marina as the twin to their twenty-one-footer chased them, slamming through swell after white-capped swell.

"That sonofabitch is starting to piss me off," Johnny sputtered as Yao and his men were gaining on them. "Bastard's taking advantage of our wake."

Yao was playing on the second-boat advantage. He'd tucked into the relatively smooth water of their wake trail.

"At this rate, he'll catch up with us in a few minutes.

What tricks have you got in your bag?" Johnny asked Savage.

"There's a limpet left in there." Doc preempted Savage as their little boat pounded against the six- and seven-foot swells that were getting rougher as the water got deeper. "Suicide mission, anyone?"

"If you yahoos don't have your life jackets on yet, do it now," Nate ordered. "This is going to get a helluva lot bumpier before we reach the freighter."

Still on his knees, Johnny buckled into his vest. He glanced behind them as the city skyline grew distant and Yao's speedboat drew closer. He grabbed his bag, dug around inside. "Somebody do something to keep them busy."

Savage and Green had already shouldered their M-4s and were answering the rounds of AK-47 fire with their own salvos. Crystal pulled a flare gun out of its brackets on the inside wall of the boat. She rose to her knees, braced her shoulder against the side of the boat, and held the flare gun in a two-handed grip.

"Duck!" she yelled, taking aim and firing.

Whomp!

A trail of flame-red smoke arrowed toward the chase boat, shattered the windshield, and smashed through the broken glass. Yao's boat sat down dead in the water and disappeared inside a deep trough.

Green and Savage whooped out a laugh as Johnny grinned down at Crystal. "I'd say that's damn close to shooting the wings off a fly."

"Freighter's just ahead," Nate yelled.

All eyes turned to the horizon that had flooded with light somewhere between the time they'd motored out of the harbor and Crystal had scored a direct hit on Yao's boat. And there, in the far distance, sat the cargo ship, *Bima Raya V.*

"Almost home, boys and girl." Nate glanced behind him. "Or not. Shit," he swore abruptly.

The bow of Yao's boat lifted above a deep swell and came crashing toward them again.

"Shoot that fucker!" Johnny yelled.

Green and Savage opened up with their M-4s. Johnny let loose with the couple of frag grenades he'd tucked into his bag. The first bounced off Yao's starboard bow, then blew up harmlessly in the water. The second went totally askew when a wave crashed their bow and set Johnny on his ass again just as he let fly.

Then the M-4s went silent. They'd run out of ammo. The only thing they had left to fight them off with were their pistols, which would make no impact at this range.

Oh yeah, and Doc's lone limpet mine. Short of attaching it to Yao's boat, they were up shit creek because no one had volunteered for Doc's suicide mission.

"What now?" Green asked.

"We'll never outrun them in these swells," Doc yelled over his shoulder. "Yao will continue to use our wake against us. He'll be shoving his nose up our transom before we ever reach the freighter."

"Green," Johnny said. "Hand me that rope. Savage, help me with this limpet."

The three of them got down on their knees in the middle of the boat, braced themselves against the rough water, and got down to business. Johnny tied one end of the rope to the limpet. Then things got real hairy. His hands were slippery and wet with rain and salt water that splashed across the bow every time they hit a big roller. He had to set the timer and pull the arming pin on the mine and hope to hell the jarring crash and slam of the waves didn't set it off before they got the sucker overboard.

"What are you doing?" Crystal asked as a monster wave broke over the bow and drenched them.

"We're goin' fishin'." Another round of automatic weapons fire sailed over the port side of their stern. "Doc, throttle back!" he yelled.

The boat dipped and dove into the belly of a roller that engulfed them from bow to transom. When they burst up over the crest, they slid down the far side like silk, then rocked like a baby with the motion of the water. Holding his breath, Johnny set the timer for three minutes, then pulled the pin, arming it.

"Will this do it?" He held the limpet mine up so Doc could see how it was rigged.

"Damn, you'd have made a good SEAL."

"You say that like it's a big deal."

"And the horse you rode in on," Doc grumbled.

Salt water and rain slapped him in the face as Johnny leaned over the side of the boat and gently placed the mine in the water. "Reel her out." Then he guided the mine away from the side of the boat as

Green slowly let out the rope they'd tied to the mine until it floated behind them.

"Here fishy, fishy," Savage chanted as the full twenty meters of rope reeled out.

"Give her a little gas now!" Johnny yelled as another wall of water broke over the windshield and drenched them.

Doc throttled forward so they were barely crawling into the swells; the bow of the boat rose to a seventy-degree angle as she harpooned up over a wall of white water.

"How we doin'?" Johnny asked Green.

"Another ten meters and they ought to be sitting right on top of it."

"Come to Papa, Dragon Man," Johnny coaxed as Yao's chase boat disappeared yet again inside the ever-deepening swells.

"Come on, come on," Johnny crooned.

"I can't hold at this trawling speed much longer!" Doc yelled. "This chop gets any bigger, it'll turtle us."

Johnny wiped water from the crystal so he could see his watch. "We need about one more minute. Hold her, Doc. I'll see to it you get a gold star and an all-day sucker."

"There he is!" Savage shouted as Yao's boat popped up another few feet closer. "Come on . . . just a little closer."

"Reed!" Doc's voice was edged with a warning that Johnny didn't need to have explained. They were going to capsize if they didn't accelerate and soon.

"Crystal, hold on to the cleat!" Johnny shouted when they were slammed sideways, jarring them into one another and the side of the boat. "Next roller ought to do it."

Breath caught, lives hanging in the balance, they held on as the sea swallowed them again, knocking the little craft sideways. The nose dove down so far the prop lifted out of the water roaring like a wounded bear.

"Reed . . ." Doc warned again. "I'm losing her!"

Johnny squinted toward the hole where Yao's boat ought to be. Another roller damn near threw him out of the boat. He checked his watch. Less than thirty seconds and the limpet would blow up harmlessly in open water, sealing their fate. Yao would catch them, blast them into a million tiny pieces and—

The chase boat emerged again directly behind them. Eighteen meters behind them, if he was reading the distance right.

"Come on. Come on!" he yelled, knowing this was their last hope.

Seventeen meters.

Yao ought to be sitting right on top of that sucker.

Nothing happened. Johnny stared in disbelief. The chase boat must have missed the mine. Deflated, he gaped at the crest of a raging swell that had once again swallowed Yao's boat.

So. That was that. He lowered his head in defeat.

Boom!

An explosion exactly where Yao's boat had dipped

below a monster wave sent a spectacular shower of sea foam, fire, and flying debris thirty meters in every direction.

"Sonofabitch!" Johnny punched a fist in the air. They'd done it! They'd blown that sucker to kingdom come!

Yao Long and his bad boys were gone for good. The bastard was never going to bother Crystal again.

"Punch it!" he shouted over his shoulder to a grinning Doc, who had already throttled forward and was attacking the heavy rollers with the determination of a sky jockey hoping to break the sound barrier.

Wiping salt water and rain from his eyes, Johnny turned to look at Crystal where she sat on the floor, bouncing around with the jarring motion of the boat and grinning like she'd just been named queen of the fairies. Her face was streaked with face-black; her do-rag had flown out of the boat long ago so her hair lay in sodden clumps around her face, and her clothes were drenched and clinging to every curve. All in all, he thought she was one of the most beautiful sights he'd ever seen.

The freighter, however, came in a damn close second as they approached her fifteen minutes later. She was a hulking, rusted relic with faded blue paint, about as sleek as a garbage scow and half as clean—but she was freedom.

Exhausted, beat-up, and happy as hell, they scrambled into the cargo net the seamen lowered over the side.

Doc grinned as they all lay panting on the deck. "Shuffleboard anyone?"

22

"I'dddd love to get youuuu . . . on a slooowwww boat to Veeeegas."

"And he sings, too." Exhausted, triumphant, and relatively dry for the first time in hours, Crystal laughed as she lay belowdecks in the cramped berth beside Johnny while he hummed the notes and changed the words to the old "Slow Boat to China" song. "Who knew? And who knew you'd know that old song?"

"Lotta things you don't know about me, Tink," he assured her as the big freighter cut her way smoothly through twelve-foot swells in the Java Sea, heading toward the Philippine Islands.

Yeah, she thought as the huge diesel engines rumbled and hummed beneath them, there was still a lot she didn't know. And a lot of time, she hoped, to learn all the facets of this multifaceted man.

Not the time. Not the place.

Just the other night, he'd said those words again. He'd been right. And for now, she accepted the sense of them. For now, it was enough to breathe without the tight fist of anxiety that had been knotted in her chest since she'd come to several days ago and realized she was Yao Long's prisoner.

Jakarta was behind them now. Yao was shark food. And while their quarters were confined and stuffy, she didn't have a word of complaint. She figured the other guys who were also paired up in similar small quarters weren't complaining either. Beggars couldn't be choosers. The skipper of the freighter had hustled them belowdecks immediately, then insisted they stay below until they made port in Manila. He didn't want his crew talking to them, didn't really want them on board, but he did want the money that Cavanaugh had forked over to buy their passage, and that was the bottom line for everyone.

A luxury cruise, this was not. Didn't matter. They were on their way home.

"I'm not dreaming, am I? We really did escape."

"No, you're not dreaming." He pressed a kiss against her temple. "But I'll breathe a helluva lot easier once we reach the U.S. embassy in Manila."

"Where we'll get to wait out the red tape while they process my duplicate passport before we can even think about catching a flight back to the States," she surmised.

"Gotta tell ya, Tink," he said, playing with her hair, "never thought I'd look forward to wading through endless, tedious hours of bureaucracy, but after the past few days, boring—and safe—sounds pretty damn good."

Yeah, right. Johnny Reed couldn't do boring if his

life depended on it. She also understood that it was her safety he was concerned about, not his.

She closed her eyes, and the images that swamped her were of a violent, fiery sea, of Yao's boat going up in flames, of Yao and his men disappearing in the midst of rain and whitecaps and fire.

She shivered involuntarily. "He's really dead, isn't he?"

"Yao and Davy Jones are probably having a set-to right now."

"I . . . I keep thinking that I should feel remorse."

"He was a bad guy, Crystal. A really bad guy. The world's a better place without him."

"I know. I agree. It's just . . ."

"It's just that you hold all life sacred. Even the life of a scumbag like him. That's one of the things that makes you different from the Yaos and the Bin Ladens of the world. But trust me on this, darlin'. He's not worth your regrets."

Trust. That word had come up a lot lately. A word she'd once thought would never apply to him.

"Thank you." She turned in his arms and faced him on the tiny bunk. "Thank you for keeping your promise and getting me out of there."

For a moment, his eyes darkened and she saw the same relief and fear and horror that she felt when she thought of what would have happened to her if he hadn't come for her.

The moment went as fast as it came, and those incredible blue eyes transitioned back into flirt mode.

"About that. Seems, early on in all this, there was some talk about a gratuity . . . a little sumthin', sumthin' to make all this trouble worth my while."

The man never quit. "Yeah, there was talk about that, wasn't there?"

His big hand skated slowly down her back, lingered at her hip and caressed. "I don't know about you," he whispered, dipping his head to kiss her, "but I've got a whole lot of time with a whole lot of nuthin', nuthin' to do. You could start making good on that promise now, if you want to."

Oh, she wanted to. She moved in to him, opened her mouth to accept his tongue, sucked it gently, and reveled in the heat of his erection pressing against her belly.

"Do you think there's something wrong with us?" She lifted her hips and helped him strip off her pants. "I mean, it seems like every time we're alone together, we end up—" She gasped when he caught her earlobe between his teeth.

"Fucking like bunnies?" he suggested.

She choked on something between a laugh and exasperation and lust. "Well, I wouldn't have put it quite that way but, yeah. We end up doing that."

"Yeah." He caught the hem of her shirt and dragged it up and over her head. "Something is definitely wrong with us. Probably ought to see a . . . oh God, yeah. Touch me there . . . see a . . . shrink or someone about it."

She giggled. "You're not taking me seriously."

He reached for her hand, guided it to his lap. "It doesn't get more serious than this, darlin'."

She laughed again, because he made her want to laugh. He made her want to do so many things. But most of all, he just made her want.

She rose above him, careful not to hit her head on the bulkhead, and took him eagerly inside. Took him deep inside. Where she wanted him the most.

Where she would always want him the most.

The search and rescue party, dispatched by the Jakarta coastal patrol, sectioned off the sea in quadrants after receiving the distress signal twelve hours earlier. Their search had been delayed by storms and high seas. But as quickly as the low-pressure system had moved in and spawned the deep-water swells and heavy rain, a high-pressure system replaced it. Blue sky broke through the thunderheads. And the search went on.

The patrol boat *Angin Tukang*, with Captain Superman Alatas at the helm, had been systematically searching back and forth across its designated quadrant. Now Alatas changed course, headed for the coordinates just radioed in from one of the S&R helicopters. The chopper's crew had spotted something that looked like wreckage.

Slowly, Captain Alatas piloted the *Angin Tukang* toward the oil slick. Overhead, the chopper hovered less than thirty meters above the Java Sea, its searchlight illuminating ink-black water and the source of the distress signal that had been picked up earlier in the day and subsequently lost.

"There."

Alatas followed his first mate's pointing finger, squinted into the dark, and finally saw what the first mate saw. A length of white. The transom of a boat, he realized as he throttled the twin engines back to idle.

He grabbed the mike on his radio and notified the chopper. He then asked the pilot to pull back as the rotor wash was whipping the water into a foaming, whitecapped frenzy.

The bird backed away. The waters calmed.

Alatas ordered the floodlights lit and trained on the water off the starboard bow. And there, clinging to the jagged remains of what had once been a speedboat, was a man.

The fog of war. It had been a state of mind Crystal could conceptualize but not identify with until now. After four—or was it five—days of running on adrenaline, self-preservation instincts, and a healthy dose of fear, everything had become a fog to her. The remainder of the trip as they lay belowdecks on the freighter was a blur. At last docking at the port of Manila, then waiting until after dark before they were finally allowed off the ship—another blur. One more night in a cheap motel, a blur.

It wasn't until they arrived at the U.S. embassy and she stood on the steps outside the building with the guys the next morning that clarity returned and reality kicked in again.

"You're leaving? Now?" she asked, stunned when Nate pulled her aside to tell her good-bye.

"Reed will stay with you all the way home," he assured her. "The rest of us are just extra baggage now. It's best we avoid the speculation we'll raise if we all traipse into the embassy together."

Yeah, collectively, they were quite the spectacle. Even individually, they would raise a few eyebrows. Her hair was a mess. Her clothes were wrinkled and dirty. Reed's hair and beard had grown beyond scruffy to suspect, but she was beyond being fazed by any of it. The guys—well, if she didn't know them she'd be wary as hell to be seen in such rough company.

The realization that they were actually leaving, however, cut through the numbness brought on by exhaustion and days of living on the edge. Her reaction was knee-jerk and immediate. She wrapped her arms around Nate Black's neck. Hugged him hard. "Thank you. I . . . God. That sounds so inadequate."

To her embarrassment, her eyes filled with tears when Nate made an awkward attempt to comfort her by patting her on the back. "Listen," he said, stepping away. "You more than pulled your weight, Crystal. I'd feel safe with you watching my back any day."

He was being kind, of course, but she loved hearing him say that anyway. And because he looked so uncomfortable with her display of emotion, she tried to put him at ease. "Well, if you're ever in the market for a new team member, you know who to call."

She'd hoped the ludicrous idea would make him smile. Instead, he regarded her with a thoughtful look, then dug into his pocket and pulled out a business card. "If you ever decide you're serious about that, call me when you sort this all out."

She was too stunned to reply. Was he serious?

Yeah, she realized when he turned, gave her a "think about it" nod, then stood aside while one by one, Green, Savage, and Colter hugged her good-bye and wished her luck.

She was still holding Nate's card when they piled into a waiting cab that would take them to the airport to catch a flight to Buenos Aires.

Johnny joined her on the sidewalk. "You and Nate had quite the chat."

"Yeah," she said, avoiding his fishing expedition. He wanted to know what she and Nate had talked about. She wasn't sure she wanted to tell him. Heck, she was still processing Nate's offer, still stunned by his suggestion as the cab pulled away. "We did."

She looked down at the card, then back at the street as the cab disappeared into the stream of heavy traffic. *Quite the chat.*

"Come on," Johnny said, taking her elbow. "Let's see what we can do to convince the guards you're an American citizen in need of a duplicate passport."

As it turned out, it took a lot of convincing. So much convincing that Johnny finally gave up, pulled out his cell phone, and placed a call to Ann Tompkins at the Department of Justice. Although Ann had no jurisdiction, she did have connections, and the fact that she vouched for Crystal went a long way.

Things happened pretty fast after that even though it

was a full eight hours before they were buckled in and lifting off the runway at Ninoy Aquino International Airport and headed for home.

"You can breathe now," Johnny said when they'd reached cruising altitude and the Fasten Seat Belts sign dinged once, then went dark.

Breathe. She turned her head to look at him. "Yeah. I'd almost forgotten what that felt like."

23

"Hey Shortstuff!" Johnny swooped Tina into his arms when she flew out of the ranch house and ran toward him. "How's my favorite cowgirl?"

"What'd you bring me?"

Johnny laughed. "You're like a broken record, you know that? Just once, I'd like to hear, *Hi, Johnny, I missed you*," he teased.

"Hi Johnny, I missed you." Tina's impish little nose wrinkled; her eyes twinkled with pure orneriness. "So, what'd you bring me?"

"Brat," he sputtered, and dug into his pocket for the sheriff's badge he'd picked up at the Las Vegas airport gift shop as soon as he and Crystal had stepped off the plane.

"Cool." Tina wiggled out of his arms to inspect the shiny piece of tin.

"I wondered what you were going to do with that." Crystal grinned as Tina trotted off with her new prize possession.

"If you wanted one too, all you had to do was say so," he said with a lift of his brows.

"Tina Marie," Sam warned as he eased his foot, still bound in a cast, out of the truck.

Tina stopped short and turned back to Johnny. "Thanks, Uncle Johnny. It's just what I always wanted."

"You're welcome, darlin'."

Abbie burst out the door just then. "Crystal!"

Johnny knew enough to get out of the way as Abbie barreled past him and enveloped Crystal in a hug that started out with both of them laughing and ended up with both of them crying.

"Woulda made book *that* was coming." Sam limped up beside Johnny and watched the women alternately laugh and cry and hug, then laugh and cry some more. "Hormones," he added with a shake of his head. "I feel like I have to test the wind every morning so I'll know whether she needs TLC or distance."

"Good luck with that." Johnny was sympathetic but only to a degree.

"Come on." Sam headed toward the ranch house. "Don't know about you, but I could use a cold one right about now."

Yeah. Johnny could use a beer. It had been almost sixteen hours since they'd left Manila. They'd changed planes in Tokyo and again in LA before finally touching down in Vegas. He'd called Sam from LAX to let them know they were back in the United States, and Sam had insisted on coming to pick them up.

"Johnny."

Abbie's voice stopped him just when he reached the front door. Her eyes were still teary and red as she reached for him, hugged him hard. "Thank you for bringing her back."

"Hey, hey there." He patted Abbie's back, uncomfortable with her distress. "It's okay. She's okay now. We're all okay. Okay?"

Lot of okays there but they didn't seem to do much to turn off the tap.

"Yeah," Abbie sniffed. "I was so afraid for both of you."

"Well, now you're just going to make me feel bad," he said gently, and made another awkward attempt to pat her back.

"I'm sorry." She laughed. "I'm . . . I'm just so . . ."

"Pregnant?" he suggested carefully.

"Yeah. That." She laughed and gave a dismissive wave of her hand. "Go. Go get that beer. I'll get this under control. And don't look at me. I don't cry pretty."

"I think you look beautiful," he said, feeling warmed by all this crying over him.

Which just made her cry some more.

He looked over Abbie's shoulder at Crystal, feeling helpless and a little panicked and appealing to her for help.

Yeah, that wasn't happening.

Crystal was having her own problems. Her lashes were spiked with tears as she met his eyes with a look so tender and trusting and approving that he felt it clear to his bones.

He knew that look. He saw it on Abbie's face every time she looked at Sam. He'd seen it on Jenna's face every time she looked at Gabe Jones.

Once upon a time, seeing *that look* directed at him would have sent him running so fast in the other direction, he'd have broken land-speed records. More than a whisper of that ingrained panic tugged at him now, warning him to run before it was too late. Too late to analyze, too late to turn back, too late to wonder if he was really ready for this. This . . . whatever was happening between him and Crystal that was starting to walk like, talk like, and look a whole lot like love.

Love. He mulled the word over as he followed the two women into the house. What the hell was love anyway? Sam seemed to think he knew. Gabe, too. But then, Sam Lang and Gabe Jones were two of the most stand-up men he knew. They knew the score, knew their own minds, knew a good thing when they saw it.

Crystal was a good thing. Yeah, he could see that. And that, bottom line, was the real problem here. She was too good for the likes of him.

And yet he didn't want to walk away from her. Wanted to take that good thing and keep it, which proved he was one selfish sonofabitch.

God, he was confused.

He tuned out Abbie and Crystal's happy chatter, and as he had been doing since they'd boarded the flight home from Manila, he rehashed all the things that had been working on him in varying degrees. He had to get a handle on this; trouble was, he didn't know what to latch on to.

As real as the past few days had been, the adrenaline highs that had fueled both him and Crystal were behind them. The true reality was here and now. And in the clear light of day, unclouded by Yao's threats and the boys with AK-47s, this true reality presented a new level of danger for both of them.

After all she'd been through, could Crystal possibly know what she was feeling? Could he?

She was out of danger now. Soon, she'd slip back into the routine of her life. Where the hell did he fit into that anyway? He wasn't a nine-to-fiver. Hell, he didn't know the first thing about the *"Hi, honey, I'm home"* routine, and that's what she'd expect. Hell, that's what she deserved.

He stopped in the kitchen doorway, watched in silence as Abbie and Crystal got comfortable on the sofa, and Abbie begged Crystal to tell her every detail.

"You got awful quiet all of a sudden," Sam said, handing him a beer.

Johnny looked up. Nodded. "A little beat, I guess."

Sam gave him a shrewd look. "Yeah. That must be it."

Sam wasn't buying his line but he didn't ask any more questions. Which was good, because Johnny didn't have any answers.

He felt caged in suddenly. Antsy. He should go. He should . . . hell, he should just go. He needed to think. He needed to think really, really hard. And he needed to do it without the distraction of a certain green-eyed pixie who glanced up at him and smiled a smile that made him melt and squirm and want to swallow her whole and get out the old vampire cross at the same time to ward her away.

"I need to borrow your truck," he said, abruptly.

Sam considered him for a long moment. Finally, he dug into his pocket and fished out his keys. "You okay?"

Johnny nodded. "I will be. Just need a little decompression time." With a quick glance at Crystal, who, fortunately, was looking the other way, he headed quietly out the door.

He drove straight for Vegas. Where he planned to drink the city dry.

Crystal had never thought much about the texture of air before. Several days sweating and dripping in the cloying tropical heat and humidity of Indonesia, however, had given her a new appreciation for the clean, arid heat of Nevada.

She especially appreciated it tonight. Or should she say this morning? It was closing in on two a.m. as she sat in the swing by herself in the courtyard fronting Sam and Abbie's ranch house. The blistering heat of late afternoon had given way to a soothing coolness, made all the sweeter by a soft breeze that delivered the scent of hay and summer for the paltry price of a deep breath.

Above her a night sky littered with stars and a three-quarter moon shed enough light that she could clearly make out the face of the man climbing slowly out of the truck he'd just parked in the driveway.

And it was, after all, the man—not the air quality—that had her up this time of night, wondering how much she should be worried about his disappearing act earlier today.

Out here, away from the city and the white noise of traffic and air conditioners and the constant rumble of thousands of conversations, the night was pristine with quiet. She watched Johnny take pains to soundlessly close the driver's-side door before he turned around, leaned back against it, and tipped his head back to face the sky.

"Beautiful night," she said.

He lowered his head, squinted through the dark in her general direction. "That you, Tink?"

"One and the same," she said. And then she waited, not quite sure why her heart was thumping, not quite certain she wanted to know.

"What're you doin' up so late, darlin'?"

The slight slur of his voice confirmed what she'd thought. He'd been drinking. Johnny Duane Reed had gone out and tied one on. She didn't kid herself about the reason why. He was scared. Of her. Of them. For that matter, so was she.

"You should have called," she said. "I would have come and driven you back."

He pushed away from the truck, walked slowly toward her. "You think I'm drunk? Nah," he assured her with the conviction only a drunk can muster. "I'm fine."

He walked on up to her.

"You waiting up for me?" He eased down beside her on the swing. Spreading his long arms along the seat back, he planted his foot and started rocking them back and forth.

She lifted a shoulder. "Couldn't sleep." Because she couldn't stop thinking about him and his disappearing act.

"I get that problem, too, sometimes. After an op," he said, head back, eyes closed. "Everything . . . just keeps rewindin', you know. Every shot. Every near miss. I look back. Wonder how I could have done things better."

"So what do you do when that happens?"

"Well, I do what I'd planned to do tonight," he said, grinning without opening his eyes.

"And drinking helps?"

He drew in a deep breath. Let it out. "Sometimes."

"But not tonight?"

He lifted a shoulder. "I guess a guy would have to get drunk to find out."

Ah. So he hadn't been drinking after all. That, too, was interesting.

They both grew silent then. The swing creaked under their weight as he continued to push it back and forth. A tiny, startled nicker sounded from a far pasture. A baby had lost its momma in the dark. A chuckling whinny answered back as the mare assured her little one that she was close by and all was well.

"You don't know me," Johnny said out of the blue. He finally opened his eyes, met hers in the dark. "You realize that, don't you? You don't have a clue who I am."

She probably should have been more surprised by his non sequitur but the truth was, she'd been expect-

ing something like this. More than once during the
past few days he'd made reference to what he perceived
as her muddled thoughts and skewed perspective about
him—or more specifically, about them.

"Guess that goes both ways," she said, because if he
could play this game, so could she. "You don't know
me, either."

"The hell I don't." He sat forward, jerking the swing
to a stop in the process. "You're smart, brave, a helluva
shot, and I'd count on you in a pinch anytime."

"Same goes," she said, meeting the challenge in his
eyes. "You're also compassionate, kind, and for some reason, you think you know what's better for me than I do."

"I *do* know what's best for you," he insisted. "But we'll
get back to that after I straighten you out on a few things.
First, I am *not* kind. And I'm not compassionate."

Did he really think that about himself? "I saw you
with Dina. And with Mary. You were wonderful with
them."

"I was doing my job."

"Yeah," she agreed. "You were. But you didn't quit
there. You gave them respect. They needed that. You
knew they needed it. That was kind. That was an act
filled with compassion."

He closed his eyes again. Shook his head. Started to
say something, then apparently changed his mind.
"You don't know me," he said again, sounding weary
and sad and right.

As she had so often, she thought back to a night
when she'd point-blank asked him, "Why the act?"

Keeps expectations low.

Father? Mother? A woman? Who had disappointed him so and led him to believe he was a disappointment, too?

"Someone, somewhere along the way convinced you that you were less instead of more, Johnny Reed. Who was it?"

He drew a deep breath, squared his shoulders, and for a moment, she thought he wasn't going to respond.

"Like I already told you, he's no one who's important anymore."

He. His father. That's what she'd figured. And yeah, he was important. A father was always important, even if that father had done irreparable damage to a little boy who had grown into a remarkable man in spite of him. "He was wrong," she said simply.

He tipped his head back, smiled at the night sky. "Takes one to know one, they always say, and my old man was a sonofabitch. Ask anyone. They'll tell you. And then they'll tell you I'm just like him."

"Sam would tell me that? Green? Savage? Nate? Would they tell me that, too? I don't think so. Those guys love and respect you every bit as much as you love and respect them. And those men—those are *fine* men. They consider you an equal."

He still wasn't buying it. "You just want to believe the best. That's because you're a good woman. A real good woman, Crystal. Too good for me."

"Oh cry me a river," she sputtered before she could stop herself. "If I thought you really believed that I might believe it, too."

Surprise turned into a glare but she didn't let that stop her.

"You know what your problem is?"

"I don't have a problem."

"You're scared," she said, in spite of his determination to deny the truth.

He snorted. "Of *you*, maybe."

She shook her head. "You're scared of *us*," she said, not letting him get by with trying to joke his way out of this. "Well, I'm a little scared, too, okay? I've never been good at relationships. I've got this little trust issue."

His eyebrows drew together. "Some sonofabitch was stupid enough to cheat on you?"

It was her turn to snort. "They stand in line to cheat on me." Her voice softened. "You would never do that. You wouldn't cheat. You wouldn't lie."

The hard lines of his mouth tightened. As he sat there with the moonlight casting shadows on his face, a vulnerability he hid behind his warrior ways was as clear and present as her own breath.

"You got that right. I would never cheat. Never lie to you. Never. But—" He stopped, swallowed, then shifted his gaze to his hands where he'd clasped them together between his widespread knees. "I don't know if I have it in me to be everything you need."

Oh, Lord, would you look at him. How did a man who looked like this, who was as capable as he was, as loyal, brave, and true, get such a distorted sense of his own worth?

The old man was a sonofabitch . . . and I'm just like him.

She hated his father at that moment and she didn't even know the man.

"I need honesty," she told him, because it was the simple truth. "You're giving me that. It's a good start."

He shook his head, conflicted and troubled and uncertain. "Startin's the easy part. Stickin'—now that's when it gets tough. I'm not . . . I'm not like Sam. He digs this domestic stuff, you know? Me . . . I don't know the first thing about belonging to someone."

"And you think that's what *we* would be about? Me owning you? Trust me, I'm not interested in the care, feeding, and domestication of Johnny Reed. And I don't want to own you. I just want to be with you." There. She'd said it. And she didn't know who was more scared now that it was out in the open.

His Adam's apple bobbed when he swallowed. "That's the problem, Tink. I won't be here. I can't be here. You need more than that. Hell. You deserve more than that."

It was her turn to hesitate. To wait out the sudden dive of her heart. She'd been mulling over what Nate Black had said to her when he'd pulled her aside in Manila and given her his card. Maybe it was time to make that leap.

"You can't be here. I got that. So . . . what if . . . what if I went with you? What if I went to Argentina?"

24

Johnny jerked his head around so fast it made him dizzy. "Argentina?"

"Yeah. I could go there."

He shook his head. "What the *hell* are you thinking?"

"I'm thinking about being with you," she said, that little chin of hers lifting ever so slightly. "And I'm thinking about something Nate said to me in Manila."

Jesus, oh Jesus. He didn't like the sound of this. "What did Nate say?"

"He told me to call him. We'd talk about the possibility of me coming to work for him."

He felt all the blood drain from his face. Work for Nate? At Black Ops, Inc.? Was Nate crazy? Did he want to get her killed? "He wasn't serious," he insisted. He couldn't have been.

"He was," she stated with a confidence that damn near leveled him.

God, Nate, why would you ever plant that stupid idea in her head?

"Okay, then *you're* not serious," he insisted. Please, God, don't let her be serious about this. She couldn't go down there. She couldn't sign on to the team. It would be like signing her death warrant. She wasn't trained or prepared for what she'd have to face on the kind of ops they worked. And hell, he'd just gotten her out of a dragon's nest. The thought of something happening to her on a mission . . . Fuck. He couldn't think about it.

"I might be," she insisted, and he could see she was working on trying to decide if she was disappointed in his reaction, insulted, or just plain pissed. "Look. I know I'm not experienced the way you guys are."

He made a choking sound. "Ya think?"

"But once you weren't experienced either," she went on.

"Jesus, Crystal. We were in the military. All of us. All of us were Spec Ops. We've spent our entire adult lives training and fighting bad guys. It ain't fun and games. It ain't pretty. And it ain't for you."

Damn. He wished he had gotten drunk. Wished he was flat-assed, shit-faced, cockeyed drunk so he wouldn't have to deal with this. The look on her face went far beyond insulted to angry, then further than that to hurt. She'd wanted him to be happy that she was considering this. Happy that she would be with him.

And Lord God above, he did want to be with her. He could dodge and fade and lunge and evade but drop-dead bottom line, he wanted to be with this woman.

He just didn't know how to make that happen and

keep her safe. And he would keep her safe because dammit, if ever he were going to prove the old man wrong, he would prove it where this woman was concerned. A man wasn't a man if he couldn't protect his own woman, even if he had to protect her from himself.

The only way to do that was to keep her the hell away from him. Lucky for him, he had a lot of practice being an asshole where women were concerned.

He sucked it up, made himself get it done.

"Okay, Crystal," he said, the voice of wisdom, reason, and rat-bastard creep. "I think maybe it's time we got a few things straight here. I've been, you know, trying to avoid saying this outright because . . . well, because I really like you and I don't want to hurt you."

When she went perfectly still, he screwed up the guts to continue with this line of the stinkiest bullshit he'd ever spewed.

"You're . . . hell, you're a really good time, you know? Great time. But the fact is, darlin', you're taking this ball and running just a little too far with it. I mean, yeah, we're good together. Damn good." He grinned, put a dose of sleazy sexual innuendo in his smile, and almost buckled under the weight of the pain he saw in her eyes.

"Awe, Tink . . . don't look so sad. Man, girl, look at me. You didn't honestly think we had more than fun and games on the agenda, did you?"

She sat back, crossed her arms over her breasts as pain transitioned to anger in the form of a glare that could have blistered paint.

That was good. That was damn good, he thought, and built on the BS factor. "For God's sake, pixie, you don't want to mess up a good thing by thinking it's more than, well, a good time, do you? I mean, sure, I've had women follow me before—'stalk' might be a better word—but the idea of you following me to Argentina? Well now. That's takin' stalkin' to new heights."

Nothing. Nothing but that quiet, accusing stare. He wasn't sure what that meant. But he was sure that he needed to turn the screws and put this to bed.

"Hey, no hard feelings, right?" His heart was pounding so hard he swore she could hear it. "I know that in Jakarta, well, a lot of stuff happened. Some things got said. Things that sometimes get said in the heat of battle, you know? A man thinks he's gonna die—he might want to go out thinkin' someone cares about him. Then the heat's off, reality sets in, and cooler heads prevail. That's all I'm sayin'."

"Promise?" she asked after a silence that rang with disappointment and anger and regret.

"Promise?" He wasn't following.

"Promise that that's all you're saying?"

"Ah. Yeah. Well. I guess that about says it all."

"No," she said, her green eyes flaring fire in the night. "I think this says it better."

Then she told him to do something that was anatomically impossible—and while he was at it, to do it sideways.

* * *

"No." Abbie laughed into the receiver the next morning as Crystal told her about Johnny's big "it was fun and it was real but it was just real fun" soliloquy. "He didn't *really* say that."

Crystal had gotten up early, breezed out of the ranch house, and borrowed Abbie's car to drive to her apartment because if she stayed, she wasn't sure she could resist the urge to make good on something she'd promised herself she'd do back in Jakarta and cut off Reed's dangly parts.

"Oh, yeah," Crystal assured Abbie as she thumbed through the stack of mail that had accumulated during her unscheduled absence. "He said it."

"So was he drunk?"

"Sober as a boy scout."

"Well, I've got to tell you, he's moping around here like he lost his dog."

"Good." Crystal walked on into her kitchen on bare feet. "I hope he's suffering."

Abbie chuckled. "Not nice to kick a man when he's down."

Crystal made a sound of disgust, poured herself a glass of water, and returned to the living room. "If I was still there, I'd do a lot more than kick him. Can you believe he actually thought I'd buy that ridiculous line of bull?"

"We love them even though they're stupid." Crystal's sudden silence prompted Abbie's soft, "And you do love him, don't you?"

Crystal sank down on her sofa, sighed. "Guess he's not the only one cornering the market on stupidity."

"Oh, sweetie. It's not stupid. It's just love. I'm happy for you."

"Yeah, happy that I love a big macho jerk whose idea of loving me is pushing me away so he can protect me from his big bad self."

And that's what Johnny's speech had been all about. She'd seen through him like a piece of plastic wrap. He was so afraid she might come down to Argentina and get hurt, he'd decided on the spot to convince her that he didn't want her there because he didn't love her.

"If it hadn't been so pathetic, it would have been laughable," she told Abbie. "God. You should have heard him. 'I've had women follow me before'"—she lowered her voice and poured on a Texas drawl—" 'but following me to Argentina? That's takin' stalkin' to new heights.' *Urgg*. Give me a break."

"So," Abbie said, sounding both amused and sympathetic. "What are you going to do about him?"

Crystal threw a leg up over the arm of the sofa, slumped back until she was lying down. She stared at the ceiling. "Give him some room, I guess. Maybe if he thinks about things for a while he'll figure out he screwed up."

"I could talk to him."

"Oh, please. Spare yourself the effort. Look. Don't worry about me. I'm fine. Maybe it's best if I get out of his face for a while. And in the interest of his health, it's a damn sure thing he's better off if I don't see him right now." Something had been working on her, though. "When is he due back in Argentina, do you know?"

"Not for another week or so. Nate told him to take some time off. Look. Sweetie. He's an amazing man. A little confused about things right now but he'll work through it. Just tell me you're not going to give up on him."

"Give up? Do those two words even remotely sound like something I'd do?" she asked with a smile in her voice.

Abbie laughed. "Right. What was I thinking? Okay, listen. I've gotta go. In the meantime, I'm sure it'll all work out," Abbie assured her. "I mean . . . look at Sam and me."

Yeah, Crystal thought. Look at them. When they'd first met, Sam had thought Abbie was a thief and had tricked her into thinking he was interested in her. Turned out he was, of course, but it had taken a wild and dangerous chase across Honduras where they'd almost gotten killed to bring them both to their senses.

"Speaking of Sam," Crystal said, "tell him thanks again for all the groundwork he did back here while we were busy staying alive in Jakarta."

"I'm so glad Johnny got you out of there." All the desperation Abbie had to have felt while she'd waited for word was in her voice.

"Well, you can quit worrying now," Crystal assured her. "Just take care of you and Baby Lang."

"So, what are you going to do today?"

"I don't know. I might go to a doctor and see about

getting this brand removed from my wrist. Or I might go down to the police station. See about getting things straightened out. Who knows. Maybe I'll drop by the casino, see if I've got a job. Or maybe I'll try to track down Mom and Dad in Italy." She'd been thinking about them a lot this morning. The *I need to talk to my mommy and daddy* kind of thinking. "Guess this big girl is still a little girl at heart."

"Well, tell them all hi for me, okay? In the meantime, why don't you just take it easy today? It's not like you haven't been through the wars."

Yeah. She'd been through the wars and Abbie knew exactly how it felt. Abbie had been through the wars in Honduras. One night over popcorn and a late movie, she had confided to Crystal that she'd had to shoot a man. It had been kill him or he would have killed Sam. No choice. None. Still, Crystal knew that the harsh reality that Abbie had taken a life still haunted her.

"Lotta haunting going on," Crystal said under her breath after she'd hung up. She was haunted by Mary's and Dina's faces. By the countless but faceless women, children, and girls who had been caught up in the sex-slave trade.

She'd almost ended up one of them. Would have been one of them if it hadn't been for Johnny Reed.

"You had to go and fall for him, didn't you?" she muttered.

Well, thems the breaks.

She didn't want to think about him now. Not that what she wanted had anything to do with what she did, because no matter how hard she tried to banish thoughts of that blue-eyed boy and his hey-baby smile, he was never very far from her mind all day.

Neither, for that matter, was Yao Long. She kept seeing him. That first night in the casino. In that sleazy room in Jakarta when he'd had his men hold her down and he'd "prepared" her. In the sleek white speedboat chasing them, then being blown up, bits and pieces of him and his men scattering to the four corners of the earth.

Yao Long was dead. He deserved to be dead. For what he'd done to her. For what he'd done to Dina and Mary and so many, many others. And yet, Crystal understood why Abbie still had difficulty dealing with the fact that she was responsible for taking the life of another human being.

Honor. Above all else, Yao Long valued honor.

His had been taken. Stolen by a whore. His disgrace could not be measured. It would, however, be avenged.

He was the dragon.

He was invincible.

Bullets could not kill him. Americans with bombs could not destroy him. Even the Java Sea, angry and vengeful and alive with peril, could not devour him.

He had lived for a reason: to destroy those responsible for leaving him adrift, bleeding and injured, battling the elements and clinging to life on a four-by-two-foot piece of fiberglass transom.

For twenty desperate hours, he'd clung to life. Hours

in which he had vowed to avenge the honor that had been stolen if he survived.

He had survived.

Now he would make good on his word.

The Gulfstream G550 cruised at 41,000 feet. He glanced out the starboard porthole, sipping slowly from his personal blend of black tea that he had imported directly from Sri Lanka. He drank only the finest Ceylon tea brewed from leaves harvested from the misty hills and valleys of a centuries-old plantation. Just as a wine connoisseur appreciated grapes nurtured and grown in specific areas of France, Long treasured the unique flavor of the tea grown in Sri Lanka.

He closed his eyes, breathed in its earthy scent as the soft strains of a *gu zheng* played gently in the background. The melodious notes from the seven-string zither soothed him, led him gently into meditation that would prepare him for the business he intended to complete upon his hasty return to the arid lewdness of Las Vegas.

The whore must be dealt with. While not alone, she was ultimately responsible for the chaos and erosion of a network he had devoted his life to assembling.

Honor. This quest was more about honor than retribution. That a woman—a being born to be a servant and whore—had been instrumental in the depletion of his revenues, the crumbling of his empire, but more important, the theft of his respect and standing in his business community, could not be tolerated.

She must die, of course. He had given her an oppor-

tunity to serve him. An opportunity she had chosen to
spurn. She deserved to die for that alone. But for leaving him to the sharks in the Java Sea, she warranted a
slow and painful death.

The others, he would deal with in his own time.

"He's got a nice stride on him," Johnny said as Sam
kneed a sleek, flashy buckskin into a jog trot.

Johnny stood with his arms crossed on the top board
of the white fence surrounding Sam's outdoor riding
arena. The Nevada sun beat down hot and dry, stirring
up the dust in the paddock as Sam made another
round.

He'd give the big guy credit. Sam knew how to sit a
horse. He'd been astride the big gelding for the past fifteen minutes, warming him up, putting him through
his paces. Kind of made Johnny itchy to get in the saddle again. Been a long time since he'd felt that much
controlled power between his legs.

Of course, he was kind of itchy to do anything—
anything but head back to Argentina, which made
about as much sense as Sam riding the day after the
cast had been removed from his foot.

"Your doctor release you to ride?" he asked when
Sam breezed by again.

Sam reined in, walked the gelding back in front of
Johnny. The familiar and pleasant scent of horse sweat
and saddle leather reminded him of Texas. The scowl
on Sam's face as he leaned forward in the saddle reminded Johnny that maybe he might be wearing out

his welcome. "Don't you have a job to get back to or something?"

Okay. So he was being a PITA. And yeah, he had a job to get back to. But he also had a woman he couldn't get out of his head. A woman he had sent packing with a trumped-up pile of horse manure.

He hadn't heard squat from that quarter since his big rat-bastard speech two nights ago. Figured that meant he'd done a pretty good job of convincing her he wasn't worth the powder to blow him into the next area code. That was good. That's what he'd wanted. To scare her straight. Straight away from him.

Love hurt. Yeah. Doing the right thing hurt.

Cry me a river.

"Can I take him for a few rounds?" he asked.

Sam grunted and dismounted. "Be my guest. Just don't mess him up. I've been working on his right lead and he's just now coming around."

"I know how to handle a mount," Johnny grumbled as he vaulted over the fence and grasped the reins when Sam handed them over.

Then for the next hour, he let the horse have his head, eased him back in when he took a mind to get too frisky, and for all of sixty minutes, thought about something other than the woman he was going to have to leave behind.

25

"Pathetic, isn't he?"

Sam glanced over his shoulder as Abbie approached him with a tall glass of cold lemonade. "Thanks." He took a long, savoring swallow.

Abbie joined him by the fence and for a few minutes they both watched Johnny ride as though he were running away from a pack of angry wolves.

"Never thought I'd see the day when that randy bastard got all moon-eyed over a woman."

"Yeah. He's pretty lovesick."

"Why doesn't he just go after her?"

"Because he's stupid," she said simply. "God love him, the boy just hasn't figured it out."

"Figured what out?"

She smiled up at him, wise and knowing and so beautiful his breath caught. "He hasn't figured out that it's too late. He still thinks he can run from this. Just like you thought you could run."

Sam grinned down at this woman who had brought so much to his life. A future, trust, hope. All things he'd never even known he'd wanted. But most of all she brought love. And laughter. "It's like a game to you women, isn't it? Reeling us in? Messing with our heads? Bringing us to our knees?"

She leaned into him, tipped her face up to his kiss. "Yep. We live to terrorize and torment."

Sam hugged her hard. "Lucky for us."

"Lucky for *us* that you're all so easy to dupe."

Sam just shook his head, knowing he was the luckiest SOB on the face of the earth as she shot him a smug smile and walked back to the house.

None of them were smiling two hours later, after he received Nate's phone call.

"Tina, sweetheart, go find Johnny, okay?" Sam flipped his cell phone shut. "And tell him to step on it."

"What is it?"

He glanced at Abbie as Tina shot out of the kitchen. "That was Nate. We've got a problem."

"What?" Johnny glanced from Sam's grim face to Abbie's clear distress as he raced into the house. He'd been mucking out stalls in the barn when Tina found him. He'd needed to do something physical or he was going to go crazy.

"Tina, us grown-ups need to talk, okay?"

Not good, Johnny thought. *This is definitely not good.*

"Does that mean I can watch *Hannah Montana*?"

Abbie forced a smile. "Yeah, that's what it means, sweetie. I'll bring you some lemonade in a sec, okay?"

As soon as Tina left the kitchen, Johnny shifted all of his attention back to Sam. "What's going on?"

"Nate just called. Savage heard from his buddy Cavanaugh."

"And?"

Sam glanced at Abbie, who was nervously pacing the floor. "And Cavanaugh just got wind that a search and rescue operation fished Yao Long out of the Java Sea a couple of days ago. Alive."

Johnny felt like the air had been sucked out of his lungs. Like someone had taken a bat and hit him dead center in the breadbasket. "No way. I saw the boat blow. There wasn't anything left."

"Apparently, he was thrown clear."

"Fuck."

"Worse than that." Sam headed for his office. "Yao's private jet landed in Vegas three hours ago."

Jesus. Jesus! The bastard was coming after Crystal.

"We need to call her." Johnny followed Sam, knowing exactly what he was going after.

"Already tried. Both landline and cell go straight to voice mail." Sam opened his center desk drawer and tossed Johnny a set of keys.

"Then call the LVPD." Johnny's hands were shaking as he unlocked the gun safe that occupied a good portion of the corner of Sam's office.

"Did that, too. Dispatch said they'd send out a cruiser to check on things."

Check on things. Which meant they do it in their own good time. "Yao's too smart to let them catch him."

He reached inside, pulled out an H&K MP-5 and a mini Uzi. He tossed the H&K to Sam along with a Kimber Tactical Pro 1911 A1 pistol. The Uzi he kept for himself along with a Sig Sauer 9mm. When he closed the door to the safe he was also carrying ammo for all four weapons.

"Let's roll."

Abbie's face was pinched with concern when she met them at the office door. "Be careful."

Sam kissed her hard, then followed Johnny out of the house. Abbie's worried voice trailed them outside. "Call me. As soon as you can, call me."

Some days it was all about the zone. Today was Crystal's zone day. Comfort zone. Chick-flick zone. Zone-out zone. After Jakarta, she figured she was entitled.

Earlier, she'd turned off her phones and indulged herself in a long, leisurely bubble bath. She'd shampooed and conditioned her hair, then slathered herself with body butter from her favorite bed-and-bath store. After almost taking a header into the tub when she slipped on the wet bathroom floor, she'd made a mental note to contact her landlord—*again*—about doing something about the impossibly slick tile. She'd gotten comfy in a pair of very girly lavender baby doll PJs. Then she'd treated herself to a pedicure and a manicure.

Smelling fantastic, feeling fantastic, and looking beyond fantastic, she'd popped a big bowl of popcorn, drenched it in butter, and slipped *Pirates of the*

Caribbean into the DVD player. Then she'd settled in on the sofa for a two-hour escape with Johnny Depp.

Nothing like a good shot of Johnny D to perk a girl up. Problem was, another Johnny D—namely, Johnny Duane Reed—kept nosing his way into her carefully constructed no-fly *zone* and throwing a world of turbulence into her perfectly idyllic afternoon.

She glanced at the clock as Captain Jack Sparrow's ship sank beneath his feet and he calmly stepped off the crow's nest and onto the wharf. She'd always loved that part.

And she would always love Johnny Reed.

Where in the hell was he?

She'd given him two days to stew in his own juice. It was time he figured out he was as wet as the rudder on Captain Jack Sparrow's sinking ship and came to tell her he loved her and couldn't live without her.

So far, that wasn't happening.

"Should have cut off his dangly parts when you had the chance," she muttered, then paused the DVD when her doorbell rang.

Her heart did a little shuffle. Maybe it was him. Maybe all this primping and shaving and polishing hadn't all been for naught after all because, damn, hard as it was to admit, she'd done it with him in mind.

Popcorn bowl in hand, she walked barefoot to the door as the bell rang yet again.

"Coming. I'm coming." She peeked out the peephole. Surprised, she unlocked the door and opened it a crack. "What can I do for you, Officer?"

"Everything okay here, ma'am?"

She frowned. "Fine. Everything's fine. Why? Is something going on?"

The LVPD officer was young, clean-shaven, starch-stiff proper, and cute as a button in a Boy Scout, God and country sort of way. "Dispatch got a call that there might be a problem at this address. Just checking things out. You're sure you're all right?" he asked, his gaze drifting over her head and into the apartment.

"Hunky-dory," she assured him. "But I'll be sure to give you a call if I need anything."

"All right, then. Have a good afternoon, ma'am."

Ma'am. What, was she his grandmother? "You too." She smiled brightly, then shut and locked the door behind him.

"No clue," she sputtered, walked back to the sofa, and punched the remote again.

Captain Jack was just about to dive in after Keira Knightley when her doorbell rang again.

Another trip to the door. Another look through the peephole. Her friendly local police officer slash boy scout was back again.

She unlocked and opened the door, peeked her head around from behind it so he couldn't get a full view of her in her baby dolls. "Forget something?"

He smiled, kind of shy and sweet. "My card. In case you ever need me . . . um . . . need *my* services . . . or something." He held out an LVPD business card with his name on it.

She read the front, then flipped it over. He'd written

both his home and his cell phone number on the back of the card.

"Afternoon, ma'am." He flashed her a quick, self-conscious smile, then turned and walked away.

"Holy mother of God. I've just been hit on by a toddler," she muttered, closing and locking the door behind him again. "Take that, Reed. There are lots of fishies in the sea. Yeah. And some of 'em are even old enough to vote," she added on a big sigh.

One more time, she grabbed her popcorn, snuggled into the sofa, and picked up the remote. Captain Jack was in the middle of a swan dive into the drink when the doorbell rang again.

"Oh, for crying out loud," she grumbled, stomped over to the door, and jerked it open.

Yao Long and two of his Ninja pricks stood on the other side.

"Still not answering." Sam flipped his cell phone shut again as they flew down the highway with Johnny behind the wheel.

"Watch it!" Sam warned when Johnny swerved to avoid a length of rubber tread from a blown-out tire.

The rear end of the truck fishtailed, slid off the side of the highway, and spun gravel behind them in a sky-high rooster tail as Johnny struggled to right the truck again.

"Why do you have to live way the hell and back from civilization?" he grumbled as the speedometer topped 105. He wasn't looking for an answer. Sam didn't bother to give one.

He was looking to get to Crystal. Hands sweating on the wheel, knuckles white, he punched the gas pedal as far as it would go, laying on the horn every time he approached a vehicle, then whipping around them like an Indy 500 racer.

"We end up roadkill, we aren't going to be able to help her," Sam pointed out with a calmness in his voice Johnny knew neither of them was feeling.

"We don't get to her before Yao does, it won't matter." Every cell in his body was focused on and geared toward getting to Crystal before—*Jesus*. They had to get to her. That was the bottom line.

"Dial her again," he said.

"Nothing," Sam said, after trying both numbers.

They had to keep trying. They had to do something. Something other than sweat bullets and pray they got there in time.

Time stopped when Crystal saw Yao. An instant of shock froze her in place before her fight-or-flight instincts kicked into high gear. She slammed the door hard in his face.

He blocked it, pushed hard on the door, and banged it wide open, knocking her back into the room. The blow threw her off balance. She stumbled backward, peripherally aware of popcorn flying as Yao and his men stormed inside and closed the door behind them.

She ran behind the sofa, using it as an ineffective barrier between Yao and the two burly slabs of muscle he'd brought with him.

"You're supposed to be dead." She couldn't help herself. The words came out on a disbelieving rush even as her mind raced through a list of possible weapons she could use to fight him off.

"I am sorry to disappoint," he said in perfect English as his two goons fanned out on either side of him and began closing in on her.

She grabbed a bronze candlestick lamp, jerked the cord out of the socket, and smashed the shade against an end table until it fell off. Then she held the heavy metal lamp like a club, the jagged glass from the broken lightbulb making the two men hesitate. It wouldn't hold them off for long but she could do a lot of damage before they got hold of her.

"You continue to surprise me," Yao said, watching her from ten feet away. His left eye was swollen shut. He had a huge white bandage over the left side of his forehead. Both eyes were black and blue. Broken nose, she figured if the swelling and the splint told the tale.

"This building is protected by an alarm system," she lied. "If I don't key in a code on a hidden wall panel within thirty seconds, this place is going to be crawling with police."

"You are a very resourceful individual, Miss Debrowski," Yao said, his expression never changing as the two heavyweights closed the circle a little tighter. "But any security system that might be in place has been disabled."

"Doesn't matter," she argued. "The police are watching the building. They were just here. They'll be back."

"And I will be gone by then. In the meantime, I do regret that I will not have the time to enjoy your many charms. It is unfortunate for both of us that you were not wise enough to accept your position as my personal whore. I would have provided well for you."

"Yeah—like you provided for Dina? I'd die before I'd let you touch me again."

"Oh, yes," he said. "You will die. In good time. In my time." He nodded toward his men. "Take her."

They were within a yard's reach of her when they both lunged. With a scream that came from someplace primal deep inside, she swung the lamp, felt it connect all the way to her shoulders, heard the grunt of pain as Ninja One went down and cracked his head on the side of her coffee table.

He lay prostrate on the floor, blood pooling from the wound on his temple.

"Take her!" Yao ordered again when the second man hesitated.

Crystal faced off against the remaining wall of muscle, wielding the lamp like a baseball bat. She waited, timed her swing just as he dove for her, surprising her when he went for her knees. Her swing went wide of the mark and the lamp flew out of her hands and sailed across the room, crashing into the wall as he tackled her to the floor.

She landed with a teeth-rattling jolt, hitting the end table as she went down. A sharp, stabbing pain knifed through her hip. Still she fought him, kicking, gouging, and clawing to get away.

He was too big and too strong, and no martial arts skills in the world were going to help her against a man who outweighed her by over one hundred pounds. He slapped her hard across the face when she made one final lunge to escape. Then straddling her hips, he flipped her onto her stomach, jerked her hands behind her back, and manacled them there with one big, bruising hand.

She could feel the shift of his weight as he reached for something. Her other lamp. He jerked the electrical cord from the base of the lamp and used it to bind her wrists behind her back.

Exhausted, tasting her own blood, she had no choice but to let him drag her to her feet.

Yao approached as she stood there panting and determined not to let him see her panic and her pain.

He grabbed a handful of her hair. Jerked her head up so she was forced to look at him. Then he got right in her face.

"Because of you, Wong Li is dead. Because of you, I have lost my most lucrative operations. I have lost face. I have lost honor."

He was inches away. And she could see in his eyes that he was going to kill her. He was mad with the need to kill her.

A wise woman might have pleaded for her life. At the very least, a smart woman might have begged for mercy. Maybe . . . . maybe it was time to bite that bullet.

Or maybe not.

Crystal looked him in the eye, swallowed hard . . . then

reared back and head-butted him right in his broken nose.

Yao staggered back on a howl of pain. His hands flew to his face as he screamed in agony. Blood gushed between his fingers like a geyser.

Heart bursting in her chest with a wild, erratic rhythm, Crystal drew a deep breath, squared her shoulders, and waited for the blow.

It wasn't long in coming. Seething in anger, Yao staggered back up to her. Blood soaked his pristine white shirt as he drew back and punched her hard in her left breast.

She doubled over in pain; nausea pooled in her belly. She sucked air in huge, gasping gulps.

"Slow and painful," Yao promised between labored breaths. "Take her to the bathroom. Fill the tub with cold water. Let us see how the whore takes to a slow and orchestrated drowning—much like she left me to drown in the Java Sea.

"I think, however," he added, using one of her white kitchen towels to stanch the flow of blood from his nose, "that she will not be as fortunate as I. The whore will not survive."

26

Johnny had been shot. He'd been beaten. He'd been knifed.

He'd lost friends in battle. Lost them in the steamy decay of the jungle. In the ice-cold ridges of barren mountain ravines. He'd felt helpless, hopeless, and questioned his motives, his own purpose and his reason for living.

But he'd never had his heart ripped out and sliced to shreds—until today.

Neither had he had to test his will and his patience and his mettle as they were being tested now, as the speedometer on Sam's truck hovered at a law-abiding thirty-five miles per hour.

"I fuckin' hate this!" he ground out between teeth clenched so tightly that his jaw throbbed with pain. On a frustrated breath, he pounded a fist on the steering wheel as he slowed at the oncoming intersection, then waited for the light to turn green.

"Yeah, you'll hate it more if we get pulled over for a routine traffic ticket and we have to explain the heavy artillery."

Johnny knew Sam was right. There wasn't an explanation in the world plausible enough to talk their way
out of a drawdown if the LVPD caught them with the
illegal firepower stowed in the front seat beside them.
They'd be spread-eagled and facedown on the street, a
SWAT team en route before any officer with an IQ
above 40 would bother to listen to a word they had to
say. By then it *would* be too late to save Crystal.

If it wasn't too late already.

"Almost there," Sam assured him as Johnny pulled
away from the light.

Four more blocks. Four blocks that felt like four
thousand miles.

Finally, her apartment building came into view.

A black SUV with rental plates sat on the opposite
side of the street.

Johnny said nothing as he pulled to a stop. He
slammed the transmission in park, unbuckled his seat
belt, and slipped outside in one fluid motion.

He shoved the Sig into the back of his waistband and
slipped a plastic grocery bag over the Uzi. Already out of the
truck, Sam did the same with his Kimber and the H&K.

Without a word, they headed up the sidewalk and
into the building.

Yao enjoyed seeing the whore thrash and struggle and
fight for her life. But he did not want her dead yet. She deserved to suffer more for what she'd done to him. For what
she had cost in not only revenue but manpower. Shen lay
dead on her living-room floor. Another man lost.

"Bring her up again," he ordered as Zhang Meng held the whore on her back, submerged under the water. He'd taken her to the edge of death three times before. Each time she'd fought like a warrior.

It was a pity she was not a man. She would have proven a worthy adversary.

Gripping a handful of her short hair, Zhang drew her upright. Water sloshed violently over the side of the tub and spilled across the tile floor as she emerged, gagging and coughing and gasping for air. Her incredible breasts strained against the soaked cloth of her pajama top as her chest heaved with the effort to draw life-sustaining oxygen into her lungs.

"It is a true pity that you have brought yourself to this," Yao said, dabbing a towel to his still throbbing nose. "Your body should be enjoyed."

"G . . . go . . . f . . . fuck . . . y . . . yours . . . self," she gasped between gulping breaths.

"You will learn respect before you die." He nodded to Zhang.

Again, she fought like a tiger, but with her hands bound behind her back, she merely thrashed ineffectually. Her body slid down into the water. Zhang lost his balance against the slippery tile floor; he struggled to right himself and dragged her up again in the process.

She twisted to her stomach, drew her knees under her, then reared up with a great explosion of water that poured over the side of the tub.

"End it," Yao ordered, then stood back to watch her die.

* * *

"Anything?" Sam asked as Johnny, his Uzi locked and loaded and gripped in both hands, pressed the side of his face against Crystal's apartment door.

"Someone's in there. All I can hear are muffled sounds."

Then a scream of rage shattered the silence and they didn't have to wonder any longer if Crystal was inside.

"Stand back!" Johnny rammed the door with his shoulder. The wood gave with a savage crack.

He raced into the room, peripherally aware of Sam on his heels. A man lay dead in a pool of blood on Crystal's living-room floor.

"Where is she?" Sam asked.

Another scream of rage shattered the silence.

They both raced toward the bathroom.

Tiny pinpricks of light danced around in the dark. Crystal's lungs burned like fire. Her throat felt raw. Her head spun. She needed air.

And she was not, by God, going to die today. Not with this bastard lording himself over her.

She was beyond thinking. It was all about animal instinct and survival now. She fought with a wild, frantic power she didn't know she had. She kicked, she bucked, she rolled in the water to her stomach, wrenched her knees up under her, and reared hard until she broke out of the water, balancing on her knees.

Air! Oh God, air!

She sucked it in, in huge, gasping gulps as behind her, Yao's paid monkey lost his hold on her hair, slipped and toppled sideways into the tub, struggling to regain his balance. Her shoulders ached with the weight of him falling on her; the impact wrenched her arms against their sockets, strained her wrists against the electric cord that had steadily loosened as she'd struggled.

She felt a slight give. Nanoseconds passed as she jerked against the cord, worked it over her hands, and in one hard jerk, slipped one wrist free. On a howl of triumph, she rose to her feet, clutched her tormentor's shirt front, and dragged him down into the water. Groping blindly for a weapon as he struggled to right himself, she latched on to the showerhead.

On another gasping scream, she heaved her arm back and brought the heavy piece of metal down on his head. She hit him hard, screaming her rage and pain and fear, until he stilled and fell facedown in the tub.

In the same instant Yao lunged for her. She stepped aside and swung the showerhead at the back of his head as he slipped and fell forward. His head cracked against the ceramic tile wall. Blood smeared in a trail over the white tiles as he slid down, then dropped like a stone across his minion's dead body.

That's how Johnny and Sam found her.

Soaking wet. Weaving on her feet. Chest heaving. Eyes glazed. A chrome showerhead gripped in her hand like a crusader's sword.

Alive.

Gloriously, miraculously alive—with Yao and his

henchman dead in the blood-red water that swirled around her knees.

"Crystal." Johnny shoved the Uzi in Sam's general direction. He took a hesitant step toward her. "Tink. It's over, darlin'. It's over."

Eyes wild and unfocused, she slowly shifted her gaze from Yao's prostrate body to Johnny.

"There you go, baby. It's Johnny. Johnny and Sam. You're okay now. You're really okay now."

He saw the instant she came back to herself. A long, slow blink. An acute awareness of where she was, of what she'd done and who she'd done it to.

"He can't hurt you anymore," Johnny said in a slow, soothing voice as he took another step toward her, held out his hand.

"Come on, Tink. Let's get you out of here, darlin'. Let's get you—"

She flew into his arms, knocking the breath out of him and cutting off his words. He locked his arms around her wet, trembling body and dragged her flush against him as he staggered backward. "It's okay. You're okay," he murmured into her hair, and lifting her off her feet, carried her out of the bathroom.

"He . . . he . . . tried . . . t . . . to . . ."

"Shh. I know, baby. I know. S'okay. You can tell me later. Right now, just hold on. Just hold on."

Then he rocked her while she trembled.

Hold on. Hold on.

Yeah. She held on. *He* held on. And he was never, by God, *ever*, going to let her go again.

27

"You sure she's okay?"

"She's fine, Abbie. The ER doc wouldn't have released her if she wasn't."

It was going on six hours since Johnny and Sam had burst into Crystal's apartment, ready to draw blood, maim, kill—whatever it took to save Crystal—only to find that Crystal had saved herself.

Johnny's hands still shook when he thought about what would have happened if she hadn't been so resourceful—and so slam-bang, dead-on determined to survive Yao and his murderous men.

"What about the mess in her apartment? I should come and help her clean it up."

"Abbie," Johnny said gently. He understood. Abbie felt helpless. She wanted to do something, *anything*, to help her friend. And it was driving her crazy that she hadn't seen her yet. "It's still a crime scene, okay? The cops have sealed the apartment until they close their investigation."

"Oh God. They aren't going to charge her, are they? Surely, they aren't going to—"

"No, listen, sweetie, settle down," Johnny cut in. "You're getting yourself all worked up over nothing. They aren't going to charge her. They just need to get all their ducks in a huddle so they can close the books on this, okay? No one is disputing the fact that Crystal was attacked and that she killed them in self-defense."

And damn, had she defended herself. LVPD's finest were still shaking their heads over the fact that Tinkerbell had put it to three trained killers. But then they made the connection that she was Phil Debrowski's daughter, and they weren't shaking their heads anymore.

"Toughest SOB ever wore the uniform," one of the officers on the scene had said. "Stands to reason his daughter could handle herself."

She'd handled herself, all right, Johnny thought. The woman was amazing. For the rest of his life, he would hold the picture in his mind of Crystal soaking wet, shaking like a leaf, with Yao and a big bruiser of a badass lying dead at her feet in the water. Just like he'd never *ever* forget the stark terror and helplessness he'd felt when he thought he was never going to see her alive again.

He forced away the thought and tuned back in to Abbie.

"Why didn't you bring her out here to the ranch?" Abbie persisted.

That had been Johnny's suggestion, too. But Crystal had been adamant.

"I don't want Abbie or Tina to see me like this," she'd said.

While she could have used a little of Abbie's TLC, Johnny understood. Crystal's poor lower lip was cut and swollen. She was covered in bruises.

"Head butt? You head-butted Yao?" he'd asked in disbelief when he'd asked her about her black eyes.

"Well, he made me mad."

God love her.

He wouldn't have stopped hugging her for that act alone if the police hadn't arrived. Sam had placed the call—after he'd locked their weapons in the toolbox in the back of his truck.

"Johnny?" Abbie's voice brought him back to the present. "Why didn't you bring her out to the ranch?" she asked again.

Nothing for it but to come clean. "She's a little banged up," he finally admitted. "She's fine," he assured Abbie again when she sucked in her breath. "But, well, there are bruises . . . she didn't want to take a chance on upsetting Tina."

The big thing, however, the really big thing that had convinced him Crystal was right, was the look in her eyes. Shell shock. Battle fatigue. Call it what you wanted but Crystal was struggling with what had happened to her and what she'd had to do to survive.

So, after the police and the EMTs had done their thing and hauled away the bodies, Johnny had grabbed a few of Crystal's things and stuffed them into a piece of luggage. After a stop at the emergency room where the doctor had ordered her to stay in bed for the next twenty-four hours, he'd checked her into a hotel.

"Oh God." Johnny could tell that Abbie was going to start crying again. "I knew it was worse than what Sam told me."

He dragged a hand through his hair, hating that she was so upset but at a loss as to what to do about it. "Sweetie. Put Sam on, will you?"

"I know, and I'm trying," Sam said when he came on the line, already anticipating Johnny's "Can't you do something with her?"

"She'll be okay," Sam assured him. "I'll take care of her. You just take care of Crystal. How's she doing by now?"

"She's sleeping. I slipped her one of the sleeping pills the ER doc prescribed. She thinks she took an aspirin."

"Good. Sleep will do her more good right now than anything else. Listen. You need anything, call."

"Roger that. I'll be in touch. Thanks, man." Johnny hung up and walked into the bedroom of the suite he'd insisted on when they'd checked in. He didn't want her to feel closed in in a single room. When she crashed— and she would crash—he didn't want her to feel cornered.

He tucked both hands into his rear jeans pockets as he leaned a shoulder against the doorjamb and watched her. Just stood and watched her sleep.

He could have lost her.

Tears burned his eyes.

Jesus.

Jesus.

He drew in a ragged breath, pinched his eyes with his thumb and forefinger to try to stop the flow.

Didn't work. Didn't stop a thing.

Jesus, he thought again as he slid to the floor, lowered his head between his knees, and bawled like a baby.

Crystal awoke with a start to soft light, a strange room, and the heat of a naked man wrapped around her body.

Johnny.

Anchoring her. Protecting her. Taking care of her. Even as he slept sound and deep beside her.

She closed her eyes again. Drifted for a moment, making herself stay here. Right here. Right now. In this moment, with this man.

But another man encroached. A monster.

Her eyes flew open. Her heart rate ratcheted up to triple time. And her breath, no longer steady and deep, backed up in her chest, stalled with pressure in her lungs.

Dead. Yao Long was dead.

She'd killed him.

She'd killed a man. Hot, burning tears formed, leaked out, trickled down into her hairline. Three men. She'd killed three men.

They'd been breathing. Now they weren't.

It could have been her. It *would* have been her if she hadn't done what she'd done.

And killed them.

Beside her, Johnny stirred, nuzzled his face deeper into the curve where shoulder met neck.

Alive.

Vibrant. Magnificent. Alive.

His heart beat strong and steady against her body. His skin felt warm and amazingly soft molded against hers. His breath, where it feathered across her shoulder, was life sustaining and vital.

Like he was vital to everything that mattered, to everything that was.

She turned her head on the pillow, whispered his name.

His eyelids fluttered open. Fluttered shut again. Flew open wide when he realized she was awake.

"Hey," he murmured, all sleepy and Texas soft. "Hey, Tink. How you feelin'?"

"You're here," she whispered, and lifted a hand to touch the silk of his hair. "So I'm fine."

On a deep breath, he raised up on an elbow. Searched her face. His gaze lingered on her bruised lip before returning to her eyes. "I thought I'd lost you."

She tried, she really tried but in the end, she couldn't stop the emotion from welling up inside of her. Her throat felt thick, her eyes burned with tears. "I . . . I thought you had, too."

"Don't. Sweetheart. Tink. Please. Please don't cry. 'Cause then I'm gonna start crying, too. You don't want that. I don't want that. I'll get all slobbery and wheezy and my lips puff up, you know? And the whites of my beautiful blue eyes, well, hell, they'll get all red."

A laugh bubbled out. How could she not laugh? And how could she not cry again when she saw the tears in his eyes and knew without a doubt that this big, brave warrior had already cried for her.

"Well, as colorfully patriotic as that sounds, we can't have your beautiful blue eyes getting red," she said on a quivering breath. "Not good for the image. Not good at all."

"There ya go," he murmured, then lowered his head to gently kiss her.

"Again," she whispered, looping her wrists around his neck and guiding him down into her arms.

"Again," he agreed and kissed her.

And kissed her until kisses weren't nearly enough.

"I need you." She shifted her hips and made room for him between her thighs. "I need the strength of you. The goodness of you."

She sighed his name when he touched her there, there where love and desire and need pooled to make this physical act the most achingly emotional connection she had ever known.

His gentleness stole her breath. His intensity made her heart race. But it was his love that made her whole again . . . and again . . . *and again* as he sank in and out of her body, bringing hope and the life force necessary to take her beyond the horror of Yao Long and everything he had stood for.

She cried out when he took her over the edge, clung to him as he joined her there. No risk. No danger. Only love greeting them on the other side.

"You're a good man, Johnny Duane Reed. A good, good man," she whispered as they lay in the aftermath, breathing in each other and the wonderful promise of tomorrow.

If it took her the rest of her life, she was going to convince him of just how good he was. "And you're the best thing that ever happened to me."

He kissed her brow. "I've never . . . never been anyone's best thing before."

Humbled. She'd humbled him. She could hear it in his voice. See it in his eyes. Just the way she could see that dark shadow of his father's legacy lift from his shoulders.

"Well, get used to it, cowboy. Because you're going to hear it a lot. You're stuck with me, you know that, don't you?"

He brushed his nose over hers, taking care of her bruises. "Damn. I guess I'm in trouble now."

Crystal couldn't remember the last time she'd been this nervous. A date. Johnny was due in five minutes to take her on a date. A real date. Not an exchange looks, rush to the bedroom, clothes magically fall off date, but a special date with eight o'clock dinner reservations.

She scrutinized her makeup one last time. Her bruises were a week old—at the zenith of color, wouldn't you know—but she'd followed the tips the girl at the makeup counter had given her when she'd bought new concealer today. A person had to be looking for bruises, she decided, studying her reflection one final time.

Johnny would be that person. Tonight, she didn't

want him thinking about what Yao had done to her. She didn't want to see that look come over his face that started out as concern, then transitioned to anger before he got control of himself again. Yeah, she loved that he cared, but she hated it that he still worried.

Her dress ought to do the trick, she thought, walking out of the bathroom and checking herself out in the full-length mirror in her bedroom.

"Oh, yeah," she said on a grin. The dress—and the four-inch black stilettos—would definitely do the trick.

It was fun dressing up like a girl again. Just like it had been fun dropping a wad at Victoria's Secret today, then scooting over to her favorite boutique and trying on several hot little numbers before finally settling on this one.

The soft jersey silk was sleeveless, cut in a deep V at the neckline, and hit her just above the knee. The rich, saturated blue made her green eyes pop, made her pale skin glow, and she figured it was guaranteed to make a certain smooth-talking cowboy stumble over his words.

She drew a satisfied breath. The makeup, the dress, the sparkly little cleavage piece that warmed between her breasts wasn't just about making Johnny Reed's gorgeous blue eyes fog over. It was about a show of strength. It was about sending a message to him—even to herself—that said, "I'm okay. I am really okay."

It was also a message that said life was far too precarious and too precious to spend the rest of it mired in residual fear and hesitation and doubt.

That's why, against his wishes, she'd moved back

into her apartment yesterday and insisted that she spend her first night back alone. He hadn't wanted her to come back. Hadn't wanted her to face the scene of horror and violence alone, even though it was exactly what she'd needed to do.

She needed to deal with it and put it behind her. There was no looking back. She was moving on. Johnny, mired in his worry over her ordeal, hadn't completely grasped the concept yet, but she was moving on with him.

Tonight was the night she was going to tell him. She was finished waiting around for him to take that next step and admit that he needed to plan out the rest of his life with her in it.

"It's you and me now, cowboy. Get used to it."

Her doorbell rang.

And her heart leapt. Like a teenager's, she thought with a happy grin. She quickly dabbed a sultry, smoky scent between her breasts, on both wrists, and on a few strategic spots in between, then hurried out of the room.

"Hello, cowboy," she said, a huge, look-how-strong-I-am smile in place, when she swung open the door.

"Oh . . . m . . . my," she murmured, doing a little stumbling over her own words when she got a look at him standing there.

The cowboy cleaned up good.

Johnny Reed wearing faded jeans, bed-head hair, and a scruffy beard was enough to give a woman heart palpitations. But Johnny Reed in a suit and tie, blond hair perfectly styled, and clean-shaven was cause for a full-blown heart attack.

"Hey," he said, all soft and slow and judging from the look in his eyes, every bit as wowed by how she looked as she was wowed by him. "You . . . man. Crystal. You look so . . . pretty."

"So," she said, when she recovered her power of speech, "do you."

He grinned then. She did, too. Then she finally had the presence of mind to step back from the open door and gesture him inside.

"For you," he said, holding out a slim gift-wrapped jewelry box.

She looked from the pretty silver package with the snowy white bow to his blue, blue eyes and felt tears form in hers. A gift. He'd brought her a gift.

It was sweet. It was . . . old-fashioned. And if the uncertainty that she suddenly saw cloud his gaze was any indication, he was also second-guessing his choice.

That just made her tear up more. "Thank you." She hugged the gift box against her breasts. "It's wonderful."

Uncertainty transitioned to amusement. "You don't even know what it is."

"Doesn't matter. It's from you. That makes it wonderful."

He lifted a shoulder, all that trademark self-confidence slipping away again. "I . . . um . . . I don't know much about picking out something for a woman."

Yeah. He was worried that she wouldn't like it.

She reached for his hand, walked him with her to

the sofa, and sat down. "You ever hear the expression 'it's the thought that counts'?" she asked, carefully sliding the ribbon off the box, then just as meticulously slipping a fingernail under the tape so she wouldn't tear the paper when she opened it.

"Okay, not that I have much experience with this, but aren't you just supposed to tear into it?" he asked, sitting down beside her. "I mean. Isn't that the fun of opening a present?"

"The fun is in savoring every moment," she informed him and finally pulled the paper away.

She glanced at him. He was all expectant, nervous eyes and held breath as he watched her and waited for her reaction.

Her heart fluttered in anticipation as she turned her attention back to the slim velvet box. On a deep breath, she opened it.

"Oh. Oh, Johnny." Her breath caught.

A delicate crystal miniature of Tinkerbell lay inside, suspended on a fine silver chain.

"It's . . ." She looked up at him, tears blurring her vision.

"Kind of silly, I know."

He'd really thought she wasn't going to like it. If she wasn't already in love with him, in that exact moment, she'd have fallen hard and fast and forever.

"What it is," she said, lifting the necklace out of the box and holding it up to the light where rainbow colors danced along the exquisitely crafted, multifaceted crystal, "is absolutely perfect."

She met his eyes again as Tinkerbell swayed in the light between them, winking and twinkling and casting her magic fairy dust in a spiraling arc that encompassed them both.

At least that's how it would have played out in the movies. And that's how the moment felt. Magical. Wonderful. Too perfect to be real as Johnny leaned forward and touched his lips to hers in the most gentle kiss.

"If there's anything perfect here, it's you," he whispered against her parted lips.

"Damn," she said, leaning into him and absorbing his heat and his strength and every good thing about him that made him the man he was, "we're not going to make our dinner reservations, are we?"

"Oh, yes, darlin', we are," he assured her, a world of promises dancing in his eyes. "Tonight, we're doing this right."

Epilogue

"Don't look now, but I think Colter's putting the moves on your woman."

Johnny looked up from the chessboard in Ann and Bob Tompkins's family room, then smiled into Gabe Jones's eyes. "I put you in check so now you're trying to distract me? Sinkin' pretty low there, angel boy. Besides, were I you, I'd be the one worried about the way *your* woman always ends up hanging around Doc when we get together."

Gabe glanced over his shoulder where, sure enough, Jenna sat on Doc's left while Crystal sat on his right. Both women had tucked unlit cigars into the corners of their mouths, mimicking Colter, as he dealt poker hands around the table.

"That redhead is crazy for five-card stud," Gabe admitted.

"*Which* redhead?" Johnny asked with a grunt, because Crystal was just as into the game as Jenna was.

"As long as they fleece the sucker, they can hang on him all they want." Gabe moved his bishop and bought himself a little more time on the board.

Johnny sat back, studied Gabe's latest move, and worked on his game strategy as he thought about the two people who had brought them all together again. Ann and Bob Tompkins were the only paternal elements in his life. Well, they had been until Crystal had taken him home to meet her parents last month.

No doubt about it, Tinkerbell was Daddy's little girl. And Daddy, after making it clear that anyone messing with his darling daughter had him to answer to, had welcomed him to the family. No reservations. No conditions. No holding back.

It took a lot to make him humble, but Phil Debrowski had done it in spades. So, over the past couple of months, had Phil's daughter. Crystal had not only met with Dina Stornello, she'd appeared with Dina at a Senate hearing on sex-slave trafficking in the United States, lending her support. Crystal was also in the process of setting up a website and a hotline where individuals could leave tips about possible victims of the sex trade.

Once the LVPD had sorted through Yao Long's international rap sheet and cleared her of the charges at Bali Hai, the casino had offered Crystal her old job back. She'd told them no, of course, and gotten a lot of pleasure doing so, because yeah, she'd come with him to Argentina.

Crystal Debrowski was now the first BOI who was a girl. Officially, she had relieved Mendoza as their internal securities and communication specialist and had done a damn fine job reconfiguring and updating their systems. Unofficially, she did a lot of work with Nate and Dr. Juliana Flores, who had been active rescuing victims of the human trafficking trade in Argentina for several years.

"So, can you see Sam burping a baby?"

Johnny glanced up at Gabe again, surprised by the tone of his voice, if not the question. Sam and Abbie's baby was the reason they were gathered at the Tompkinses today. A baby shower, for Pete's sake. *Keeerist.* Leave it to Ann. Hell, who would ever have seen this coming? The BOI team—including Mendoza, Savage, Green, and yeah, even Nate Black—had all shown up in Virginia at Ann Tompkins's request to participate in a baby shower for Sam and Abbie's little boy, who was due three months from now.

Blue booties, baby powder, and blankies—all gifts from guys much more comfortable with guns, ammo, and RPGs. And now Gabe Jones—the baddest of the bad—was talking about burping.

"You ask that as if you have a special interest in the subject." Johnny studied Gabe's face, which he'd arranged in a pretty good imitation of indifference. Not good enough, though. "Don't tell me you and Jenna are expecting a little tricycle motor."

Gabe shook his head, looking thoughtful. "No. We're not pregnant."

Next to Sam and Bryan Tompkins, their fallen brother who had brought them into his family's fold, Gabe was the only other man Johnny had ever considered an actual brother. "But you're thinking about it?"

A look very close to panic crossed Gabe's face. "It scares the hell out of me."

Johnny rubbed his hands over his cheeks. Un-freakin'-believable. Gabe Jones had faced the fire, walked through the fire, survived the fire. He'd lost a leg while saving Jenna from a madman; he'd saved not only Johnny's ass but the lives of most of the men in this room. And he was afraid of the idea of a baby.

"You know," Johnny said softly, "I've always had a lit-tle thing for your wife."

Gabe nodded. Smiled. "Yeah. I know. But since you've always had a little thing for breathing, too, I knew you'd never act on it."

"Right. Look. Jenna is amazing. If anyone could pull off this motherhood thing, well, next to Abbie" — he glanced at Sam's wife where she sat in the corner talking with Ann and the Tompkins's daughter, Stephanie— "it would be Jenna. And don't ask me why, but I can actually see those big scarred mitts of yours handling a smelly baby thingy."

"Smelly baby thingy? You mean a diaper?"

Johnny shrugged. "Yeah. That."

"What about you?" Gabe asked.

"Whoa." Johnny moved his queen. "Easy, big fella. I'm just getting used to this monogamy thing."

Gabe grinned from Johnny to the board and knocked his bishop out of play. "Checkmate."

Fuck. Gabe had gotten him so rattled over the prospect of being a papa Johnny'd lost his concentra-tion. "You dirty dog. You suckered me into that."

"If you can't run with the big dogs, you'd better stay home, bro."

Home, Johnny thought as Gabe rose, made a big show of dusting his hands, and headed for the bar. Yeah, he knew what that was now. Home was Crystal.

"Hold up. I've been carrying this around. Keep forgetting to give it to you." He stood, fished the butterfly knife that he'd taken off the street thug in Jakarta out of his pocket.

Gabe lifted a brow.

"Long story. Sometime when you've got an hour or ten, I'll tell ya about it."

Gabe nodded his thanks. Johnny watched him walk away and his throat thickened with pride, as it always did when he thought of all Gabe had gone through and all he'd overcome. His limp was barely detectable. He may have lost a limb, but he hadn't lost one bit of his edge. It had been less than a year since the surgery, and Gabe was back on board with the BOIs full-time.

The BOIs. He looked around the room. This place and these men were the closest thing to home he'd ever had, until that pixie with the Tinkerbell tattoo had welcomed him into her heart and changed his world.

Speaking of which, here she came. Big eyes. Big smile. Big, big love.

"Gabe beat you again, did he?"

He held out his hand as the crystal Tinkerbell necklace she was never without winked at him. "He cheated."

She grinned. "That's what you said the last time."

"What about you? How much you take Colter for?"

"Between Jenna and me? He's down around fifty bucks."

He pulled her down onto his lap. "That's my girl."

"Ann and Bob are amazing," she said, looking across the room where the two of them were making sure everyone was filled up with food and drinks. "Bryan must have been very special."

Johnny nodded, thought of his fallen brother who had bled out in the heat and the jungle in Sierra Leone while they all stood by, helpless. "Yeah. He was."

She kissed him, a sweet, tender kiss, to help make the hurt go away. "Raphael Mendoza seems to think Stephanie is something, too," she added with a nod toward Mendoza.

Johnny followed Crystal's gaze across the room where Raphael had managed to work his way to Stephanie's side. Again. "You picked up on that, did you?"

"I think everyone but Stephanie has picked up on it."

"Never figured Mendoza for a shy guy around the ladies."

She looped her arms around his neck. "I can see why shy would be a concept that would escape you."

He leveled her a look. "There's a dig in there somewhere."

"No, sir. There's a world of gratitude for the fact that there's not a shy or retiring bone in your body. Or that 'no' is a word you have never been able to comprehend."

Yeah, he thought. If he'd backed away every time

she'd laid that word on him in the beginning, they wouldn't be together today. And he wouldn't be the man she'd helped him become.

"I love you," he said, straight out, plain and simple.

The most amazing look came over her face. Tears filled her eyes. "Well, it's about damn time."

He blinked. "What? You didn't already know that?"

"I knew it. I just wasn't sure that you did."

She was serious. "Are you kidding me?"

"A woman needs to hear those words."

Damn and damn again. She looked like she was really going to cry. It broke his heart. "I say them all the time!"

"Yeah, when we're *naked*."

"You mean that doesn't count?"

She slugged him. "You can be so dense sometimes."

Yeah. He could. Especially when he had the chance to get her riled this way. When she figured out he was baiting her, she slugged him again.

"You rat. You're just trying to get a rise out of me."

"Tantrum. I was hoping for a tantrum. Your tantrums make me hot."

She expelled a sigh thick with the suffering he made her endure. "Everything makes you hot."

Laughing, he held her on his lap when she attempted to get up. "No, baby. Just you. You make me hot.

"Okay. Okay." He lifted his hands, surrendering when she shot him another glare. "I'll get serious."

A roll of her eyes told him how much stock she put in that notion.

A pressure in his chest made him relent. It was his heart. Swelling. "I love you, Crystal. I can't imagine ever not loving you."

When she realized he wasn't playing any longer, her lower lip quivered and damn, if his eyes didn't sting a little when a tear slipped down her cheek.

"I love you," he said again, pressing his forehead to hers, no fun, no games, just honest, open emotion. "I will always love you."

She sniffed, pushed out a groan. "You had to do this now? You had to get all serious and romantic and make me get sloppy in front of your friends? Your timing really sucks, you know that?"

He wrapped her tightly against him. "So, then I guess now would be a really bad time to ask you if you wanted to, you know . . . make it permanent?"

She pulled back. Looked at him through misty eyes that had grown round and wide, like she didn't trust what she'd just heard. "Permanent?"

He shrugged, felt his heart slamming away like thunder because, wow, this was heavy stuff. Good stuff. The best stuff. "Yeah. Permanent."

"Now *that*," she murmured with the softest, most beautiful smile. "*That* counts. Big-time."

Dear Readers,

While *Whisper No Lies* is a work of fiction and meant purely to entertain, the issue of human trafficking is very real. Over 800,000 individuals find themselves victims of the sex trade annually—a figure that is as staggering as it is tragic.

For more information on this deplorable reality, please go to www.acf.hhs.gov/trafficking or call the National Human Trafficking Resource Center at 888-373-7888.

All my best,
Cindy Gerard

Catch up with love...
Catch up with passion...
Catch up with danger....

Catch a bestseller from Pocket Books!